The Cliff Hangers: Not, Not Guilty

A Cliff Ford Mystery

TERRY TOLER

Cliff Hangers: Not, Not Guilty
Published by: BeHoldings, LLC

Copyright ©2022, **BeHoldings, LLC**
Terry Toler
All Rights Reserved

Book Cover: BeHoldings Publishing
Editor: Donna Toler

For information email: terry@terrytoler.com.

Our books can be purchased in bulk for promotional, educational, and business use. Please contact your bookseller or the BeHoldings Publishing Sales department at: *sales@terrytoler.com*

For booking information email: booking@terrytoler.com.
First U.S. Edition: August, 2022
Printed in the United States of America

ISBN 978-1-954710-16-0

OTHER BOOKS BY TERRY TOLER

Fiction

The Longest Day
The Reformation of Mars
The Late, Great Planet Jupiter
The Great Wall of Ven-Us
Saturn: The Eden Experiment
The Mercury Protocols
Save The Girls
The Ingenue
Saving Sara
Save The Queen
No Girl Left Behind
The Launch
The Blue Rose
Body Count
Save Me Twice
Cliff Hangers: Anna
Cliff Hangers: Mr. & Mrs. Platt
Cliff Hangers: The Quarterback
Cliff Hangers: Macy
Cliff Hangers: The Book Club
Winter Deceptions: Triggers

Non-Fiction

How to Make More Than a Million Dollars
The Heart Attacked
Seven Years of Promise
Mission Possible
Marriage Made in Heaven
21 Days to Physical Healing
21 Days to Spiritual Fitness
21 Days to Divine Health
21 Days to a Great Marriage
21 Days to Financial Freedom
21 Days to Sharing Your Faith

21 Days to Mission Possible
7 Days to Emotional Freedom
Uncommon Finances
Uncommon Health
Uncommon Marriage
The Jesus Diet
Suddenly Free
Feeling Free

For more information on these books and other resources visit terrytoler.com.

Thank you for purchasing this novel from best-selling author Terry Toler. As an additional thank you, Terry wants to give you a free gift.

Sign up for:

Updates
New Releases
Announcements

At terrytoler.com

We'll send you a copy of *The Book Club*, a Cliff Hangers mystery, free of charge.

For Peggy

1

The sound of the judge's gavel pounded on the bench and reverberated throughout the courtroom like lightning striking a house.

"How could I have gotten it so wrong?" Cliff muttered to himself.

Up until seconds before, he didn't think he had. Now he wasn't so sure.

The words from the judge sent his confidence out the window even though there were no windows in the courtroom. Whatever energy he'd felt inside had left him as he struggled to catch his breath which had left him faster than air from a punctured balloon.

That's what it felt like. Somebody had figuratively stuck a dagger in his heart.

"I declare you innocent," the judge said. The words rang in Cliff's ears like the echo in a canyon. Never in a million years did he think the judge would make this decision.

"It's a travesty. I'm ashamed of what has happened to you," the judge said to the defendant, Henry Lee Clay, who stood at the defendant's table. Tears streamed down Clay's face. His lawyer's hand rested on his shoulder.

The excoriating words that came next were meant for Cliff.

"We have the greatest judicial system in the world," the judge said. "But sometimes it fails. Sometimes it makes mistakes. In this case, what occurred wasn't a mistake. The conduct of the investigator was appalling."

What?

Cliff couldn't believe the words coming out of the judge's mouth.

Henry Lee Clay confessed!

"I find that the confession was coerced," the judge said bitterly.

A witness placed him at the scene.

"The eyewitness testimony was unreliable."

The DNA proved he was at the scene.

"I find it likely that the DNA evidence was planted or tainted by the investigator. Either way, it's not reliable."

I would never plant evidence and it wasn't tainted. I was careful!

Who was on trial here? Cliff wanted to shout his innocence at the top of his lungs. He had to bite his tongue to keep from doing so.

The arguments swirled around in his head. The District Attorney had vigorously defended Cliff and his actions. The judge didn't agree. His ruling was clear. Henry Lee Clay would go free. After ten years in jail.

Judges were all powerful. The truth was whatever they said it was.

"The investigation was lacking," the judge opined.

I investigated the case thoroughly.

"This was a rush to judgment."

Cliff could feel his knees weaken even though he was sitting down. His Lieutenant had warned him this might happen. The judge was anti-police. He'd once sentenced a rapist to probation because the woman had dressed a little too provocatively. She had deserved it, according to him.

His bias was evident in his rulings. He was notoriously lenient on defendants and tough on cops.

Normally, overturning convictions by a jury was a rare occurrence. The D. A. had fought over the last two days to have Henry Lee Clay's conviction upheld, but a lot of factors worked against them.

"Mr. Clay, you deserve better than this," the judge said with a noticeable scowl on his face. A look of disdain. While he didn't look in Cliff's direction, Cliff knew the vitriol was intended for him.

"You are to be commended, Mr. Clay. You never lost faith. You were lucky the *Not Guilty Group* took your case. Your lawyers are to be commended."

Clay had gotten lucky. He had exhausted his appeals. Two years before, he wrote a letter to a local news reporter looking to make a name for herself. Shannon Roberts. Clay proclaimed his innocence in the letter. He'd been writing similar letters for eight years. To no avail, until Roberts took up the cause.

She went to high school with a famous actress, Anna Quinn. Roberts was the maid-of-honor at Quinn's high-profile wedding. The two beauties brought attention to Clay's case. Convinced of his innocence, the women took up the cause like rabid dogs. The media followed them around like they were on leashes.

The women tried first to get Clay a pardon. When the Governor rejected their plea, the *Not Guilty Group* took the case. Clay would've spent at least another ten years in jail if not for them.

"I can't give you your ten years back," the judge said. "All I can do is apologize to you, sir. Nothing can ever repay you for your suffering."

What about Tessie's suffering?

The victim. She couldn't get the last ten years back either. Never will. She's dead.

"I wish I could order the city of Chicago to pay you for your damages," the judge said. "But I can't."

Highly inappropriate statement for a sitting judge.

The Lieutenant, Cliff's boss, had warned him about that as well. If the conviction was overturned, a civil suit would follow. Henry Lee Clay would get millions of dollars in a settlement, which the city would be quick to offer.

The ramifications would be far reaching. All of Cliff's prior convictions would be questioned. There'd be dozens of motions for new trials from murderers Cliff had put behind bars over the years. The D.A. 's office would be inundated.

This reversal would affect Cliff's current and future cases. This verdict would undoubtedly be brought up at all future trials by skilled attorneys. Used to create reasonable doubt in the juror's minds.

Cliff's reputation was at stake. This judge was convinced that Cliff had planted evidence. The worst charge that could be leveled at an investigator. The *Not Guilty Group* argued that Cliff either planted the evidence or was incompetent.

A bunch of hogwash.

Admittedly, Cliff had been new to the job. He'd only been an investigator for less than a year when this murder was dropped in his lap. A horrendous crime. A young girl. Kidnapped off the sidewalk while walking home from school. Forced into a shed behind a vacant house and brutalized in unspeakable ways for several minutes before her throat was slashed.

A neighbor saw Henry Lee Clay running away from the house. The elderly woman was certain at the time.

She died four years ago so she wasn't able to testify this time around. Her daughter testified that her mother began to have doubts later in life. The D.A. argued that her testimony was hearsay. It was, but the judge had already heard it.

You can't "unring" a bell in the courtroom. Once the judge heard the daughter's testimony, he might rule it inadmissible, but human nature was what it was. How could he disregard it entirely like he was required to do by law?

A pound of the gavel brought Cliff back to reality.

"You are free to go," the judge said emphatically. "Mr. Clay, I hope you are able to get some semblance of your life back. Go with my deepest apologies."

Henry Lee Clay hugged his lawyers for a second time. The *Not Guilty Group* had a half dozen lawyers in the room. Clay had some of the best defense attorneys in the United States representing him. They were no doubt chomping at the bit to get outside and in front of the many cameras.

Clay's case had captivated the city of Chicago. The national news media had picked it up on it as well. The Cable News outlet talked about it almost nonstop.

Cliff approached the prosecutor's table. He sensed the coldness. The agony of defeat. They'd put forth their best arguments. They'd defended

Cliff vigorously. But he could tell the difference. The judge hadn't believed their arguments.

Cliff had been the one on trial and had been found guilty. As much as the D.A. and his Lieutenant didn't believe the arguments, now it didn't matter.

They lost.

Like the football team who loses the Super Bowl because the kicker missed the game winning field goal. Cliff was the kicker. They didn't want to blame him to his face, but they'd never look at him the same way.

The allegation that Cliff would plant evidence bordered on ridiculous. In more than ten years as a homicide detective for Chicago P.D., he'd never done so and wouldn't even consider it.

The confession wasn't coerced. He'd read Clay his rights. But the kid was only sixteen. A juvenile. Even though he was eventually tried as an adult. The interrogation was videotaped, but someone had forgotten to turn on the volume. Cliff wasn't the one who made the mistake even though he was accused of it. All that could be seen on the video was Cliff questioning the kid for four hours.

The interrogation had been rough, but that's Cliff's job. He was convinced Clay was the killer and had gone after him with a vengeance. Angrily. A twelve-year-old girl had been killed. Cliff had seen the girl's body and his heart broke for her and her parents.

Cliff had been under extreme pressure to solve the case. Not from the Lieutenant. Not from the department. But from the victim. Tessie. He always felt it. That little girl deserved every ounce of energy and skill he could bring to finding her killer.

The victims had always motivated him. That's why he got into the profession to begin with.

He'd had a stellar career. Solved many high-profile cases. Cliff Ford was considered the most senior in the department, even though others had been there longer. He was given the most difficult cases to solve.

Would that still be the case tomorrow morning?

If the mood of the Lieutenant and the prosecutors were any indication, it wouldn't. He could tell they looked at him differently. He was a wounded animal. They were like a lion pack, trying to decide if it was worth fighting off the pack of hyenas to save one of their own.

They might cut their losses. They hadn't said as much, but Cliff wondered if that's what they were thinking.

Would he lose his job over it?

The Lieutenant put a hand on Cliff's shoulder as a slight olive branch. A minimal gesture of support. The Lieutenant probably would fight for Cliff. There was only so much he could do though. The court of public opinion was behind the sixteen-year-old boy, tried as an adult, wrongfully convicted, and put in jail for ten years.

By a crooked cop, the most cynical believed. An incompetent newbie by the rest who tried to give him the benefit of the doubt.

"The DNA was what killed us," Ed Armitage, the D.A. who had argued the case said. He was clearly licking his wounds as well. This was a stunning defeat for his office.

"Yep," the Lieutenant said. "That's unfortunate."

The DNA evidence was missing from the evidence locker.

Clay's DNA had been found at the scene. A positive match confirmed it. That was the final nail in Clay's coffin at the time. Cliff's case had been airtight. A jury found Clay guilty in less than four hours of deliberation. A tough judge oversaw the trial. Sentenced Clay to life in prison with the possibility of parole after twenty years.

The *Not Guilty Group* had a heyday with the missing evidence. In the press and in the courtroom. The judge had been furious when the prosecutor admitted it was missing. No one knew where it was.

The beginning of the end.

The case began to unravel. The *Not Guilty Group* lawyers were masterful. They wove a twisted tail of fiction. The missing DNA was damning. A cover-up was argued.

The original DNA results were still a problem for the defense that they had to overcome. They had to come up with a plausible reason for the positive results. So, they attacked Cliff's handling of the scene.

Even though Cliff didn't handle the evidence, they said he planted it.

A DNA sample was one of the first things obtained from Clay after he was arrested. The *Not Guilty Group* argued that Cliff went back to the scene and planted the DNA there.

Cliff did go back to the scene. To take pictures of Tessie's body. He wanted to show Clay. To pressure him into a confession.

Not to plant evidence.

The cross examination of Cliff had been brutal. The *Not Guilt Group* slung accusations at Cliff faster than a hundred mile an hour pitcher throwing at a batter. Cliff answered them calmly for the first few hours. Eventually, they got under his skin. He got argumentative. Which made him look defensive.

Clay's attorneys were grasping at straws, but how could Cliff prove a negative?

When did you quit beating your wife? When was the first time you planted evidence? When did you decide to take the DNA back to the scene and plant it?

Unfair questions.

"How did Clay's DNA get under the victim's fingernails?" Cliff had argued. "How would I put it there without anyone seeing me do it?"

The defense attorney had feigned outrage. He never answered the question. He doesn't have to. He can hurdle accusations with few limitations.

"What about the scratch on Clay's neck?" Cliff had said.

"Objection. We'll ask the questions," the attorneys argued, and the judge agreed.

"Detective, I'm not going to tell you again," the judge said angrily. "Limit your responses to the questions asked you by counsel."

It hadn't gone well. Still, Cliff thought no upstanding judge would overlook the mountain of evidence. You had to set aside all common sense to make the leaps the defense was asking the judge to make.

And yet, that's what he had done. Cliff was stunned.

The judge left the bench. The sudden movement startled Cliff. He didn't even remember rising for him.

Henry Lee Clay walked out of the courtroom. Not before glaring at Cliff. If looks could kill, Cliff would be dead.

None of it made sense.

Cliff tried to plead his case again to his colleagues.

"I didn't plant any evidence and I didn't steal the DNA out of the evidence locker," Cliff said defensively to the group standing at the prosecutor's table.

"We know," the Lieutenant said.

The prosecutor nodded.

It wasn't a ringing endorsement.

His boss would have to circle the wagons. He'd still support Cliff, but now the proverbial cat was out of the bag and rearing its sharp claws. Clay would probably get ten to twenty million dollars in a settlement the Lieutenant had estimated.

After all, what was ten years of a young man's life worth?

Clay's high school years were taken from him. He never got to go to his prom. Go to college. Get married. Have kids. His life was ruined. The conviction would be expunged from his record, but the stain would follow him for the rest of his life.

All because of Cliff.

Was there any chance Cliff had gotten it wrong? Did he rush to judgment?

Cliff never considered any other suspects. It's called tunnel vision. Investigators are accused of it all the time. Focusing on one person and then making the evidence fit.

Clay had an alibi. He was with his girlfriend. She testified at the original trial.

"He was with me at the time," Misty Matthews had said.

She moved away from Chicago and was married now and didn't want to get involved in a new trial.

What if she'd been telling the truth? Clay didn't have a record and was a good student. Came from a decent family. He didn't fit the profile of a killer.

The DNA.

What if Cliff's clothes were contaminated? He'd handled Clay's arrest. Clay's DNA would have been on Cliff's clothes.

But Cliff never touched Tessie. How could he get the DNA under her fingernails?

What does it matter now?

Clay was free. Double jeopardy applied. He could never be tried again anyway. Even if Cliff had been correct and he was guilty.

What about justice for Tessie?

Clay did ten years in prison. Some people got less than that for rape and murder.

The case would be reopened as an unsolved murder. Cliff wouldn't handle it for obvious reasons. No investigator in the office would give it more than a cursory look.

If Clay didn't kill the girl, how could they ever prove who did it? If they did find another suspect and arrested him, the man's attorneys wouldn't have to be that skillful to create reasonable doubt. They'd just point back to the conviction of Henry Lee Clay.

"Time to move on," the Lieutenant said to Cliff soberly as they walked out of the courthouse and into a waiting car. "Nothing we can do about it now."

Cliff knew that was correct. The sooner he put it behind him the better.

***

Henry Lee Clay walked out of the courtroom a free man. For the first time in ten years. The bitterness overwhelmed him like a cancerous tumor.

The last ten years had been a living hell.

He'd been the target of the other inmates. They didn't think much of someone convicted of raping and murdering a child. His treatment had been brutal. He'd been savagely raped and beaten more times than he could count.

All because of Cliff Ford.

The homicide detective.

His hatred for the man knew no bounds. He'd had many nights in the stir to think about it. Every time he ate one of the horrid meals. Every time he laid down on the steel-cold bed. When he heard the sound of the prison bars closing around him. When he was forced to spend night after night in the small concrete cell like a caged rat.

He glared at Cliff Ford as he left the courthouse to face the press.

His attorney had his arm and led him out of the courtroom. As the large and burly prison guards had been doing all those years.

He was free but it still didn't feel like it.

Clay went through the courthouse doors and was greeted by bright sunshine that caused him to squint. He didn't see the sun much in prison.

He was greeted by a cheering crowd and felt like a rock star. Dozens of members of the media snapped his picture.

A podium was set up with a throng of reporters surrounding it. Clay wouldn't speak. His attorneys would do all the talking. Maybe he'd do an interview at some point. His attorneys were demanding a hundred grand for exclusives. They'd probably get it according to the lead attorney.

He might get a book deal. With his strikingly handsome looks, his attorney told him he might have a future in television.

Whatever. He wasn't interested in the limelight. He was just glad to get out of that prison hole.

His attorney was peppered with questions from reporters.

"Henry Lee Clay is an innocent man. Not guilty in the eyes of the law." His attorney orated in a deep booming voice that didn't need the microphones.

"Justice was done. The system finally worked," he added. "We are relieved that Henry Lee Clay can go home tonight to his family."

In spite of his ordeal, Clay did feel relief.

His attorney kept repeating the "not guilty" phrase.

Clay forced back a smile.

His attorney saw it and put his arm around him and pulled him toward the podium.

"Look at this smile," the attorney said. "The smile of an innocent man finally found not guilty."

Henry was laughing on the inside.

His attorney had no idea.

He had raped and killed that girl. And would probably do it again.

2

Six months later

Henry Lee Clay received a settlement from the city of Chicago for his "so-called" wrongful conviction. The attorneys for the *Not Guilty Group* had been hoping for five million. Clay got sixteen.

The settlement offer came quickly after Clay related the harsh treatment he'd endured at the hands of the prisoners and guards at Northern Illinois State Penitentiary. Much of which was already documented by his frequent visits to the hospital and the long stints in solitary meant for his protection from the other inmates.

The ten years had been horrendous. Clay made a daily vow never to go back there. The alternative to prison was death. He realized that.

Henry Lee Clay wasn't long for this world.

He would kill again.

The compulsion inside him was too great. The voices in his head were too strong.

He'd eventually get caught.

But he could never go back to prison. He'd die first. Suicide by cop was an option or he'd kill himself if and when he got back in that situation.

So far, he'd been able to resist the urges to kill and was enjoying his freedom and money.

Even then, Clay spent his money carefully. He only splurged on two things. An expensive car, a nice condo on Lake Michigan, and designer clothes. That's it.

The clothes and car were two necessities for picking up women. The Porsche 911, Carrera 4 GTS two door red coupe, turbo, was all he needed to entice the members of the opposite sex. The fact he was good looking and dressed to the nines only helped sell the persona.

His ten years in jail were never mentioned. Occasionally, someone recognized him from the news reports. He quickly moved on from those women.

There were plenty to choose from.

Any night of the week, he could go to a bar, mention his car, offer a pretty girl a ride, and he'd be back at her place within hours.

Not to kill her. That wasn't his aim. The devil inside drove him to young girls. Sixteen and under. For whatever reason. His carnal desires drew him to older women. Early to late thirties. More experienced. Less drama. No complications. Just sex.

His M.O. was well established. He'd go back to their place one time. Have fun. Take their numbers when offered. Then never call them back. On to the next woman. He was getting pretty good at it.

Tonight, he'd made an exception. Most of the time, he only saw the woman once. Less complicated. He didn't want a relationship anyway. Just a night of uninhibited pleasure.

Then he met Summer.

Asian. Dark hair and eyebrows. Silky smooth skin. High cheekbones. A full and luscious bottom lip. Thin upper lip. Surprisingly, the lips worked well together despite the differences in size.

Summer was as passionate and hot as her name. He'd seen her three times now. Tonight would be the fourth. This was getting close to being considered a relationship.

For whatever reason, he couldn't resist her. Even though he'd tried various times to lose her number and put her out of his mind.

Summer was falling for him as well. He could tell. At some point, he'd have to cut it off. For now, he'd continue to enjoy it while it lasted.

Henry stared at himself in the mirror of his bathroom. Applied the last bit of gel to his hair. Satisfied with what he saw although he wished he was taller. Five-five made him feel like less of a man.

The inmates had mocked him incessantly about his height. He was no match physically for the brutes in prison.

Maybe that's why he preyed on young girls. He didn't have the confidence he could overpower a grown woman and kill her. Summer was toned and fit. He doubted he could kill her, even if he wanted to. Which he didn't.

Clay brushed his hand through his Cocker Spaniel brown hair. Then surveyed his dark thick eyebrows to make sure they were perfectly proportioned. Turned his head from side to side to look over his carefully trimmed beard. Then stepped back from the mirror to view the entire picture.

He wore charcoal black slacks, with black shoes. No socks. White shirt. Always a white shirt, unbuttoned three rungs to reveal his buff chest. That's the only good thing that came out of his incarceration. When in jail, he had nothing else to do but work out like a fiend.

He lifted weights constantly when he was in the yard. In the winters or while in solitary, he did more pushups a day than he could count.

Summer was a fitness instructor at a local gym. That's how they met. Clay had joined the gym to keep up his physique. She noticed him first. They struck up a conversation. He invited her to dinner. She already knew about the car. The gym had windows along the front facing the parking lot. She'd seen him drive up.

That's one of the things he liked about Summer. She wasn't impressed by the car. She seemed to like him for who he was. Ironically, she really didn't know him. If she did, she'd never invite him to her house.

Something she hadn't done, until tonight.

Summer was playing hard to get. She'd made him pursue her. They'd kissed a few times. Made out once in his car, but she never let it go beyond that.

It seemed like things were moving faster now. Summer was cooking him dinner. All indications were that she was ready to take things to the next level.

Clay could feel the excitement building inside of him. His whole spine tingled. He could feel the desire running down his leg.

Would the relationship survive the night? Was this their last date? Would there be more?

He had his doubts. Once the pursuit was over and he got what he wanted, he would no longer be mesmerized by her. She could never be as good as he pictured it in his mind.

It almost made him sad. He'd miss her.

Clay stopped by the store to pick up a bottle of chilled white wine. He splurged and spent too much on it. A Rombauer Chardonnay, 2018. Two hundred and eighty-nine dollars, plus tax. Over three bills. A colossal waste of money. Summer wouldn't even be impressed if he told her the price. Which he would never do. She'd think less of him if he told her.

He should've gotten a cheap wine but had asked the clerk for the most expensive white wine. The man left his perch behind the counter and showed him a Chateau Haut Brion Blanc Pessac, 2013.

$999.99.

Clay had almost fallen over when the man quoted the price. The only reason Clay remembered the long name of the wine was because the clerk wrote it down on a card. Clay kept the card because he might bring it up tonight if the conversation lagged.

A fifteen-dollar bottle of Chardonnay was probably more Summer's style but he couldn't resist the extravagance. She deserved the best tonight. So, he splurged on the three-hundred-dollar bottle of wine and left his regrets at the store counter.

It made him feel important to spend that much on her and he wanted the night to go well. He hadn't taken the time to analyze why. Maybe he was making up for lost time. Perhaps it was because he knew the gig would be up soon.

Too bad he couldn't get rid of the urge to kill.

The sixteen million dollars was invested well and growing every day. He could keep this up for a long time.

Honestly, what good did it do to invest the money so wisely?

When he finally succumbed to his demons and killed again, it didn't matter that he'd spent too much on a bottle of wine. He'd never be able to really enjoy all that money.

That caused a sudden sadness to come over him, putting a damper on his mood.

Revving the Porsche made him feel better.

Summer lived in a modest neighborhood near downtown. The liquor store wasn't far from her place and he made it there in no time. When he stepped out of his car, the excitement was back. His heart leapt a couple of inches in his chest when she opened the door and brushed his cheeks with her lips.

"You look nice," she said sincerely. "I guess you found the place with no trouble."

"My car has navigation," Clay said.

Summer chuckled. "Didn't your own satellite come with the car?"

Maybe she was a little impressed. Which made him feel good.

"I brought this," Clay said, extending the long skinny brown sack which held the bottle of wine.

Summer took it from him.

"Come in and make yourself at home," she said as she walked away from him toward what Clay presumed was the kitchen. "Dinner will only be a couple more minutes."

Clay followed her admiring the view. Summer was understated as usual. Tight form fitting blue jeans with a red top that zipped down. Modestly. The sleeves went slightly below her elbows. She wore some kind of sparkling sandals. Her toes were painted red. Matching the slight shade of red on her lips.

Clay noticed every detail. That came from his time in prison. That's one of the ways he passed the time. Thinking about the details of his surroundings. His prison cell had one thousand four hundred and thirty-three cracks in the concrete blocks.

"Can I help?" he asked, hoping the answer was no.

He hadn't cooked a meal in his life. His mother and sisters did all the cooking growing up. Since he'd been out of jail, he'd eaten every meal out, except for cereal or a power bar for breakfast. His stove and oven were unused. His refrigerator was mostly empty. Taking a girl back there wasn't an option for a number of reasons.

Summer waved her hand dismissively. "I've got it handled. You relax."

He couldn't relax. But he did lean against the kitchen counter and folded his arms in an attempt to calm his nerves.

Summer lifted a lid off a pot on the stove and tasted the steaming liquid with a wooden spoon, then let out a moan which sent chills down to his toes. The spoon had a red stain on it. She'd made spaghetti.

"Let's see what we have here," Summer said as she pulled his bottle of wine out of the brown bag on the island.

Her lips twisted to the side in a partial grimace. A look of disappointment. His heart sank a degree. What was wrong with the wine? Did she not like that brand?

Did she know how much it cost?

"This won't do," she said.

He wasn't sure what she meant.

Summer opened the refrigerator and put the bottle of wine on the side shelf. Was it not cold enough? She disappeared into her pantry and returned with a different bottle of wine.

"Is something wrong?" Clay asked.

"White wine doesn't go with spaghetti. Red wine does."

"I'm sorry. I didn't know."

She must've seen a hurt look on his face because she walked over and kissed his pouting lip.

"No worries. I have red wine. We'll save the white for later. It needs to be chilled anyway. Red wine is good at room temperature."

I paid three hundred dollars for that bottle of wine!

He bit his lip to keep from shouting angrily at her. His cheeks felt hot.

If Summer noticed his anger, she didn't let it show.

He turned away in case she did look at him. He didn't want to ruin the evening by exploding in anger. This was the first time he'd ever felt the urge to kill an adult woman. He had to resist it.

She took his hand and led him to his seat at the table which calmed him somewhat. Once he was seated, she took his plate and went back into the kitchen and began to dish out the meal. She was back within seconds and sat the plate down in front of him.

He didn't have to wait long before she sat down across from him with her own plate filled. The conversation turned pleasant for the next few minutes.

Even jovial. She made a crack about eating spaghetti on a date. That it wasn't usually a good idea. His white shirt might be a problem, she quipped.

Clay tucked a napkin in it just in case he spilled some red marinara. He was particular about his things. Especially his clothes.

A few minutes later, the conversation turned serious. Right after he'd taken the last bite and his last sip of wine.

"I looked you up on the internet," Summer said. Almost sheepishly. Like she'd done something wrong.

Clay felt his heart skip a beat and the anger returned.

"What did you find?" he said coolly.

"You've been to prison."

He nodded as anxiety pulsed through his body like a faucet had been turned on full blast.

"I was innocent."

"I read that."

The conversation paused and turned awkward as neither knew what to say next.

"Were you ever going to tell me?" she finally asked.

"I figured I'd tell you tonight," Clay said. "It's a fourth date kind of reveal."

"Hmm. After I've fallen for you?"

"Have you fallen for me?"

"Maybe."

"It's not something that's easy to talk about."

"I get that. You still should've told me."

He tried hard to hold back the rage building inside of him. It'd been more than ten years since he'd had this feeling. The day he killed the young girl. Saw her walking home from school. It's like something took over his body. The next thing he knew, Tessie was dead.

He had that same feeling now.

He clutched the fork still in his hand. His jaw was clenched so tight it hurt.

"I was waiting until I was sure there'd be a fifth date," he said, forcing a smile on his face. He thought humor might be the best way to diffuse the situation.

"Will there be a fifth date?" he added.

"I haven't decided yet," she said with a sly grin.

Was she about to dump him?

There won't be if I kill you on the fourth date!

Clay had to be careful that the thoughts didn't escape his lips. He could easily say what he was feeling and not even know it.

"Like I said, I was innocent."

"Tell me what happened," she said softly.

"I don't like to talk about it."

"It's okay. You can trust me."

"The city of Chicago gave me sixteen million dollars."

"I know. I read about that."

"I didn't kill the girl. I was with my girlfriend at the time."

"I wonder why they think you did it then? Why do you think the jury found you guilty?"

Clay squirmed in his chair. He felt like he was being interrogated all over again and didn't like it.

"That investigator, Cliff Ford, had it in for me all along. You have no idea what it's like to go to jail for something you didn't do."

"I'm sorry that happened to you."

The words started spewing out of Clay. Like water from a broken faucet. All the anger and vitriol from the last ten years came out of him like steam from a kettle with no other place to go.

He told her everything. Most of it anyway. He left out the part about actually killing the girl.

Clay opened up about the abuse in prison. In the settlement agreement, the city of Chicago agreed to pay for counseling, but Clay never went. He'd never talked to anyone about it. He felt a release. It felt good to finally let it all out.

"I was wrongly accused."

"It was horrible. Going to jail for something I didn't do."

"I lost ten years of my life."

"I was innocent."

The words came out of his mouth so easily, he almost believed them.

Summer's demeanor changed. She was clearly moved. Tears formed in her eyes as he spoke.

When his own tears began to flow, she stood and walked over to him, and draped her arms around his neck. It wasn't the reaction he was expecting. He figured she was about to kick him out of the house.

He'd already decided he wasn't leaving there without having sex with her. Raping and killing her if he had to.

Instead, she took his hand and raised him from the chair. Then led him behind her toward the bedroom.

He still felt the rage. But he had an outlet for it.

They ravaged each other like two wild animals.

So rough, it almost frightened him while it was happening. He was afraid he was hurting her.

When they finished, Clay was sweating profusely, and all his emotional and physical strength had left him. He collapsed on the bed. Out of breath.

She seemed equally spent.

A sense of dread suddenly came over him.

He was right. Things did change between them. Immediately.

Now he hated her. She knew too much about him. He felt it. She had judged him.

"I wonder why they think you did it?" she had said. "I wonder why the jury found you guilty?"

Almost like she was mocking him.

Like she wasn't sure he hadn't done it. She probably read about the trial. Knowing her, she poured through the evidence. She knew about the confession and the DNA.

She knew he was guilty. He could sense it.

Why did she take him into her bedroom?

For the danger of it. Girls liked being with bad boys.

His mouth almost flew open. She felt sorry for him.

He didn't need her pity.

Clay had to get out of there. Summer got out of the bed and went into the bathroom giving him the opportunity he needed. He retrieved his clothes which had been practically torn off of him.

Things had happened so fast they didn't have time to use protection.

One button was missing on his shirt. Which made him angry. The shirt cost two hundred dollars. Less than the wine, but it was one of his favorite shirts.

Summer's eyes widened when she returned to the room wearing a tee-shirt and saw him dressed. She was walking gingerly. He had hurt her.

"Where are you going?" she asked.

He made up a lame excuse.

"I have a doctor's appointment in the morning."

"Oh."

He walked out of the bedroom, and she followed him.

The wine.

He wanted to ask her for it. Then thought better of it. He didn't want a confrontation. He had to get out of there before he did something he regretted.

"Did I do something wrong?" Summer asked, almost apologetically after partially opening the front door.

"No. It's me. I have to go."

She took his arm, but he pulled away.

"I said I have to go."

Summer opened the door all the way and he bolted through it like a cat let out of a cage. He got in the car, started it quickly, revved the engine, and sped off.

Summer stood at the door with a stunned look on her face as he drove off. She forced a slight wave. He ignored it.

Clay forced himself to breathe when he was to the next block.

He hadn't felt like this in ten years. Not since the day he killed that little girl.

***

A shadowy figure stood behind a bush next to the driveway and watched the man drive off in the Porsche. A fiery rage burned inside of him.

Summer, his ex-girlfriend, stood in the doorway. Half dressed.

His imagination was running wild. Had been for more than two hours. Ever since the man arrived.

He knew what she'd done. Cheated on him with some rich guy.

When Summer closed the door, Wayne Bowman emerged from behind the bushes, and walked around to the back of the house.

He took the knife out of his pocket and waited.

3

Later that night

Ever since the Henry Lee Clay fiasco, it seemed as if the late-night calls to Cliff came more often than before. Like he was being punished. Cliff was already in bed when the text alert went off on his phone. His wife, Julia, who never went to sleep before eleven, had to rouse him by the shoulders. He almost slept through it.

Homicide. Woman. Upper West Side.

The address followed.

Cliff rubbed his eyes to get them working again. The life of a homicide detective in downtown Chicago was stressful enough. Now, it seemed more so for Cliff, as his rank in the department had been, for all practical purposes, yanked down a notch.

Not officially. In practicality. While no one said they blamed him for the sixteen-million-dollar cost to the city, his name would forever be associated with the largest wrongful conviction settlement in Chicago's history.

Henry Lee Clay case.

An embarrassment to everyone involved.

Cliff had sucked it up and soldiered through it. Worked his cases with the same care he did before. Maybe even more so. He was tired because he not only had to work his cases, but was constantly being pulled into the D.A. 's office to discuss old cases.

Motion after motion for new trials had been filed by inmates who he'd put behind bars over the years. Most didn't go anywhere and were dismissed. But Cliff still had to provide an answer to each one.

He had to deal with the most absurd allegations.

That he manufactured evidence.

Coerced a confession.

Failed to Mirandize a suspect.

A couple of desperate low life scum threw in police brutality for good measure.

The mountain of new motions along with his normal case files weighed on him. So much so, he'd even considered changing professions.

The Lieutenant had talked him out of it. As had his wife, Julia. He was born to be a detective and was good at it, she had argued. The Lieutenant had been even more adamant. If Cliff gave up, then Henry Lee Clay cost the city of Chicago a lot more than sixteen million dollars. It'd cost the city its best detective.

The sentiment should've felt good but it didn't.

Cliff didn't quit though. If he did, cases would go unsolved. Murderers would be loose to murder again. He'd invested too much in this career to give up now. And what else would he do? Be a security guard at a department store?

Investigating murders was in his blood and he was good at. His conscience was also clear. He didn't do any of those things Henry Lee Clay accused him of.

That's why Cliff dragged himself out of bed night after night and put his suit and tie back on and trudged over to a house on the upper west side of downtown Chicago. A middle-class house in a respectable neighborhood. Murders happened all over Chicago with regularity. Not so much in this neighborhood.

A crowd had already gathered outside.

Probably neighbors. Some were still in their pajamas. The blue lights of one of the patrol cars were still flashing drawing attention to the scene. Cliff told one of the cops monitoring the crowd to turn them off.

Cliff walked under the yellow police tape and up a small incline to the porch and through the already opened door. No need to flash his badge. The cop guarding the door knew who he was.

A pang of insecurity crept down Cliff's arm. The feeling kept coming over him when he arrived at a crime scene or went to work in the morning.

Did the cop know who he was? Had he heard about the Henry Lee Clay case?

It felt like people were judging him. Thinking about him. Questioning his judgment. That they didn't respect him like they used to. No one had ever said anything. He was probably imagining it. The feelings were real anyway, and he couldn't seem to shake them.

The same thoughts flooded his mind each time he felt this way.

Were the cops on the scene watching me closely to make sure I didn't plant any evidence?

Stupid.

His angst was unnecessary. Most cops stuck together. Circled the wagons for their own. If the cop was thinking anything, he was probably glad he got a good investigator like Cliff assigned to the case. Some of Cliff's colleagues were difficult to deal with and treated the beat cops like their lap dogs.

Cliff had always treated them with the utmost respect if they deserved it. They were the ones on the front lines. He found them valuable. He needed their observations. They were the first ones on the scene. More often than not, they saw something that was helpful to his investigation.

Cliff went inside the house to find the one in charge. So far, it looked like everything had been done by the book. He knew why once he saw George Strunk. A decorated veteran with years of service. Strunk would be retiring soon.

A big smile came on Strunk's face when he saw Cliff which seemed out of place considering the bloody room Cliff had just entered. Crime scenes had a smell and Cliff's nose crinkled slightly.

"Strunk, I thought they put you out to pasture already," Cliff quipped.

The two men were close enough friends to shake hands or even hug, but this was a crime scene. Cliff never touched anything or anybody once inside the house and once he had booties and gloves on.

"Not yet," Strunk said. "I got until the end of the year. Then I'm done with all you donut belly paper pushers. Especially you, Ford. I can't wait."

"Looks like you've had a few of those donuts yourself lately there partner," Cliff said, playfully pointing to George's belly which was slightly protruding over his belt. Surprisingly, since Strunk always scored the highest in the annual fitness tests even though he was usually the oldest.

Strunk let out a grunt of acknowledgement but let the remark pass. Instead, he pointed at the body of a woman lying on the living room floor.

Cliff let out a sigh.

Seeing a dead woman always sent a little shock through his system. That and little girls. Like Tessie. The girl Henry Lee Clay killed. The image of that girl's body still haunted Cliff at night sometimes.

"Do we know who she is?" Cliff asked.

"Summer Lange. Here's her I.D."

Strunk took it out of his pocket and handed it to Cliff who looked it over.

Summer Ann Lange.

An Asian woman. Five feet two inches tall. Thirty-two years old. Weight 106.

Address. He was standing on it.

Cliff studied her picture, then bent down to get a closer look at the body. The face of the woman lying on the floor was unrecognizable. Beaten to a pulp. Stabbed multiple times. A violent attack.

"Somebody she knew," Cliff muttered. Mostly to himself but loud enough for Strunk to hear.

"Prob'ly," Strunk said. Chicago beat cops rarely pronounced all the syllables of their words. Especially the Italian ones.

Cliff knew everything he needed to know from looking at the body. At least until he got the autopsy and crime lab report. Likely a crime of passion. Probably from a current or former lover. It looked like she'd been raped. She was half dressed. Her clothes ripped off of her. He noticed bruising on her inner thighs.

Signs of a struggle. A lamp was knocked off a table. The carpet on the floor was curled up like she'd tried to run away, and she'd struggled with the assailant on the floor. Several of her manicured nails were broken. Cliff wondered if they'd find DNA under them.

Henry Lee Clay's face flashed into Cliff's mind. He beat it away. Clay's DNA had been found under Tessie's nails. He still got off. Cliff might not ever get over it.

"Who called it in?" Cliff asked.

"A neighbor. Vivian Keller. She heard screams and called 911."

Ms. Keller was likely the woman standing outside with another cop. She'd be the first person he talked to after he looked through the house to see what he could see.

"I want to talk to her," Cliff said, even though it was unnecessary. Strunk nodded.

Cliff walked toward the kitchen which made up one large area along with the living room. A dining room table separated the two rooms along with an island. In these instances, Cliff let his instincts take over. He had no rhyme nor reason when he searched a crime scene. He was led wherever his feet and eyes took him. For some reason, it started him in the kitchen.

Cliff instinctively looked over at the back door which led off the kitchen to the backyard.

"No forced entry," Skunk said, anticipating Cliff's next question. They knew each other well enough to know what the other was thinking most of the time.

"Do I smell spaghetti?" Cliff asked, sticking his nose in the air and breathing in, noticeably.

Strunk was Italian. His nose was as big as a caricature artist at a carnival might draw on a piece of paper.

Strunk breathed in then exhaled. "I smell garlic and basil. Some kind of Italian dish. Not lasagna. Marinara. Probably spaghetti. Reminds me that I haven't had lunch yet."

Working the evening shift, Strunk would take lunch at midnight.

Cliff opened the dishwasher. Steam poured out. Probably one of the last things the victim did on this earth. Load the dishwasher, turn it on, then fight for her life.

"Dang it," Cliff said. "I was hoping those dishes were dirty. Maybe she was entertaining a man. Fingerprints and DNA aren't on the dishes anymore if she did."

"I'll have my men check the trash out back," Strunk said. "Maybe she threw something away that might be helpful. Empty wine bottle if we get lucky. Can't have spaghetti without red wine. You can, but what's the point?"

Cliff nodded and opened the refrigerator door. A bottle of white wine sat in the door. Cliff picked it up and held it up to the light.

"There are fingerprint smudges on this," Cliff said, as he carefully replaced it. "Maybe the murderer brought it for dinner."

"Not if they were having spaghetti. White wine doesn't go with marinara sauce."

"Maybe they don't know the rules for eating Italian cuisine."

"Guyasabbu," Strunk said in his most Italian voice.

Cliff knew from working with him that it meant "who knows" in Italian. Strunk used it often.

The investigative wheels were spinning in Cliff's mind.

Did the victim have a date? A friend over? Most people didn't go to the trouble to make spaghetti and then eat alone.

"Have you been in the bedroom?" Cliff asked. "Anything to see in there?"

"My partner went in there when we cleared the house. I haven't seen it, but he said I needed to. I just hadn't gotten around to it. Follow me Murudda."

"What did you call me?" Cliff asked as they started to walk toward a hallway off the living room.

Strunk had all kinds of nicknames. Italian words he used to describe people when he didn't want them to know what he was saying. Chooch was one he used often. It meant jerk. Scooch meant the same thing. Gidrul meant you were crazy. Disgraziat was his most common. Usually reserved for the perps. It meant dirtbag or scumbag.

Murudda was a new one Cliff hadn't heard before.

Cliff thought he saw a discernible smile on Strunk's face as they turned down the hallway to the back of the house. He didn't tell Cliff what the word meant.

Cliff's mouth flew open when they walked into the bedroom and made him forget about the banter.

"It looks like a tornado hit that bed," Cliff said.

"Maron," Strunk muttered.

An Italian curse word if Cliff remembered correctly.

The bed was in all kinds of disarray. Like two sumo wrestlers had a match on it.

Was this where she was attacked? Then the body moved? Or did she run away into the living room where the killer caught her and killed her?

Was she into rough sex?

A lot of questions flowed through his mind. Considering how clean, neat, and organized the kitchen was, it seemed unlikely Summer Lange wouldn't make her bed in the morning. Something happened in that room. Cliff could feel it.

He could almost feel the man's presence in the room.

Cliff assumed the killer was a he. Based on the nature of the woman's wounds. Deep and violent. Blows struck with power behind them. Unlikely that a woman generated that level of force.

He heard noise coming from the other room. From the sound of it, forensics had arrived.

Cliff went out to greet them and give them instructions.

He wanted to get out of their way. Now seemed like a good time to talk to the neighbor.

Strunk was already off doing other things, so Cliff left the house and went outside. He walked directly toward the older woman standing next to the policeman.

"Are you Ms. Keller?" Cliff asked.

"Mrs. Keller."

"Yes ma'am."

"My husband's passed, but I still go by Mrs. Keller."

"Of course."

Cliff noticed she did have a wedding ring on her finger. An older set. Looked to be antique. They'd probably been married for many years.

Vivian Keller looked to be pushing ninety. A twinge of guilt came over Cliff for making her stand out there that long.

She seemed tired, but so was he. Not weak or feeble though. Not like a woman her age. She was thin and wiry and seemed to have a strong constitution.

He introduced himself.

"Mrs. Keller. My name is Cliff Ford. I'm a senior homicide detective with the Chicago Police department."

Special emphasis on *Mrs.* for her benefit.

"Is Summer dead?" she asked. Her voice cracked as she said it. She looked past him toward the front of the house.

Cliff looked around. No reason to avoid the question. They'd eventually bring Summer Lange's body out of the house in a black bag.

"I'm afraid so. Yes."

He paused to let that sink in.

"I'm told that you're the one who called 911," Cliff said. "Why did you do that?"

"I heard screams."

Cliff's heartbeat accelerated as it usually did when clues started to develop.

"What time was that?"

"At nine-thirty," Mrs. Keller said. Then touched her forehead. "No. Exactly, nine thirty-one."

"How do you know that was the time?"

"I was in bed. I hadn't fallen asleep yet. You know. I watch my shows at night. Then go to bed and read."

"Which house is yours?"

She pointed to the one across the street. It sat up on a hill.

"Where is your bedroom? The front or back of the house?"

"It's in the front. Right over there."

It's possible she could hear screams from that vantage point. They'd have to be really loud, though. Cliff wondered about her hearing considering her age. Was she already looking out the window? Spying on her neighbor?

A nosy neighbor seeking out gossip for the neighborhood pipeline.

"Go on, please," Cliff said. "You said you heard screams."

"That's right. I heard a woman scream and I got up and looked at the clock."

"What did you see?" Cliff asked.

"Nine thirty-one."

"Not on the clock. That's not what I meant. Did you look out your window?"

"Yes. That's what I did. I looked out the window. I heard the screams. Then I looked at the clock. Then I looked out the window."

"Did you see anything?"

This woman might be a problem on the stand if it came to that. Her testimony might be considered unreliable. She had lost some of her cognitive skills which was to be expected.

"I can't believe Summer is dead," Mrs. Keller said instead of answering the question. "She's such a sweet girl. Pretty as a butterfly. I just love her. She brought me stuff. The other day she bring me some peach cobbler. My favorite."

Mrs. Keller dabbed at her eyes. Then wiped them on her sleeves.

"Did you see Ms. Lange when you looked out the window?" Cliff asked.

"No. I don't believe I did. All I saw was her porch light on and lights on in her house. I didn't see her."

"Did you see anyone else? Anyone leaving the house."

"No sir."

Cliff's heart sank a little. Mrs. Keller didn't know much. She'd never be called to the stand. Maybe to establish the time of death. That's about it. So she heard screams. Didn't mean anything if she didn't see anything. Summer Lange probably did scream at the top of her lungs. Somebody had violently attacked her.

"Thank you, Mrs. Keller, for your time. You can go home now."

He didn't bother getting her phone number. He knew where she lived and could probably look it up.

As Cliff was walking away, Mrs. Keller said, "I saw a car."

Cliff stopped in his tracks and was back to her side immediately.

"When did you see a car?"

"Earlier this evening."

"What time?"

"About seven thirty."

"What kind of car?"

"One of those fancy ones."

"Big or little?"

"A little one."

"A sports car?" Cliff asked.

"Yeah."

"What color was it?"

"Red."

Cliff did get her phone number.

4

Cliff sent George Strunk to notify Summer Lange's family that she was deceased and to ask them to meet him at the station at nine.

He fell into bed around three in the morning. Utterly exhausted. Crime scenes took a lot out of him. Some detectives were as stone cold as the Great Wall of China. No emotion whatsoever. They were like robots. Incapable of feeling anything other than the normal frustrations of a job.

Even after all these years, Cliff couldn't turn his emotions on and off. He was concerned that if he did turn them off to the tragedies he saw everyday in his job, he'd eventually shut down the feelings he had for Julia and his daughter, Rita. The staff shrink said he should learn to compartmentalize. He didn't know how to do that.

So, he decided a long time ago that he wouldn't. He'd rather feel the sadness and empathy for the victim, than risk becoming a disengaged and aloof husband. Those people became uncaring. Turned to alcohol or drugs to mask their real feelings. The divorce rate for homicide detectives was twice the national average.

Cliff wanted to stay as normal a person as possible. No small task considering the nature of his business.

Those emotions for Summer were what propelled him to find the killer anyway. He drew on them. Summer's face reminded him every day to do his job.

She was someone's daughter. Sister. Friend. Those people were feeling tremendous grief at that moment. And they were counting on him.

Cliff was the only one between Summer and justice. He was tasked to find the killer. The only person in Chicago P.D. with that assignment. If he didn't come through, the killer went free. He had no way of relieving himself of that burden other than by doing the best job possible. Caring about the victim. Practically obsessed with leaving no stone unturned to find her killer.

Those thoughts left him with many sleepless nights.

Since he couldn't sleep, Cliff was up early. The crime scene scenarios were already playing out in his mind like a movie on the television.

The killer knew the victim. Violent crime scene. Probable rape. Crime of passion. All precaution was thrown to the wind by the killer. Red sports car seen leaving the scene around the time of the murder.

He'd bet his house it belonged to the killer.

Cliff expected to find a treasure trove of information in the forensics. Fingerprints. DNA. Fibers. Evidence of sexual assault. This case would likely be solved by the physical evidence and autopsy. It'd take a couple of days to get those results.

Most people were killed by someone they knew. Most women by a boyfriend, husband, or ex. Occasionally by a third party in a love triangle. The odds were that Cliff could narrow the suspect pool within hours of investigating.

Hopefully, Summer's parents or friends would shed light on who might've done it and he could solve the murder before the test results were completed. Cliff already had a picture of the man in his mind. Now he only needed a face to put with the faceless figure.

Only a matter of time. Cliff was optimistic this murder would be solved quickly.

He showered and went to fix himself some breakfast. His wife Julia was a step ahead of him. Often the case when he had a late night. She stood over the stove frying eggs. They'd be over medium. The way he liked them. Two pieces of sourdough toast were already on a plate sitting on the counter. Grape jelly was on the table. Along with a glass of iced tea.

Julia knew him well.

"Good morning, honey," he said as he kissed her on the cheek and gave her an affectionate squeeze of her arm.

Rita must still be asleep. Julia would get her up soon and ready for school. She was in a summer preschool program. She'd be starting kindergarten in the fall.

It warmed Cliff's heart that Julia wanted to make sure he was fed first. Before she did anything else.

"Late night last night?" Julia said or asked. Could be perceived either way. "I heard you come in."

"I'm sorry if I woke you."

"You know I'm a light sleeper. Don't worry about it. I went right back to sleep."

Julia began to stir the eggs vigorously. Occasionally, she made him scrambled eggs instead of fried. When the yokes broke, or she had overcooked them.

"I wish I had been able to go back to sleep," Cliff said. "These late-night murders are the worst. I can't sleep after going over a crime scene."

"You know what they say," Julia said, with her head down and her arm beating feverishly. The eggs looked almost done.

"It's like sitting in traffic because of a car wreck," she continued. "It could be worse. You could be the one in the car. In this case, the one murdered."

Cliff nodded. "I'd rather be the investigator than the victim any day of the week," he said.

"That's my point. Who's the unlucky victim?"

"Woman. In her thirties."

Julia let out a slight groan. Cliff didn't mention that Summer was about her age.

"Probably raped," Cliff added soberly. "Stabbed a hundred times."

Julia looked up from what she was doing on the stove.

"Not a hundred," Cliff said. "But a lot. Maybe a hundred."

"Any forced entry?"

"Nope."

"Someone she knew," Julia said. "Current or ex."

"Yep."

Julia could be a detective. Her instincts were that good. Although, it didn't take a rocket scientist to know the killer was likely a current or former love interest. Strangers only accounted for sixteen percent of female homicides in Chicago last year.

"Was she pretty?" Julia asked.

"Hard to know since she was beaten to a pulp."

Julia glanced his way and grimaced.

His wife was so beautiful. He couldn't imagine someone doing that to his wife.

From the driver's license, Summer was beautiful as well. Not stunningly gorgeous like Julia, but pretty in her own way. Julia was Cuban and had jet-black hair and dark features. Eyes that were penetrating. A hot body considering she'd had a baby.

"Yeah, she's pretty," Cliff said. "I saw her driver's license."

"Poor girl. Why do the pretty ones always get involved with the wrong guys?'

"You're a pretty one."

"My point exactly."

Cliff chuckled.

"I'm kidding," she said. "Kind of like a car wreck. I'd rather be dating the investigator than the murderer."

"Dating?" Cliff said with a huge smile on his face. "Do I need to remind you that we've been married for seven years? As of next Friday."

"Next Thursday."

Cliff did the calculations in his head. It was Thursday.

"We're celebrating on Friday," Julia said. "That's why you're confused. Thanks for the effort though."

"You're welcome."

Julia scooped the eggs onto his plate. Then handed it to him after she set the pan back on the stove.

"Seven years," Cliff said in a playful manner. "Seems like thirty."

"I don't know if I should be offended by that comment."

"No, ma'am, I meant it in a good way. What I meant to say is that I don't remember my life without you."

"That's sweet. I don't want you getting the itch."

"What itch?"

"The seven-year-itch."

"What's that?"

"More couples get a divorce at year seven than any other year."

"I didn't know that."

"Look it up. It's a fact."

"I don't have any itches," Cliff said.

"Good to know."

"You're stuck with me."

"If you get any itches, let me know. I'll scratch them."

Cliff laughed out loud.

"Every once in a while, I get itches between my toes. You know. Athlete's foot."

"Eww. You're gross."

"I'm just saying."

"You know I don't touch feet."

"How did this conversation get so far off the rails?"

"I don't know."

"What were we talking about before the banter turned to disgusting chatter?"

"The dead girl was stabbed a hundred times by her boyfriend," Julia said.

"We really need some new conversation topics," Cliff said as he walked over to the table and sat down to eat his eggs before they got cold.

"Why don't we talk about things normal people talk about? Like, what's the weather going to be like today? What's for dinner tonight? How is our daughter doing in school?"

"We were talking about picking the wrong men," Julia said.

His mouth was full, so she continued.

"Not me. I got a good man and I intend to keep him."

She sat down in the chair next to him.

"But, I do see it all the time at the shelter. These girls keep picking the wrong men. We help get them out of a bad relationship, and they go right back into another one in no time."

"Or back in the same one," Cliff said.

"Right. I don't know which is worse."

Julia was the director of a women's shelter. She worked with battered and abused women and young girls. She was experienced in what Cliff encountered the night before. Maybe not murder. But she'd seen her share of women beaten to within an inch of their lives.

If Cliff didn't solve the case right away, he might run the facts by her. Julia had often helped him with cases. He sometimes picked her brain. More often than not, she had incredible insight that helped him solve his cases.

He probably didn't need her on this one. His instinct told him he'd have the case solved before the day was over. Within forty-eight hours for sure.

Julia kissed Cliff on the forehead and left the room to get Rita up and ready for school. With his thanks.

An easy case to solve.

Even Julia knew Summer Lange likely had a romantic connection with the murderer. Either a current boyfriend or ex-boyfriend. Cliff scarfed down his breakfast. He wanted to get to the station early and prepare for the interview with the parents.

Hopefully, they'd know who their daughter was dating.

***

Except for the red eyes and the tissues she clutched in her hands, Mrs. Lange could be going to a business meeting. Not an interview in a cold and sterile police station interrogation room.

Mr. Lange was in a dark suit, wearing a red tie. Cufflinks. Polished black shoes. Not a hair out of place.

Cliff had on a black suit with a blue tie. He wore blue when he met with the victim's family. Red if he was interrogating a suspect. Blue conveyed warmth. Red gave out an intimidation and power vibe. He'd read that once. He wasn't sure if it worked, but he'd take every advantage he could get.

Mrs. Lange wore a navy blue business pantsuit, with an off-white blouse and multi-colored scarf. Her hair was dark and clearly coiffed by a professional. Her nails and eyelashes had been recently done.

The power couple appeared to be in their early fifties.

Mr. Lange stood when Cliff entered and extended his hand. Cliff shook it matching his firm grip. Mrs. Lange made no motion toward him and Cliff did nothing but acknowledge her with a nod of the head and a faint smile.

"My name is Cliff Ford. I'm a senior homicide detective for the Chicago P.D."

Mrs. Lange dabbed at her eye with the tissue when Cliff mentioned the word homicide.

"I will be investigating your daughter's death. Let me start by saying that I'm very sorry for your loss."

Cliff was a no-nonsense investigator and came across as such. Julia had been trying to get him to exude more warmth. It didn't come naturally for him. The sadness and anger he felt inside each time a new murder came across his desk rarely made it to the surface. If his demeanor couldn't express his sympathy, at least his words could.

Maybe he did compartmentalize to some extent. At least he controlled what others saw from him in the way of emotions.

"Thank you, detective," Mr. Lange said. "What can you tell us about our daughter's death? The police sergeant didn't give us much information."

Mr. Lange spoke with a slight Asian accent. With perfect diction. This was a man of substance.

Cliff liked Mr. Lange immediately. He was calm and in control. Obviously stunned, but not abrasive or demanding at all. Some family members demanded answers immediately and became belligerent if information wasn't forthcoming.

Sometimes Cliff didn't know the answers to their questions. Other times, he didn't want to say for investigative reasons. Mr. Lange appeared to be giving Cliff the benefit of the doubt for now.

It made things easier for Cliff.

"I will tell you what I know," Cliff said. "I'm treating your daughter's death as a homicide. Her body was discovered last night around ten o'clock. When was the last time you spoke to your daughter?"

Mrs. Lange answered. "I spoke to her yesterday. She was at work.

"Where did Ms. Lange work?" Cliff asked.

"She works at a law firm. Downtown. As a paralegal."

Cliff asked for the name of the firm and was given it. He didn't sense the slightest bit of hesitancy on their part. They were going to be forthcoming. At least it appeared that way.

Cliff was familiar with the firm. Big firm corporate litigators. To his knowledge, they didn't handle criminal cases. The thought occurred to Cliff that the murder could be related to a disgruntled client at the firm. Not likely, once he knew the name of the law firm.

"Did your daughter seem distressed at all?" Cliff asked.

"No," Mrs. Lange said. "She seemed normal to me. A little stressed work wise. But she was normally that way when I called her at work."

"Did she seem concerned about anything? Has she spoken to you recently about something that might be troubling her?"

"No," Mrs. Lange said.

Cliff didn't like asking yes or no questions. He preferred open-ended questions which gave the person an opportunity to elaborate. He'd hoped Mrs. Lange would do so without prompting. So far, she was holding herself together pretty well, but not filling in the blanks. Maybe rapid-fire questions would be more effective.

"Did she have any financial problems?"

"Oh. I don't think so," Mr. Lange said. "She had a good job. We taught our daughter how to handle her money."

"Have you noticed a change in her behavior? Something different in her routine?"

"No."

"Did she have a boyfriend?"

"No."

"Would she have told you if she did?"

"I think so. I don't believe she was seeing anyone at this time."

"Do you know of anyone who might have a reason to kill your daughter?"

"There is one person," Mrs. Lange said.

Cliff felt his eyebrow raise.

"Who's that?"

"Summer has an ex-boyfriend."

Cliff felt his heart jump in his chest.

"Do you know his name?"

"Wayne Bowman."

"Tell me about him."

Good question. Not closed ended. She'd have to elaborate. Cliff sat forward in his seat. He hadn't opened his black book yet, but it was on the table in front of him along with a pen.

"My husband and I didn't approve of the man," Mrs. Lange said.

"We only met him once," Mr. Lange interrupted. "I stopped by my daughter's house one afternoon. Dropped in unexpectedly. He was there."

"We didn't make a big deal about it," Mrs. Lange said. "You know. We didn't want to drive her further into his arms by forbidding her to see him."

"And she's an adult," Mr. Lange said. "We had to trust that she'd come to her senses. And she did."

"Can you describe him to me?"

Mr. Lange answered. "He's a rather large man. Disheveled. Ragged beard and long hair. Tattoos on his arms. Not the kind of man my daughter usually dated."

"She didn't date him for very long," Mrs. Lange said defensively. Like she was defending her daughter.

"When was this?" Cliff asked.

"About six months ago," Mrs. Lange said. "That's when they broke up."

"Why do you think he might have a reason to kill your daughter?"

"My daughter was afraid of him," Mr. Lange said. "I could see it the day I came to her place."

"He was violent with her one time," Mrs. Lange said. "She eventually confided in me. After she broke up with him. But I already knew. I could tell."

"What do you mean by violent?" Cliff asked. "Did he hit her?"

"I don't know. They got into a huge argument when she broke up with him. She told him to leave, but he wouldn't. She threatened to call the police and he left. But he broke one of her pictures. Threw it on the floor."

"Did she ever call the police?"

"I don't think so. But he showed up at her work once. Not at her work, but in the parking garage. She got away from him as fast as she could."

"The man was stalking her for a while," Mr. Lange said. "To my knowledge, she never let him back into her life."

"What kind of car does Mr. Bowman drive?"

"I don't know," Mr. Lange said. "I've never seen it."

Mrs. Lange nodded in agreement.

Cliff questioned them for twenty more minutes.

"Can we see our daughter?" Mr. Lange asked.

"Not at this time," Cliff said. "I'm sorry. The coroner is still examining the body. When he's done, she'll be released to you."

Summer's bruised and battered face popped into Cliff's head. He couldn't keep them from seeing their daughter, but he'd strongly discourage it. At least not until a funeral home had a chance to work on her. Even then, the funeral director would probably recommend a closed casket.

No reason to share with them that information at this time.

Mrs. Lange's eyes began to water more heavily. She dabbed at them. Mr. Lange had a somber look on his face. His shoulders had drooped. The confidence he'd entered the room with had taken a hit.

Cliff could feel their pain.

"If you think of anything else, please give me a call," Cliff said, standing, then handing Mr. Lange one of his cards.

Cliff wasn't good at expressing warmth, but he was good at bravado. Reassuring families. So he said, "Mr. and Mrs. Lange, I want to assure you that I will do everything in my power to find out who did this to your daughter and bring him to justice. You have my word on that."

"Thank you. Please find... our daughter's killer," Mr. Lange said. His voice cracked for the first time.

"I will."

They walked out of the room.

Maybe Cliff already had found the killer. Wayne Bowman seemed like a prime suspect. Former boyfriend. Proclivity toward violence.

Stalker.

Cliff intended to pay him a visit.

First thing.

5

Tracking down Wayne Bowman was harder than Cliff had expected it to be. He went to the usual sources first. Bowman had no criminal record other than an assault charge which was dropped after the victim refused to press charges. According to the police report, Bowman got into an altercation with a man at a bar over an unnamed girl.

Summer?

According to witnesses, both of the combatants were equally at fault in starting the fight. Bowman was arrested because he was the better fighter and the bigger man. He broke the other man's nose and threatened him with a broken beer bottle.

Bowman spent the night in jail, made the thousand dollars in bail the next morning and pled not guilty when arraigned. That's as far as it got. A note in the file said he paid the bar a few hundred dollars for the damages.

He also had a record as a juvenile, but those files were sealed. Cliff found his driver's license and an address. He went by there, but Bowman had moved a couple of years before. No one had a forwarding address.

Something about the picture wasn't making sense anyway. Based on the neighborhood and residence, Bowman didn't appear to have the wherewithal to own a fancy sports car. Unless he somehow came into money after he moved.

According to Summer's parents, Bowman worked as a mechanic at a local grease pit in Cicero. They didn't know the name. Cliff went to three garages until he found someone who knew him.

Bowman hadn't worked there for several months. They had an address, but Cliff had already been by there. He did take the opportunity to interview the man who knew Bowman.

"What kind of car did he drive?" Cliff asked.

The most pressing question. He felt like the red sports car was the key to cracking the case.

"He didn't drive a car. He rode a motorcycle. A souped-up Harley Davidson Fatboy. Raised handlebars. Nice ride."

Cliff could barely hide the disappointment. The old woman who heard Summer scream and saw the sport's car wasn't totally reliable. Maybe she mistook a sedan for a sports car. A jacked-up Harley, on the other hand, could never be confused for a sleek sports car.

"Did he ever own a sports car?" Cliff asked.

The manager chuckled. "Bowman wouldn't be caught dead in a wine car."

"What's a wine car?"

"A car a preppie boy drives. That's what Bowman called them."

"You work on sports cars here," Cliff said. "So Bowman obviously knew his way around one."

"Yeah. But he made fun of 'em all the time. I can't see him ever owning one."

"What about in the wintertime? Can't ride a bike in the snow."

Cliff had a motorcycle before he met Julia. A good way to navigate traffic in Chicago. When they got married and she became pregnant with Rita, he agreed to sell it. Too dangerous. His work was dangerous enough. Julia didn't want to worry about him dying in a motorcycle crash, so he reluctantly sold it. Now he was glad. He preferred his Volvo SUV.

"Tiny owned a van," the man said. "White. Souped up as well. He liked to take older rides and restore them."

Cliff had seen a white van in the DMV records. He had the license plate but no valid address. He didn't put out an APB, an All Points Bulletin, on Bowman and the van, because he didn't have enough to go on. Probable cause was required. Which meant more evidence than Bowman dated Summer six months ago.

"Did you call him Tiny?" Cliff asked.

"Yeah. We called him that. Not to his face. The man is a giant."

The driver's license said six foot four, two hundred and eighty pounds. Big enough to do serious damage to a hundred-and-six pound female.

"Did Bowman ever show any violent tendencies?"

"Oh yeah. You didn't want to mess with Tiny. He'll knock your block off if you cross him. Don't get me wrong. The dude was as gentle as a kitten if he liked you. In fact, he had a soft heart for animals and kids. A stray showed up at the shop one day. Tiny took him. Fed him and nursed him back to health. Like I said, he was a softy. But if you made him mad, look out."

"Did you ever see him strike anyone?"

"Nah. He threw some tools around. He got in a guy's face one time. One of my employees. I thought they were going to come to blows. But the men in my shop knew better than to get in a fight with Tiny. So nothin' came of it."

"Have you ever seen this girl?" Cliff asked, as he shoved a picture of Summer in his face.

He looked it over.

"Nope. Never seen her before in my life."

"Did Tiny have any girlfriends?"

"Not that I know of. I'm sure he did. He was a hound. Like most of us single guys."

"You ever go to a bar with him?"

"A few times after work. For a beer."

"Did you ever see him talking to other women?"

"Yeah, man. Of course. I suppose. Why not? Not that girl, though. I'd remember her if I'd seen her before. She's a looker. You don't see girls like that at the bars Tiny and I go to. More biker chicks."

Like Julia pointed out, sometimes girls went for the bad guys. It didn't make sense. Wayne Bowman certainly didn't seem like Summer's type. Maybe Summer was going through a "sow your wild oats" phase. Apparently, she came to her senses and dropped Bowman before it became too serious.

Not soon enough, obviously, since Bowman didn't take it well and started stalking her.

Cliff was beginning to think this was a dead end anyway. Bowman didn't drive a sports car. Didn't have a known address or a job. As far as Cliff knew, he could've left the area months ago.

Cliff handed the man his card. "Call me if you think of anything or if you hear from him."

The mechanic stuck the card in his pocket. Cliff figured the card would be in the trash can before he was out of the parking lot.

"Was Mr. Bowman a good mechanic?" Cliff asked.

"The best."

"So, you'd hire him back?"

"In a second."

"Thank you. You've been helpful."

Cliff got in his car and left. He had one more lead to follow up on. Bowman had gotten a speeding ticket eighteen months before. The officer listed a different address on the ticket. Since it wasn't on any of the public records, Bowman must've given it to him.

As Cliff was driving to the location, his wife Julia called.

"Hi honey," he answered.

"Are you busy?"

"Sort of. I'm running down some leads. But I'm good. I'm in the car driving to my next stop. So, I've got a few minutes. What's up?"

"We've got a problem."

"What kind of problem? Animal, vegetable, or mineral?"

Julia laughed. Cliff wasn't even sure why those words had come out of his mouth.

"Definitely animal," she said. "Since it involves your daughter Rita."

Julia's tone was casual, so Cliff tamped down any concern that had tried to rear its ugly head. When someone at work called and said,

"We've got a problem," it meant that a witness was dead. Or a suspect had fled the area. Something that really was a problem.

Whatever problem Rita was having was probably related to her smart mouth. Which she got from her sassy mother.

"I got a call from Rita's preschool principal."

"Really?" Cliff said. His heart rate ticked up slightly. "Is she okay?"

"Yes. Sorry. I guess that came out wrong."

"Don't give me a heart attack."

"No. Nothing like that. The principal wants to meet with us."

"Did she say why?"

"No. I told her I could meet with her when I pick Rita up. Can you make it? I'm heading that way soon."

"I'm running some leads on that murder case I was telling you about."

"Don't worry about it. I can handle it."

"No. I'll be there. Unless something comes up. I'm curious now."

"Me too. She wouldn't say, but it sounded serious. Like Rita was in trouble or something."

"If she is, it's your fault."

"Ha. Ha. Very funny."

"If I don't make it, go ahead without me. I'll be there if I can."

"Go arrest a bad guy."

"I'm trying. Love you."

"Kiss. Kiss."

The drive took about fifteen minutes with moderate traffic. The house was in another rough neighborhood. Cliff parked in front of the two-story wooden structure that needed several coats of paint and some landscaping.

He got out of his car and looked around. For whatever reason, he touched the gun on his hip for reassurance.

The driveway was filled with cracks. The number of blades of grass on the dried and barren ground could be counted without a calculator.

The step leading to the porch was nothing more than a couple of concrete blocks. The porch itself had a number of loose boards.

If Bowman had a sports car, it was worth more than the house.

A white van was parked in the driveway. No sign of the motorcycle. A quick check confirmed that the plates on the van matched the information Cliff pulled from the DMV. It looked like he might have finally found Wayne Bowman.

Cliff stepped up on the porch cautiously. He rapped loudly on the door. Probably shouldn't hit it too hard or it'd fall in. He listened carefully for any signs of life coming from inside.

When he heard nothing, he knocked again and waited.

Looking inside the windows wasn't an option. Even walking around to the back was a stretch. He could do so if he wanted but didn't want to step on a rusty nail or trip over some junk. It wasn't worth it at this point. Cliff didn't get the feeling that Bowman was his man.

As Cliff exited the porch, a man across the street caught his eye. He was outside watering his lawn with a water hose. That house was out of place. It really did have a lawn. The nicest in the neighborhood.

The house was freshly painted. The lush green lawn was accented with various colorful plants. A striking contrast compared to the barren ground Cliff had to walk across to get back to the street where he could cross to the other side.

Cliff flashed a smile and then his credentials when he approached the man. "Good afternoon," he said in his most friendly voice. "My name's Cliff Ford. Chicago P.D."

"Are you finally going to give him a ticket?" the man said abruptly. Pointing at what Cliff presumed was Wayne Bowman's house.

"A ticket? I'm not following you."

"Are you a cop?"

"I'm a detective with the Chicago P.D."

"It's about time you showed up. I've called you guys a dozen times. This is the first time anybody's come."

Cliff's curiosity was piqued. Why did the man call the police? Had Bowman threatened him? Why would Cliff write Bowman a ticket for a neighborhood dispute?

Cliff needed more information. "Do you know the man who lives across the street?" he asked.

"Yeah. I know him. He's a loser. Wayne Bowman's his name. You should already have it. I gave the name to the 911 operator."

The man's tone bordered on belligerent.

Cliff took out his black book to make it look official. He'd humor the man. He wasn't there regarding any 911 call, but the man clearly had a story to tell and Cliff wanted to hear it.

"Why did you call 911?"

The man let out a huge groan of disgust. "You should already know. I told the 911 people."

"I didn't get that information. Can you repeat it?"

"Isn't it obvious?"

It wasn't.

"Humor me. I'd like to hear it from you."

The man pointed across the street. "Look at his yard. He's got junk in the back and his yard is an eyesore. It's bringing down the value of the whole neighborhood."

Cliff wanted to rub his eyes roughly. This obviously didn't involve violence. Cliff was getting frustrated. Bowman was probably a dead end. The guy standing in front of him was obviously a jerk.

So, he took a more serious tone with the man. "Are you telling me that you called 911 to complain about Mr. Bowman's yard?"

"Dang right I did. Something's got to be done about it, don't you think? Are you going to write him a ticket and give him a big fine?"

"I'm thinking about it."

He tried to say it with a straight face. Cliff wasn't aware of any basis for writing a ticket but wanted to humor the man. He needed to get more meaningful information or get in his car and leave.

"Has Mr. Bowman threatened you in any way?" Cliff asked.

The man waved his water hose in the air dismissively. Almost spraying water on Cliff's shoes.

"Nah. I ain't scared of him. He's as big as a bull, but I'm pretty tough myself."

"I don't suggest you confront him personally."

From what Cliff knew of Wayne Bowman, he could snap the man standing in front of him like a twig. The skinny guy was a hundred forty pounds if Cliff watered him down with the hose for ten minutes.

"Is Mr. Bowman home?" Cliff asked.

The man peered around Cliff.

"I ain't seeing his motorbike. He drives one of them loud Harleys. I called you guys about that too. It makes the dangdest sound when he drives by. At all hours of the night."

"Did you hear the motorcycle last night?"

"No."

"Do you know if the white van was in the driveway last night, around nine or nine thirty?"

"I go to bed before that. I didn't hear nothin'."

"Have you seen this woman?"

Cliff showed him a picture of Summer. His eyes widened. Not in recognition, but more in a pleasurable way.

"Never seen her before in my life."

Cliff wasn't surprised. She doubted a woman like Summer frequented this part of town. Nothing about this scene made sense. If she had dated Bowman, it was an unlikely match. Cliff could see why it had ended quickly.

"Have you ever seen a red sports car at the house?" Cliff asked, even though he knew the answer.

"You mean like one of them fancy Porsch."

The man didn't pronounce the e at the end. He said Porsch. A common mistake to the unknowledgeable.

"Yeah. I mean something like that. Red color."

"Nah. Ain't nobody around here drives one of those except the drug dealers."

"What's your name, sir?" Cliff asked.

"Walter Mooney. You can call me Walt."

Cliff got his phone number and wrote his address in the book beside his name.

"Don't call 911 anymore about the yard, Mr. Mooney," Cliff said sternly. "911 is for real emergencies. The state of Mr. Bowman's yard is not an emergency. Calls like yours get tossed to the side."

Cliff was surprised a police officer hadn't shown up to warn Mr. Mooney. Frivolous 911 calls were against the law. Fines of up to a thousand dollars if Cliff remembered right.

Mr. Mooney seemed agitated.

"You worthless piece of..." Mooney muttered the rest of the sentence under his breath so it was unintelligible.

Cliff had better leave or he might say something he'd regret. He thanked Mr. Mooney, even though it was for nothing. Then walked back across the street.

He stood by his car with his hand on the hood and stared at the white van. He decided to walk over and give it a once over.

His phone dinged before he could. He looked down at the screen. The message was from Julia.

Headed to the school.

He got in his car and started it.

On my way. See you soon. I wonder what the principal wants?

Me, too, Julia responded.

***

Wayne Bowman watched the four-door government issued undercover police car drive up. The man in the suit looked like a detective. He watched him from an upstairs window. Behind a curtain.

The man pounded on the door and woke him up from a deep sleep. Once Wayne got his bearings, that's when he had looked out the window and saw the vehicle.

Wayne thought he was going to jump out of his skin.

He hadn't had a chance to clean the blood out of the van.

Summer's blood.

He'd gotten it all over him the night before. He had to kill her. If he couldn't have her, no one could.

He had decided not to answer the door. The cop didn't have anything. Otherwise, he'd have a swarm of cops with him. He was there to question him.

Mr. and Mrs. Lange!

Thinking of them sent a bolt of rage through him. Summer's parents probably told the detective about him. They never did like him. If not for them, Summer would've never broken up with him.

Started dating that rich punk. In the red sports car.

Bowman intended to kill him next.

He was torn. Confused about what to do. If he answered the door, the cop might ask to search his premises. This wasn't his first brush with the law. He knew how it worked.

If he didn't answer, the cop might search around the van. Look through the windows. If he saw the blood, then he'd call it in.

Bowman was screwed. He'd have to get out of there.

He put on his shoes and got his gun off the end table by the side of his bed.

Checked to make sure a bullet was in the chamber.

He'd kill a cop if he had to.

He took another look.

The cop was standing by his car. Looking toward the van. Without warning, the cop got in his car and drove away.

Bowman let out a huge sigh of relief.

That was a close call.

He'd better do something about that van before the cop returned.

Then decided to wait. He might need the van. After he killed the man in the red sports car, there might be more blood.

No use cleaning it twice.

6

When Cliff walked into the principal's office at Rita's school, his daughter and wife were already there sitting in the lobby. The door with the principal's name on it was closed. A receptionist and her desk provided a barrier between the lobby area and that door.

Rita saw him and jumped out of her chair and ran into his arms. He smothered her neck with kisses causing her to laugh loudly. Cliff tried to quiet her. He wasn't sure of the proper etiquette in a principal's office. Even though he'd been there a time or two back in the day.

Usually when he got into trouble. He looked at his daughter. He wasn't one of those fathers who thought his daughter could do no wrong, but he wasn't sure what she could've done that required this big production.

What was so important that it couldn't wait? He had to take time off from a murder investigation to be there.

Was she talking too much in class? He expected that from Rita. She was social and verbal like her mother.

Was she chewing gum?

Did she beat up one of the boys?

That thought almost made him laugh. Julia had insisted that Rita start a judo class the year before. She'd argued that they couldn't start too early. Not in today's world.

The kids mostly stood around in huge pads staring at each other. Everybody but Rita, who was the most aggressive. After the class, Cliff emphasized the importance of fighting only for self-defense.

That's probably what it was. Rita probably made a boy cry.

Julia smiled at Cliff warmly, but nervously. She was obviously still worried about the upcoming meeting.

Cliff was more curious than worried.

Rita might not even be in trouble. His daughter had mentioned a show and tell at school. She wanted Cliff to come and tell the other kids about his job. The principal probably wanted to discuss a date.

"Ms. Harrell," Julia said, speaking to the receptionist, "this is my husband, Cliff."

She nodded semi warmly.

"It's a pleasure to meet you," Cliff said.

"Look at my picture, daddy," Rita said. She was at his feet again with a colored picture in her hand.

He squatted down and looked at it.

"This is beautiful, honey. Look at you. Coloring between the lines."

She had done a good job. Better than he did at that age, although he didn't remember if they even had kindergarten when he was growing up. He did remember coloring. Mostly scribbling outside the lines. Artistic expression wasn't one of his strong suits.

He complimented her again. Effusively. Rita threw her arms around his neck a second time.

"We'll put it on the wall in your art gallery," Cliff said.

They had a place where they hung up her drawings. This would be added to the collection.

The door to the principal's office opened and a woman appeared. Pushing sixty. Shoulder length highlighted blonde or slightly gray hair. The lady wore business attire. Slacks and jacket with a tie hanging halfway down her shirt.

Similar to what Cliff was wearing except his tie was snug around his neck. Seeing her tie made him want to loosen his.

Julia stood, but Cliff made sure he was the first to greet the principal

"Cliff Ford," he said. "I'm Rita's father. This is my wife, Julia."

"We've met," Julia said. "When Rita first enrolled in your school."

The woman bowed her head slightly.

"I'm Debra McVade," she said in a businesslike voice and with her hand outstretched. Cliff was holding Rita's hand, so he released it and shook the woman's firmer than expected handshake.

He matched her firm grip. The woman scowled at him slightly. At least that's how he interpreted the glare.

Cliff wondered if this was how he came across. Cold but professional. Aloof.

Ms. McVade bent over slightly and said, "Rita, honey, you wait out here while I talk to your mommy and daddy."

"She can't come in with us?" Julia asked.

"I think it's better that we have this discussion in private. Ms. Harrell will watch her."

"I want to come with you, daddy," Rita said, clutching his leg.

Cliff lifted Rita up and held her. She was getting heavier by the day. At some point, he wouldn't be able to do this.

He didn't understand. Why couldn't his daughter be in there with them? What was so serious that they couldn't discuss it in front of his daughter.

This was a tactic Cliff used with suspects. Put them in separate rooms so they didn't hear what the other was saying.

The thought almost made him laugh out loud.

He turned his attention toward Rita so the principal wouldn't think he was laughing at her.

"We'll only be a few minutes, honey," Cliff said to Rita.

She let out a whiney groan.

"How about we stop and get ice cream on the way home?" Cliff said.

Julia glared at Cliff.

"Or maybe we'll go get a pizza. Then ice cream," he quickly added.

"Perhaps you can discuss it later," the principal said.

Hey!

What business was it of hers? Did she think her time was more valuable than his? He was trying to solve a murder. What major problem had the principal solved today? Finding Joey's missing retainer?

Cliff almost laughed again. He didn't know if the school had a Joey. The thought had just popped into his head as fast as a burp. Fortunately, it didn't come out of his mouth.

Still, he didn't like this woman and hadn't known her for more than two minutes.

She seemed genuinely upset with them.

Why?

He really wanted to know.

Ms. Harrell took Rita from Cliff and sat her on the chair where she'd been sitting next to Julia. The woman had a piece of paper and some crayons in her hand.

That made Cliff mad.

What was protocol? Who had authority in the office? The parent or the principal. Cliff had half a mind to push back, and demand Rita go in the room with them. Then thought better of it. Perhaps the principal felt the need to speak freely. If she wanted that right, Cliff wanted it too.

The principal waved her hand in the air as a gesture for Cliff and Julia to enter her office. Cliff entered after Julia and before the principal who closed the door behind them.

"Thank you, for meeting with me on such short notice," the principal said in a matter-of-fact tone. A ceramic frog on the floor had more warmth to it.

She sat down behind her neat desk. Every paper was in place. Cliff and Julia sat across in uncomfortable side chairs next to each other.

He considered reaching over and touching Julia's hand as a show of affection and solidarity. Then decided against it. Julia's hands were in her lap. She was wringing them. Her jaw was clenched. Cliff had seen his wife like this before. She didn't appreciate the principal's demeanor or tone either but was controlling herself.

Cliff wasn't angry. Not yet. More amused than anything. He tried to lighten the mood.

"Rita tells me that you're having a show and tell. She wants me to come and address the kids. I'd be happy to. Let me know a good date and I'll work it into my schedule."

"I don't think that's going to be possible," the principal said.

"Oh. Why not?"

"My understanding is that you're in law enforcement."

"That's right," Cliff said proudly. "I'm a detective with the Chicago Police Department."

He left out the homicide part. Some people were creeped out by it. Or intimidated.

"I don't think that'd be appropriate for young children."

Cliff didn't understand.

"Oh," he suddenly realized something. "You don't want me to have a gun in your classroom. I can understand that."

"It's not just that. We make it a policy not to promote violence in our classroom."

"I don't understand. My job is to protect the public from violence. Not promote it. We stop bad people from doing bad things."

"That's not a message we want to send to our children. They'll get confused. I'm concerned about the safety of the children. Some kids are afraid of the police. If you come to our classroom, it might frighten them."

"All the more reason why I should speak to them," Cliff said. "To show them that they don't need to be afraid of the police."

"Some police are the bad ones."

What was happening here?

Was the woman purposefully trying to get a rise out of Cliff? To offend him. She was getting close to doing so.

"There are some bad apples," Cliff said. "That's true with every profession. I arrested a dentist for murder the other day. Are you comfortable letting dentists speak to the kids? Most kids are afraid of dentists."

If she was going to be confrontive, Cliff would match her tone.

"You're missing my point," she said. "A powerful and corrupt police state is oppressive to a civilized society. I will not allow that to be promoted on my watch."

Cliff could feel his blood boiling up inside of him.

"Sounds like you're more concerned about your agenda than safety," Cliff said. "Let a school shooter walk through your doors and I bet we'll be the first ones you call."

The principal opened her mouth to respond.

"Is this really what we were called here to discuss?" Julia said roughly, interrupting her before she could get any words out.

"No, it wasn't," the principal said, giving Cliff a glare out of the side of her hate-filled eyes.

This woman obviously had a bias against the police. He'd heard about it in the schools but hadn't seen it firsthand. He certainly didn't expect to see it in a preschool.

"Why did you want to see us?" Julia asked in a calmer tone. Obviously, trying to diffuse the situation.

Good idea. The last thing Cliff wanted was to get into a philosophical debate.

"We're seeing troubling behavioral problems in your daughter," the principal said. "She's a real troublemaker."

Cliff about jumped out of his chair. His defenses were already at the surface. It was one thing to offend him, but he wasn't going to let this woman slap a label on Rita.

"She's six years old," Cliff said strongly. "Wait until she's sixteen. Then we'll talk."

Julia reached out and touched Cliff's arm. Her way of saying for him to shut up. Cliff was still steaming about the whole bias-toward-police agenda. Now he was furious at this woman.

"What kind of behavioral problems?" Julia asked.

"Your daughter prays before her meals in the school cafeteria. We've asked her several times to stop and she won't."

Cliff burst out laughing.

"Is this funny to you?" the principal asked.

"I was pulled off a murder investigation to meet with you this afternoon. I was told it was urgent. You're telling me you're concerned because our daughter says grace before her meal. Give me a break."

"We're of the Christian faith," Julia said with more composure than Cliff could muster at the moment. "We taught our daughter to pray before she eats. Why is that a problem?"

"She asks the other kids to hold hands and pray with her."

Julia looked over at Cliff and he rolled his eyes but didn't say anything.

"That's how we do it around our kitchen table," Julia said. "We hold hands and then pray. Sometimes Rita leads it. She's only mimicking what we taught her."

"She's coercing the other kids to pray with her," the principal said.

"You said she asked them to hold hands with her," Cliff retorted. "Not told them to do it. That doesn't sound like coercion. Perhaps you don't understand the meaning of the word."

Cliff was being sarcastic now. He should probably take the higher road but didn't want to.

"The other kids feel pressured," she said.

"Pressured to do what?" Cliff asked.

"To pray."

"If they don't want to pray, all they have to do is say no. They have that right."

"It's a violation of church and state."

"No it's not!" Cliff's voice was raised now. "Freedom of religion was to prevent the school from imposing a prayer on the students. Not the students freely praying on their own."

"The Supreme Court took prayer out of school a long time ago. For good reason."

"Not for the individual. My daughter has a constitutional right to pray over her food."

Cliff was steaming now.

"That's what she said," the principal said mockingly. With vitriol.

Cliff was angry. This woman was bitter. At somebody.

"Good for Rita," Cliff said. "We've taught our daughter to stand up for herself. I'm glad she did."

"Now, I see where she gets it," the principal said. "Your daughter's attitude is belligerent. She doesn't obey her teachers."

"She shouldn't obey them. Not if they're asking her to do something that violates her constitutional right."

The debate was raging now. The tension was so thick, it'd take a chainsaw to cut through it.

"What are the teachers asking Rita to do that she's not willing to do?" Julia asked.

"We asked her to stop asking the other kids to pray with her."

"Okay," Julia said. "So did she stop?"

"Today during lunchtime, she put her hands together and prayed out loud."

"By herself?" Julia asked.

"Yes."

"Did she ask the other kids to pray with her?"

"I don't believe so."

"Then what's the problem? It sounds like our daughter did what the teacher asked her to do."

"No. She prayed out loud. So others could hear her. It made them feel uncomfortable. I got a complaint."

"Who was the complaint from?" Julia asked.

"From one of the teachers."

"A teacher is the one who felt uncomfortable? Not a student?"

Cliff decided to stay out of it for the moment. Julia was doing just fine on her own. If this was an interrogation, Julia was pointing out the principal's distorted representations of the facts.

"Yes. The teacher's aide is the one who complained."

"Let me get this straight," Julia said. "You asked my daughter not to ask the other kids to pray with her. She stopped doing it. Instead, she prayed by herself."

"Out loud so others could hear her."

"Are you telling me that an employee of the school who is here to teach my daughter, is so uncomfortable in her own skin that she would complain to the principal about a six-year-old girl voicing a prayer over her meals?"

"The aide asked your daughter to stop."

"I can't believe what I'm hearing," Cliff said.

"The aide told your daughter to stop," Ms. McVade said angrily. "She wouldn't. It was a rather long prayer."

Cliff had been present for some of Rita's long prayers. His daughter's bedtime prayers could go on for several minutes. She prayed for anyone and everyone she could think of. Including her stuffed animals. If Cliff remembered right, Rita had prayed for her teachers on more than one occasion.

"I must agree with my husband," Julia said. "I don't think Rita is doing anything wrong."

"It's disrupting lunch. It's a major problem."

"It sounds like you're the one with the problem," Cliff said.

The principal scowled at him. "Your daughter is exhibiting Oppositional Defiant Disorder."

"I take exception to that characterization," Julia said in a raised tone of voice. No longer able to control herself. Whatever the principal said had struck a nerve in his wife.

"I'll have you know that I have a degree in child psychology," Julia said.

You go girl. Let her have it.

"Kids with ODD display rebellious and hostile behaviors toward authority figures," Julia said. "My daughter is a well-adjusted six-year-old. She is generally a people pleaser. If you approach her in the correct way, she'll do what you ask her to do. I think she's confused. She doesn't understand why it's okay to pray at home but not at school."

"I don't understand it either," Cliff said. "It's the stupidest thing I've ever heard in my life."

"Your daughter needs to see a professional."

"No way," Julia said. "My daughter does not need to see a child psychologist. I will not let you or anyone else label her with some kind of disease, simply because you don't like the fact that she prays before her meal."

Julia was as hot as a firecracker now. She sat on the edge of her seat. Her jaw was clenched and she was pointing her finger at the principal.

"Your daughter is easily annoyed when told what to do," the principal argued. "A classic symptom of ODD."

"I'm pretty annoyed myself, right now," Cliff said. "Does that mean I have ODD?"

"If your child's behavior doesn't improve, she'll have to be separated from the other children," the principal stated.

"I'll pull her out of this school before that happens," Julia said.

"I see where she gets it."

"Now who's being ODD?" Cliff asked. "Look who's annoyed. Were you diagnosed with it as a child?"

"I don't think we're getting anywhere with this conversation. Obviously, you're not taking your daughter's disrespect of her teachers seriously."

"I will talk to Rita," Julia said. "I will ask her to pray privately. To simply bow her head and pray in her head. Not out loud."

"Ask her not to move her lips or cross her hands in front of her."

"Oh for heaven's sake," Cliff said with exasperation.

"I don't want her to do anything that makes the teachers or other kids uncomfortable," the principal said.

"I don't care about the teachers," Julia said. "They need to get over it. I'm sure they have bigger things to worry about."

"Insubordination will never be tolerated in my school."

"Like I said, I will talk to my daughter," Julia said. "I agree with you about one thing. Rita should obey her teacher. If the teacher tells her to do something, then she should do it."

"They don't have the right to tell her not to pray," Cliff said.

"We'll discuss that point later," Julia said to Cliff.

"I don't see how this woman can stop Rita from praying inside her head anytime she wants," he said.

"As long as Rita limits her prayers to nothing more than that, I'm fine with it," the principal said.

"I'll talk to Rita and tell her to be more respectful of her teacher's directions."

Julia glared at Cliff so he wouldn't say anything more. They were getting to a resolution.

"Thank you," the principal said. "That's all I'm asking."

Cliff stood up first. The ladies hesitated, then followed suit.

Rita was excited to show them her picture.

As they were walking out to their car, Julia said, "I have a feeling we're going to be back in the principal's office again. Sometime soon."

"I think you're right," Cliff said.

7

The next morning

Cliff and Julia both decided to work from home. Rita was off to school with instructions to keep her prayers private and to always follow her teacher's instructions.

They'd had a minor disagreement the night before about the second instruction. Julia won the argument when she reminded Cliff that people had to follow all the laws, even those they didn't agree with. Rita should be respectful of her teachers at all times. Like all citizens should be respectful of law enforcement. It's the way society maintained order.

Cliff ceded the point. It could've turned into a fight had he pressed the issue more.

In their office were two work areas, so they both had a desk and neither anticipated being on the phone, so they wouldn't likely disturb the other. They liked being together even though they had little to no interaction when they each had a lot to do.

Cliff's inbox was full of Summer Lange's murder information and demanded his full attention. The coroner sent over the autopsy report. One of Cliff's assistants pulled a list of red sports car owners in the immediate area. It'd take days to go through all the information.

Of particular interest was an email from the forensics lab. They found a fingerprint match on the bottle of wine in the refrigerator, and would send it over later this morning after all the tests were run.

Cliff could barely contain his excitement. That meant he had another suspect. He was ready to move on from Wayne Bowman. In his mind, the driver of the red sport's car bought the expensive bottle of wine.

Wine guy was with Summer right before she was murdered. The last one to see her alive. Unless he had an alibi, he was at the top of the suspect list. If his DNA was found inside of Summer, then Cliff had his rapist.

It wasn't much of a stretch to assume the rapist was also the murderer. He saw this case coming together rather quickly. As he had anticipated.

"Guess how much that bottle of wine cost?" Cliff asked Julia, who didn't seem so enthralled in her work that she couldn't be bothered. He'd just finished looking up the price on his computer.

"What kind was it?" Julia asked. "A chardonnay if I remember right."

"That's correct. A Rombauer Chardonnay. Vintage 2018."

Julia's gaze focused on the wall behind him as she was deep in thought. "Four hundred dollars," she blurted.

Cliff let out a groan. He thought she'd say forty dollars or so. "You obviously guessed high because of the way I asked the question."

"How much did it cost?" she asked.

"Three hundred dollars." Cliff said the amount slowly, emphasizing every word for effect.

A wide smile formed on Julia's face, and she leaned back in her chair. "How come you don't buy me a three-hundred-dollar bottle of wine?"

"Because I'm not stupid."

"Are you saying I'm not worth it? That'd it'd be stupid to spend that much money on me."

Cliff backtracked. "Of course, you're worth it, honey. But so are shoes on Rita's feet."

Julia laughed.

"I saw some three hundred dollar baby shoes once. Can you believe it? She'd outgrow them in a matter of months."

"Some people pay that."

"Like some people buy a three hundred dollar bottle of wine to impress a girl. "

"You have a birthday coming up," Cliff said.

"Cliff Ford, don't you dare spend that much on a bottle of wine," she said sternly, pointing her finger at him. "I wouldn't want it, even if we had the money. Which we don't. That's two weeks worth of food at the grocery store."

"It does seem like a waste considering you're going to pee it out later."

She frowned. "You're so romantic, Cliff. Haven't you ever heard the term, wined and dined? We women like that. Wine is a good way to seduce a woman."

"You're already seduced. You're a sure thing."

"I don't like being taken for granted," she said, a little stronger than she probably intended. "I wouldn't mind a little effort on your part to seduce me every now and then."

"I'll seduce you right now if you want me to." He had a silly school boy grin on his face as he said it. Not the seductive look he was going for.

"Not right now, silly," she said, waving her hand in the air dismissively. "Seriously, since we had Rita, there hasn't been a lot of romance. We could use a little spice in that area."

"By spice, you mean, some wine, soft music, candles. A bubble bath."

"I'd settle for dinner and a movie," Julia said. "Remember how we said we were going to have a date night, one night a week. After Rita was born we quit doing it. We've been slacking off. When we go out, it's with other couples."

Julia stood from her chair and walked over to Cliff's desk and put her arms around his neck while standing behind him. She kissed him on his ear. He could smell the familiar scent of lavender in her hair. It sent a chill down his spine.

If he didn't have so much to do on the Summer Lange murder case, he might try and seduce her. It wasn't the right time. He did appreciate the display of affection though. He put his hand on her forearm which was still around his neck.

"I miss our alone time," Julia said.

"We're alone now," Cliff said, seductively.

Nothing was going to happen. Didn't have to. They were playfully bantering. He liked it.

Julia broke the embrace and slapped him on the shoulder. "Your mind is a million miles away from here," she said.

"I'm going to solve Summer Lange's murder today," Cliff said. He wished he could take his mind off the murder, but he couldn't. Not right now. Not when he was this close to solving it.

Julia was right, though. They did need more romance. Things were getting a little stale. Comfortable. Part of him loved it, other parts of him missed the intense passion they had when they were first married.

"Do you think it's the guy in the red sport's car who bought the wine?" Julia asked.

"That makes the most sense."

"Why would he spend that much money if he was going to kill her?"

"Like you said, women liked to be seduced. He used the wine to gain her trust. Then he killed her."

Cliff felt a little uncomfortable saying those words so definitively. He had zero evidence that the man in the red sports car actually killed Summer. It was all based on intuition.

He didn't prejudge cases, but human nature was what it was. His job was to formulate scenarios based on the facts as he interpreted them. Sometimes those details were based on circumstantial evidence. Other times, he relied on his gut.

It always came down to what he could prove. Who he had as suspects. Right now, all he had was Wayne Bowman and the man who drove the red sports car. Cliff was convinced they were two different people.

Wayne Bowman hadn't paid three hundred dollars for a bottle of wine in his life. He seemed like the kind of guy whose idea of seducing a woman was buying a six pack and hopping in the back of his van. Which probably had a mattress in it.

Cliff decided to voice what he was thinking and keep the conversation going. Julia was good at brainstorming cases with him.

"I don't think Wayne Bowman is the guy who bought the bottle of wine," Cliff said. "I doubt he's got that kind of money."

"You'd be surprised. Harleys are expensive. Didn't the guy at the car shop say it was souped up? I dated a guy once who spent a thousand dollars on throttle valves."

"I didn't know you knew what a throttle valve was."

"I don't. I just remember the term."

"He must've left an impression on you."

Julia waved her hand in the air. She was back at her desk now. "I don't even remember his name."

"Jack Laurels."

She chuckled nervously. "You remember all the guys I dated better than I do."

"Oh well."

"I wonder what Jack is doing now?" Julia said in a voice that seemed intended to get a rise out of Cliff. If so, he wasn't about to take the bait.

"Jack is probably in deep despair about the one who got away," Cliff said with a smug grin. "He's probably homeless somewhere in California."

"He was an architect. He's probably rich."

"I don't think so. After you broke up with him, he went into a deep depression. Spent six months in a psychiatric hospital. When he got out, he was penniless. Now he lives on the street begging for bread. That's the effect you have on men."

"That's sweet. I think."

"Anyhoo," Cliff said, "Bowman doesn't seem like the kind to spend that much money on a bottle of wine, even if he had it. And he doesn't drive a sports car."

Julia swung her chair around and slid over to the edge of his desk.

"Something about the picture doesn't make sense to me," Julia said.

"What's that?"

"This was a violent murder. Am I right?" Julia asked.

Cliff had the autopsy on his computer screen. He'd read it several times and practically had it memorized.

"It doesn't get more violent than this one."

He read from it.

"According to the coroner, Summer Lange was brutally raped. She had internal and external bruising. She had deep bruising on her inner thighs and legs. She was stabbed more than a hundred times. The coroner couldn't even determine which blow was the fatal one. Any number of wounds could've killed her. I'd say that's pretty violent."

"That's what I'm saying. Summer invited the guy over to her house. For a date. She cooks him dinner. He's a rich guy. Drives a fancy car. She trusts the guy. They've been out before."

"It could be a first date."

"Nope. A woman doesn't invite a man over for dinner on a first date. First dates are for restaurants. Maybe a drink after work. A movie or a show. Cooking a man dinner is intimate. It takes effort. A woman is not going to go to all that trouble for someone she doesn't know."

"I suppose."

"And it's dangerous to invite someone back to your house."

"Obviously."

"I'd guess they were on their third or fourth date."

"Why do you say that?"

"She hasn't told her parents about him. That's a three or four date guy. They haven't been together long enough to introduce him to daddy, but they've been out enough times to where she trusts him enough to invite him home for dinner."

"I'm with you so far."

Julia continued. "He brings an expensive bottle of wine to further gain her trust. White wine. That doesn't work. They're having spaghetti. Everyone knows that red wine goes with spaghetti."

"Not everyone. The killer didn't know it. It might've added to the rage. He wasted that money."

Julia nodded. "He bought the wine to seduce her."

"Not seduce her. To rape her."

"I'm not so sure. Maybe to seduce her."

"The coroner determined it was rape."

"But why rape her? She's probably a sure thing. If a woman invites a man back to her place and is going to cook him dinner, most guys will assume that they're getting some."

"That makes sense. At least regarding her state of mind."

"I'm guessing she's been playing hard to get," Julia said. "Probably hasn't let him go further than a kiss. He goes all out with the wine. She can't say no to sex since he spent that much money on her. At least that's his state of mind."

A light bulb went off in Cliff. "Ah... The unopened bottle of wine is a clue. He brings the wrong wine. He wasted the money. She resists his advances. That makes him angry, and he rapes and kills her."

"So you're saying he didn't plan to kill her? That it wasn't premeditated?"

"I don't know. All I know is that this is an extremely violent crime. It takes a lot of rage to invoke that much punishment on someone. She was probably killed with one of the first few stabs with the knife."

"It still doesn't make sense to me," Julia said. "I can't quite put my finger on it. Do you get that angry over a bottle of wine? Just because she doesn't want to have sex with him?"

"As you know, rape is not about sex. It's about power and control. It's about violence and domination. It takes a certain rage to force yourself on a woman. Pent up anger. You can't understand it because your mind doesn't think that way. You'd never scheme to get inside a woman's home to kill her."

"That's my point," Julia said. "Why buy a bottle of three-hundred-dollar wine? He was already going into the house. Regardless. She invited him. He didn't need to spend the money on the wine. He sounds more like someone who's going to seduce her rather than rape her."

"What if she said no? Like you said, he's expecting sex. He spends three hundred bucks. He doesn't get his money's worth. That makes him mad. They get in a confrontation. He rapes her. It turns bad. He kills her because of all the women before who have teased him and then let him down."

"That's one possibility."

"I think it's the likely one. Or something similar. The guy in the red sports car has to be the killer."

"Don't get locked into one suspect."

For some reason, that struck Cliff the wrong way.

"My job is to lock into one suspect," Cliff said, roughly.

"What I mean is don't get so locked into one person that you don't consider all the possibilities," Julia said.

"I'll go where the leads take me," Cliff argued.

The tension was rising between them.

"That's how I've always done it and that's how I'll always do it," he added.

"I'm not trying to tell you how to do your job," Julia said. She must've sensed his defensiveness.

"That's good to know," Cliff said. "Cause I'm good at it."

Julia seemed surprised by the sudden turn in the conversation. She went back to typing. Cliff went back to studying the autopsy.

The coroner found DNA under the victim's fingernails along with blood. Which likely meant she scratched him. That made it easier to identify a suspect. The killer had scratches on his body. When there were also injuries to the suspect, then Cliff had something tangible. A way to exclude a suspect. Or pin the killing on him.

Motive. Alibi. Physical evidence. MAP as Cliff liked to call it.

The three keys to an investigation. Any one of the three provided a roadmap to solving a case. In this instance, it sounded like he had the physical evidence. Apparently, it was tied to a potential suspect.

From that, Cliff had to determine if the man had a motive. Then opportunity. An alibi, or lack thereof.

It hardly mattered what Julia thought at this point. The fingerprints and DNA would put all the pieces together for him.

He was glad she was focused on work, and they hadn't gotten into a fight. They didn't fight often, but it seemed like they had more tension in the relationship than they used to.

She was right. They did need some alone time together. The spark between them was still there, but needed some accelerant thrown on it. Maybe a fight would reignite the passion.

Not a chance. It'd only hurt her.

"I'm sorry I snapped at you," Cliff said.

"It's no problem," she said. "I'm not mad. I'm sorry if it sounded like I was saying you didn't know what you were doing. That's not what I meant."

"I know."

He turned his mind back to the case. After he exhausted the autopsy, he began working on a things-to-do list. First, he intended to drop by Wayne Bowman's house again. See if he was home. Nose around the van if it was still there.

Three wine stores were also on his list. He had one of his assistants call around and find stores in the area that sold the Chardonnay found in Summer's refrigerator. If the fingerprint match was from the bottle of wine, that might not be necessary. He'd already know who purchased it. At least who handled it.

For all he knew, Summer might've purchased the wine. That'd be a twist.

That reminded him. Julia was right about another thing. He couldn't prejudge a case.

Cliff clicked on his email again and his heart accelerated when he saw the email he'd been anticipating. The fingerprint match.

"The email is here," Cliff said.

Julia looked up from what she was doing.

Adrenaline started to rise inside of him which it did when he felt like he was about to break a case wide open. He opened the attachment and scrolled through the standard language until he got to the fingerprint match.

His mouth would've dropped to the floor if it wasn't attached to his neck.

He couldn't believe what he was seeing.

Henry Lee Clay was in Summer Lange's house that night.

8

Cliff stared at the computer screen. Henry Lee Clay's name stared back at him like a coiled rattlesnake.

"Oh my goodness!" Cliff said, with as much intensity as he could muster. For Julia's benefit, who was busy at work on her computer.

She stopped what she was doing and looked his way. He continued to stare at the screen for effect.

Did this mean Clay was the murderer?

Obviously.

"What is it?" Julia asked.

"You're not going to believe it."

"Tell me."

"I got the fingerprint report. The killer is the one who bought the wine. I'm certain of it."

"How do you know it's the killer?"

"Did you hear what I said? His fingerprints are on the bottle of wine."

"So. What does that prove?"

"It's the killer. After seeing the name, I know it for sure."

"Do you know him?"

Cliff clicked off the email and opened a separate email. The one with the list of red sports car owners in Chicago. He typed in Henry Lee Clay's name.

It came up. Cliff almost jumped out of his chair with excitement. Clay owned a Porsche. Red. No doubt purchased with the money from the sixteen-million-dollar settlement. Anger jolted through Cliff like he'd stuck his hand in an electrical socket.

"Are you going to tell me what's going on?" Julia asked, impatiently.

"One second," Cliff said. His hand shook as he maneuvered the mouse making it hard to get the cursor on the right line.

"The person who purchased the wine also owns a red sport's car," Cliff said, enthused.

Julia stood up. "If you aren't going to tell me I'm going to see for myself!"

She walked around the desk and looked over Cliff's shoulder. He went back to the fingerprint email and reopened it. Scrolled to the page with the name of the fingerprint match.

Cliff paused the page before he got to the name, so it was still not on the screen. He was doing it for dramatic effect. His way of teasing Julia. Once she saw it, she'd agree with him. Clay was the killer.

"What am I looking at?" she asked. "I don't see a name."

Cliff looked up at her as she leaned in closer. "The name I'm about to show you is the killer. He's the one whose fingerprints are on the bottle of wine and the one who owns a red sports car. He was there that night."

Cliff scrolled down until the name appeared on the screen.

Henry Lee Clay.

A name neither of them would ever forget. Not after what he had put them through.

Julia let out a gasp.

"Oh my goodness gracious sakes alive," she said. Her words echoed through the room like she'd said them in a canyon.

"I know!"

"Henry Lee Clay was Summer's date that night," Julia said. "That's unbelievable. What are the odds that you would get this case?"

"His fingerprints are everywhere," Cliff said. "On the front door knocker. On the bottle of wine. On the kitchen counter and kitchen table. On a coaster on the coffee table in the living room. On the powder room faucet handle. No other fingerprints were found. Summer and Clay were the only two people in the house that night."

"This is shocking."

"Clay raped her. Like he raped Tessie."

"How do you know? Do you have the DNA results back yet?"

"Not yet, but it's obvious. Clay's fingerprints are in the bedroom. That's where the rape occurred."

"What does this mean?"

Cliff leaned back in his chair and Julia moved away from behind him and sat on the edge of the desk.

"It means that I need to bring Henry Lee Clay in for questioning," Cliff said.

His mind was already spinning like a top. There were so many ramifications to consider.

"Can you do that?" Julia asked. "Given the lawsuit."

One of those ramifications.

"I'm not sure," Cliff said. He hadn't had time to think it through.

"You should ask the Lieutenant."

"He's out of the country for two weeks. On a conference for police administrators. The conference is in London. We aren't supposed to bother him unless it's an emergency."

"This might qualify as an emergency, don't you think?"

"Why? I'm running an investigation. Clay is a suspect in a murder assigned to me. I have a duty to follow up on that lead. Besides, I want to nail the low life scum. The Lieutenant might take the case from me."

"That's why it might be a conflict of interest. Clay will say you had it in for him from the beginning. Remember that he said you planted evidence."

Repeating that accusation made Cliff angry. "There's no conflict of interest. I didn't plant evidence. All I have to do is make sure everything is done by the book. The physical evidence is overwhelming. There's no way anybody could've planted Clay's fingerprints in all those places."

"Remember, Cliff," Julia said. "Just because Clay was in the house doesn't mean he's the killer."

"Are you trying to annoy me on purpose?" Cliff asked, angrily.

Julia was getting close to crossing another line. It was his job to interpret the evidence, not hers. He didn't need to be reminded of all the problems with the events of the last six months. They were firmly etched in his mind.

This was his case. He would decide when to arrest a suspect.

He'd arrested a lot of people on a lot less evidence. If the DNA results came back as he expected, and Clay raped Summer, then the case was a slam dunk.

Julia didn't say anything more. Thankfully, before things got heated between them. Cliff didn't want to get firm with her, but would if she persisted with the idea that Clay wasn't the killer.

Cliff tried to calm his heartbeat which was pounding in his chest. But it was no use. He couldn't contain the excitement he felt inside.

This was an opportunity for redemption. He knew Clay killed Tessie. Years ago. Cliff didn't plant that evidence. The DNA belonged to Clay. So what if the Judge believed something different. Judges got it wrong all the time.

Cliff had been there. Cliff knew what he did and didn't do.

That arrest was solid. Clay should've never gotten out. If he hadn't, Summer would still be alive. This was Cliff's chance to put Clay behind bars again and he wasn't going to blow it a second time.

He tore up his things to do list and threw it in the trash. No reason to go by Wayne Bowman's house. He was no longer a suspect. Going by the wine store would be a waste of time as well.

He had one thing to do. And one thing only.

Find Henry Lee Clay and arrest him.

***

Later that afternoon

Cliff took two uniformed police officers and a fellow homicide detective with him to arrest Henry Lee Clay. Overkill perhaps, but Cliff wasn't taking any chances. Too many eyes would be on this arrest after the fact. So, he made sure he had plenty of witnesses every step along the way.

He didn't necessarily need an arrest warrant to detain and question Clay, but he got one anyway. More precautions. While Julia's tone had bothered him earlier, she was right. He had to make sure he did everything by the book.

Cliff had more than enough probable cause to get ten warrants. He still filled it out carefully. Everything was detailed. Normally, he could get a warrant on his sworn affidavit. In this instance, he provided explicit evidence for the judge. The only thing missing were the DNA results. Which Cliff wished he had, but wouldn't be ready for a few days. The lab was aware of the need for a sense of urgency.

If Clay was the one who raped Summer and the DNA proved it, then this case was ready to be taken to the D.A. He had more than enough evidence. Actually, it'd be even better if they found evidence in Clay's condo. Cliff was hoping Clay was dumb enough to hide the murder weapon or bloody clothes in his personal residence. Maybe Summer's blood was in the car.

Summer's DNA in Clay's personal residence or car would be a godsend.

Even with the prior so-called wrongful conviction, Clay was going down. Cliff could feel it. Cliff didn't need the additional evidence, but wanted it. He was being greedy. Like a football coach running up the score against his archrival.

Clay was as close as it came to a nemesis for Cliff. The man's lies almost destroyed his career. When Cliff saw the posh building where Clay lived, a burst of rage went off inside of him like a fireworks display. Ill gotten gains. It chafed Cliff's behind that Clay killed a young girl, lied about it, got off on a technicality, then parlayed it into sixteen million dollars. Tax free. Now he drove a Porsche. Lived in a condo overlooking Lake Michigan.

Cliff lived in a modest house on a detective's salary. Clay lied, cheated and stole his way to his fortune. He'd never get a chance to spend it behind bars.

The need for revenge was temporarily satisfied when the tow truck arrived to impound Clay's red Porsche from the parking garage. After the vehicle was secured, Cliff would go upstairs armed with his warrant and haul Clay out of there in handcuffs. He couldn't wait to see the look in the man's eyes.

Would he see guilt? Resignation that he'd been caught. Or defiance?

Every suspect was different. Some bawled like a baby. Cliff doubted he'd get that lucky. Clay would most likely be belligerent and cocky. Spewing threats and venom. Men like Clay thought they were above the law and invincible. The last time Cliff saw Clay was as he was leaving the courthouse and Clay had glared at him.

Like he was going to come after Cliff.

Cliff looked over his shoulder for several weeks after the judge's ruling. Even Julia took precautions. It disrupted their lives for nearly three months.

Cliff wanted to wipe that smug grin off the man's face. He had to be careful. His anger could get out of control. He didn't want to jeopardize the case by doing something stupid. Give Clay a basis to claim police brutality.

The Porsche was on the tow truck. That had a certain satisfaction to it.

Cliff heard a shout.

Coming from the other side of the garage.

"What are you doing with my car?" the familiar voice said.

Henry Lee Clay. He had exited the elevator and entered the parking garage and was walking toward his car.

He saw Cliff and stopped in his tracks. Their eyes met.

Clay's eyes widened so big they looked like they were going to pop out of his head. A panicked look came over his face.

Cliff reached in his suit jacket for the warrant. Before he could pull it out, Clay turned and took off running out of the garage.

"We've got a jackrabbit," Cliff shouted. Pointing.

The officers and other detectives were slow to react. Cliff was the only one who'd seen Clay and was the first to pursue.

Cliff exited the parking garage and had to stop to see which way Clay went. He didn't see him at first. That's because Clay had crossed the busy street. Was dodging traffic causing honking and screeching of tires.

One car almost hit Clay. Clay avoided it by placing his hands on the hood. The car stopped barely in time to keep from running him over. That wasn't good. Cliff didn't want Clay splattered on the concrete. He wanted the satisfaction of hauling him away in handcuffs.

Cliff threw caution to the wind and entered the street. When a car almost hit him, he slowed down and got out of the lane of traffic. Cliff didn't want to be killed either. So, he was more cautious. Held out his hand to stop the traffic while showing the drivers his badge.

Most of the cars slowed. Brakes squealed. Thankfully, Cliff didn't hear the sound of crunching metal. The last thing he needed was an incident downtown. An accident caused by a police foot pursuit. God forbid an innocent bystander was injured.

The Lieutenant would have a fit.

The delay in getting across the street gave Clay a head start. Cliff barked instructions through his microphone on his lapel to the other officers. Although, Clay could go any number of directions.

Cliff had to hurry. Clay could get lost in the busy downtown streets of Chicago if he got a couple more blocks over.

Cliff quickened his pace.

His lungs were burning. He hadn't chased a suspect in a long time. Fatherhood had put a few extra pounds on him. He was going on sheer adrenaline.

As much as it was taxiing Cliff's body, Clay's running was the best thing that could've happened. It made the man look guilty. More proof. Fleeing the arrest might even mean Clay wouldn't get bail.

Cliff had to catch him for that to happen.

A panic came over him when Clay turned down an alleyway and Cliff lost him temporarily.

He can't get away.

A thousand horrible thoughts started running through Cliff's mind. What if Clay had prepared for this? He had the money to disappear. What if he left the country? Somewhere that didn't have extradition. It'd been six months since Clay got the big settlement. That money could be offshore by now.

The thought sent a second wind through Cliff. He crossed another busy street. It was rush-hour in downtown Chicago.

Cliff saw Clay out of the corner of his eye, and then he disappeared again. Down another side street. Cliff raced to it. Dodging pedestrians on the busy sidewalk.

It wasn't a side street. More of an alley. It ran between businesses. Cliff rounded the corner. Clay was about halfway down the alleyway.

A straightaway. Cliff put it in another gear. It'd been years since he'd run this hard and this fast.

Cliff was gaining. Close enough to shout for Clay to stop. To give him a police warning. Not close enough to pull his gun.

Clay slowed and looked back. Fear gripped his face, and he took off running again.

Cliff was on him now. His heart was pounding like a racehorse at the Kentucky Derby.

Cliff shouted for him to stop again.

They neared the end of the alleyway. Cliff radioed his position. Still kept his gun holstered. He had to bring Clay in alive.

At the end of the alleyway, Clay hesitated. Looked to the left. Then the right. Then back to the left. Unsure which way to go.

That's all Cliff needed.

As Clay started to run again, Cliff tackled him like a linebacker hitting a running back. With such force it sent them both tumbling into the concrete wall at the end of the alleyway.

Clay let out an oomph. Cliff felt his breath leave him as he fell on top of Clay.

Clay cried out in pain. His face cracked on the side of the wall. Cliff was on top and pushed Clay's face further into the street causing Clay to cry out louder.

Cliff was breathing hard. So hard, he had trouble getting the words out. Words he was so excited to say.

"Henry... Lee... Clay... You're under arrest."

It came out something like that. Between breaths. Cliff's voice cracked.

Clay moaned in pain.

Cliff was sitting on top of him. He grabbed Clay's wrist and twisted his arm behind his back. The adrenaline was still flowing, and he forced Clay's arm behind him with more force than Cliff had intended.

Clay cried out in pain again. Cliff heard the muscles and ligaments pop. He might've damaged his arm.

Cliff reached for the handcuffs and got them out of his belt while maintaining his grip on Clay's wrist.

Clay resisted when Cliff tried to secure the handcuffs on Clay's other wrist.

Cliff put his knee square in Clay's back and hyperextended the arm in the air causing Clay to cry out again. It worked. Clay quit resisting.

Instead, he spewed out a volley of expletives and threats. Like a broken sewer line.

"This is police brutality," Clay said. "I'm going to sue you again. Wait until my lawyer gets a hold of you. I'm going to take your house. And your car. I'll have your badge for this."

Clay was in handcuffs now. Cliff stood and jerked him to his feet.

The side of Clay's face was bloodied from where he hit the concrete wall and sidewalk. It had already begun to bruise. Clay's shirt was torn.

Cliff grimaced on the inside. The injuries couldn't be helped. The man was resisting arrest.

Clay had scratch marks on his neck running down his chest and disappearing under the white shirt, which was now bloodied.

"Where did you get those scratches on your neck?" Cliff asked.

"From you. You did this to me. You scratched me."

An image came into Cliff's mind. Like he was watching a movie. Summer's face was on the screen. Fighting for her life. Clay on top of her. She scratched his neck. He punched her.

A wave of disgust came over Cliff as he saw Summer's beaten and lifeless body as the next image.

The scratches were more proof.

The coroner said Summer Lange had the killer's DNA under her fingernails. Clay had marks that fit the description of a woman's scratches. Clay's DNA was already in the system. Wouldn't be hard to make a match.

Cliff stood next to Clay waiting for the other officers to arrive. Also trying to catch his breath. He waited to read Clay his rights until the other officers arrived, so he'd have witnesses. He could technically wait until he got Clay down to the station but Cliff wanted to Mirandize him immediately in case Clay said something incriminating before they got him there.

The threats that spewed out of Clay's mouth could certainly be used against him. Resisting arrest. Fleeing. Putting the other officers at risk. Not to mention the general public. The drivers of the cars who could've caused an accident by his negligence and unlawful behavior.

A number of charges bounced around in Cliff's mind like a racquetball in a spirited match. The D.A. would probably only be interested in resisting arrest. Why charge Clay with jaywalking when Cliff had Clay dead to rights on rape and murder? Charges that should put him away for the rest of his life.

The other officers arrived.

"You're under arrest," Cliff said a second time for the officer's benefit.

"What's this about?" Clay asked.

"You have the right to remain silent. Anything you say can and will be used against you in a court of law. You have the right to an attorney. If you can't afford one, one will be provided for you by the state of Illinois."

"Why am I under arrest?" Clay asked in a not so believable tone.

"For rape and murder."

Clay's shoulders slumped.

"For the rape and murder of Summer Lange."

Clay's eyes widened. Then he bit his lip. Like he wanted to say something but stopped himself.

Cliff started to lead Clay away by the arm. He'd take some satisfaction in the public perp walk. Leading Clay back across the streets in handcuffs. In full view of the pedestrians and cars on the busy street.

Then decided against it. The press might already be on their way to the scene. They'd get pictures of the bloody suspect. Cliff couldn't let them create a false narrative.

Cliff sent the two officers to get their patrol car. They'd take Clay away in the alley.

Cliff searched Clay. Pulled out his wallet, keys, and miscellaneous items in Clay's pockets. He didn't find any weapons on him.

Cliff pulled up Clay's shirt. He had scratches on his back. Deep scratches. And on his chest.

"Where'd you get these scratches?" Cliff asked again. "Did Summer do that when you raped her?"

Clay glared.

"I want an attorney," he said.

"You'll get one. Once we get you booked at the station."

Clay had a smug look on his face. Cliff wanted to slap it off of him.

When the patrol car arrived, Cliff deposited Clay into the police cruiser with instructions for them to take him to the station and book him. Then put him in an interrogation room. Cliff would be along after he searched Clay's house.

He'd let Clay stew in the interrogation room for a while. It'd give Cliff time to prepare for the interrogation and make Clay anxious.

As he walked back to the condo, Cliff tried to analyze what had happened.

What was Clay's reaction all about?

When Cliff mentioned Summer's name. He saw Clay smile.

Why?

***

Henry Lee Clay suffered all the indignities of being arrested. Including a strip search including a cavity search. He was angry at himself for being in this position again. He had vowed he'd never spend another day in prison. Now, here he was.

He shouldn't have run. It only made things worse.

If he'd known then what he knew now...

He was confused. Cliff Ford said he was being arrested for the rape and murder of Summer Lange.

Clay didn't even know she was dead. After the night at her house, Clay had avoided her. He hadn't called her and hadn't gone back to the gym where she worked. He didn't want to risk running into her again.

Why did Cliff Ford think he killed her?

He didn't kill her.

A sense of relief came over him. His attorney would be able to prove that fact.

At first, Clay thought they were arresting him for killing the girl.

The one in the park last night.

9

The body of Nancee Hale was discovered shortly before five in the afternoon behind a storage building in a residential park outside Chicago proper by a female jogger. Cliff was called to the scene.

Henry Lee Clay was processed and was in a prison cell awaiting a hearing in front of a judge to determine bail. The interrogation hadn't lasted long. He lawyered up and his lips were sealed tighter than an unopened jar of pickles.

Once a suspect requests an attorney, all questioning had to cease. Clay made the mistake of saying, "I didn't kill Summer Lange."

"Why did you run away?" Cliff asked. Clay had opened the door somewhat by making a statement. He couldn't have it both ways. Refuse to answer questions but make an argument for his innocence.

Clay's attorney wouldn't let him answer. Instead, he answered for him, telegraphing how they intended to approach that problem.

"He feared for his life," Clay's attorney said. "After the way you beat him up the first time you arrested him, he was afraid you'd do it again. Or kill him and say it was in self-defense."

"I never laid a finger on him the first time."

"You can't say that this time, can you, Detective?" the attorney said slyly.

Clay's face was swollen like a balloon. He'd have one, maybe two shiners.

Cliff didn't answer. Whatever he said could be used against him in a court of law as well. The only problematic part of his case. Clay's defense attorney would make plenty of hay about the injuries.

Clay sustained those because he ran. Had he surrendered voluntarily, nothing would've happened. Cliff also didn't cause the injuries. Not really. Clay fell into the wall. If anything, the D.A. could charge Clay with assault on a police officer. Cliff had some bumps and bruises as well.

An officer could use whatever force necessary to subdue a suspect. It was supposed to be a force that was reasonable. The suspect was never allowed to use force on an officer. Any number of crimes could be brought to bear in that instance. Like assault and resisting arrest.

Nevertheless, Clay wouldn't go down without a fight. Which was his right. Cliff presumed his attorney would use that line of defense to make bail and at trial. Clay ran because of a corrupt and vicious cop who was out to get him because of the settlement.

The judge's ruling six months before was problematic. Cliff had to hope Clay's DNA was tied to the rape. No way for Clay to distract from that fact. Claiming Cliff planted that evidence would be laughable. No way to call it consensual sex. The coroner ruled it a sexual assault. The injuries on Summer's body were too great.

Clay could level whatever accusations he wanted toward Cliff. Fine. Only a distraction. He couldn't get away from the mountain of evidence piling up against him.

Before Cliff left the station, he called Julia to let her know he'd be late for dinner.

"I arrested Clay," Cliff said.

"Really?"

"Yep. He's as guilty as sin. Took off running as soon as he saw me."

"I'm glad you caught him."

"There's another killing of a young girl. In a park. I'm headed there now. Sixteen."

"Do you think Clay is involved?"

"He'll be my first suspect."

"Like I said, don't get too focused on one person."

Don't tell me how to do my job, Cliff wanted to say but resisted. At some point, they might have to discuss this. Cliff wanted to keep running his cases by her. He really did value her input. At the same time, he didn't need to be constantly reminded of the obvious.

She was only trying to help, he told himself.

Maybe this was what the seven-year itch felt like. It seemed like they were annoying each other more than usual now than when they were first married.

Of course, they had a six-year-old as well which added to the tension. There'd been talk of another baby, but Julia didn't want one right now. She was back working at the shelter and enjoying being out of the house. At some point, the baby itch might hit her again, but for now she was perfectly content with the way things were.

Even when Cliff annoyed her which he admitted to himself was probably more than when she annoyed him.

The drive to the park took longer than usual because of the time of day. By the time Cliff arrived, forensics was already on the scene as were a cackle of reporters. They spewed out questions when they saw him.

To be expected. When the murder of a teenager came across the police scanner, the press pounded the scene like a piranha on a wounded fish in the water. Cliff ignored them and walked straight to the cordoned off area behind the yellow tape. Not before familiarizing himself with the park.

To his right was the parking lot. A couple of hundred steps from where he was now. The building could be seen from the parking lot, but probably not well at night. There were two walking and bike trails. The one closest to the building was for walkers and joggers. The one that ran through the center and out of the park and alongside the road was wider and accommodated bikes as well as those on foot.

A number of picnic tables were to his left. No children's playground was in the park.

Satisfied, he found the beat cop who appeared to be looking for him as well.

The woman had quite a bit of information for Cliff. After the usual introductions she offered them voluntarily without him having to ask for it.

"Sixteen-year-old female. Nancee Hale. Spelled with two e's on the end. Not a y. Sophomore at Riverdale High. Brown hair, brown eyes. Her throat was slashed."

Normally, Cliff liked to discover these things for himself by looking over the scene but didn't want to get in the way of forensics who were busy at work behind the building where Cliff assumed the body was located. He couldn't actually see the body from his vantage point.

"The girl was last seen last night around nine o'clock at Central Mall," the cop continued. "She went there with some friends. They split up. Nancee had a shopping bag with a tee shirt she bought at one of the stores. No sign of it here."

"How do you know all of this?" Cliff asked. He didn't see any witnesses standing around or any friends or family.

"Her mother filed a missing person's report last night, when she didn't come home from the mall. It's all in the report. I'll email it to you."

Cliff could've looked it up himself. Most cops would make him. This woman was on the ball and trying to be efficient and helpful. He appreciated it.

The officer paused to see if Cliff had any more questions. He did but didn't ask them. No reason to ask for information she was already planning on giving him.

The cop looked down at her notes. Another reason Cliff didn't ask. The one question he did ask had already gotten her off her train of thought. Fortunately, she got it back quickly. Hopefully, she didn't pass over any important information.

"The girl texted her friends that she was getting a ride home. A sick ride, the text said. She told her friends she'd send pictures of it. The text messages are attached to the missing person's report."

That seemed like an important clue to Cliff. Apparently, the picture was never sent, or the cop would've mentioned it.

"Has the next of kin been notified?" Cliff asked.

"No, sir. That's your jurisdiction. I didn't want to overstep my bounds. I'm only here to secure the scene and follow your instructions."

Cliff liked this woman. He made a mental note of her name even though he could always find it on the police report. If he had time, he'd shoot off a note to her supervisor. Actually, he'd make time. He was a young detective once. Atta boys didn't come along often in their line of work. Atta girls in this situation.

"Anything else?" Cliff asked.

"There's one other thing. I don't know if it's relevant or not."

"Let me decide that."

"Of course. Around ten o'clock last night, the 911 operator received a call from a man and woman who saw a suspicious man on a motorcycle loitering in the parking lot."

Cliff instinctively looked over at the parking lot. Theoretically, the motorcycle could've come up on the bike bath, but more than likely stayed in the parking lot.

Would a motorcycle be considered a "sick ride" by a sixteen-year-old?

Most definitely.

"Did they give a description of the man or the motorcycle?"

"Yes. It was a Harley Davidson. The couple said it had those fancy mufflers."

"Any description of the person?"

"Large man with a beard. A biker type. It was dark but they did get a good look at him."

Wayne Bowman popped into Cliff's mind. Harley Davidson. Beard. Biker type.

He dismissed the thought. A thousand different people in Chicago fit that same description.

"What was the man doing that was so suspicious?"

"They didn't say exactly. I guess you can ask them. Their names are on the police report."

"Did officers respond to the call?"

"They did. But not until after midnight. Whoever it was, was already gone."

"Thanks for the information. You've been very helpful."

"I'm happy to do my job."

"One other thing," she said. "I observed a footprint when I first arrived. On the sidewalk."

That caused Cliff's heart to skip a beat. You could tell a lot from a footprint. Not as much as a fingerprint, but he could use that information once a suspect was identified. The shoe size was definitive. If the shoe fit, so to speak.

"Okay. Show it to me."

"It's a bloody footprint."

They walked toward the activity. A sidewalk came up to the storage building from two different directions. More a walking and jogging trail than a sidewalk. A smaller concrete walkway led to the back of the building. On the sidewalk, was a clear image of a footprint. It appeared to be made from a boot. Something like a work boot or hiking shoe. Cliff estimated it to be a size twelve or thirteen. It belonged to a big man.

"I doubt the killer realized he left it," Cliff said. "Since it was dark back here."

There was no light on the side or behind the building. The walking trail was lit, but the killer probably couldn't see anything in the dark. Cliff made a mental note to see if the moon was out the night before.

"Is there anything else I can do for you, detective?"

"Have your men scour the park and see if you find anything that might be related to the crime scene?"

She gave him a slight salute with a couple of fingers and was off.

Cliff thought about talking to forensics, but they were hard at work. He observed from a distance. A nagging thought kept tugging at his psyche.

Wayne Bowman drove a souped-up motorcycle.

A Harley Davidson.

He was a big guy with a beard.

He worked as a mechanic and probably wore a boot.

If a lot of people saw someone like Bowman loitering alone in a park late at night, they'd think it was suspicious.

Cliff tried to tamp down the nagging feeling. It seemed improbable that Wayne Bowman was involved in this murder. What were the odds? A lot of people drove Harley's in Chicago. Some big and menacing. There were biker's clubs all over the city.

Cliff had hoped to pin this murder on Henry Lee Clay. It felt similar to the case several years before. The one Clay was convicted and spent ten years in jail for. That victim's throat was slashed as well, if Cliff remembered correctly.

But he'd already ruled out Henry Lee Clay. By the bloody footprint. Clay was a small man. Probably wore a size six or seven shoe. A twinge of disappointment hit Cliff. He'd have to be satisfied with pinning one murder on the man.

Cliff did a thorough survey of the crime scene, took a few pictures, then waited for the body to be taken away.

On the way home, he decided to stop by Wayne Bowman's house again. For the heck of it. He still needed to rule him out as a suspect in the Summer Lange murder anyway. He already had for all practical purposes. It'd be good for the file if he showed that he considered other suspects and didn't focus only on Clay.

Maybe he'd get lucky, and Bowman would be home.

The white van was not in the driveway.

Cliff knocked on the door. He thought he heard a sound coming from inside but couldn't be sure. That piqued his curiosity. If someone was in the house, they weren't required by law to open the door for him, but it was always suspicious when they didn't.

Not always. Some people might not open the door for a stranger. A woman or child home alone. Or someone naturally skittish. Wayne Bowman didn't strike Cliff as worried about opening the door for anyone. If the descriptions were correct, Wayne Bowman wasn't afraid of much.

Except maybe a cop knocking on his door.

That sent Cliff's curiosity a couple of rungs higher on the anxiety chart. He walked around to the back of the house. The ground was wet. Like someone had been hosing something off.

Still no sign of the motorcycle. Probably kept inside the locked shed in the back.

Cliff knocked on the back door.

No answer.

He walked back to the street and turned and looked up at the house. He thought he saw a shadow in the upstairs window. Someone was looking at him, but trying not to be seen.

Knocking on the door again would be a waste of time. Cliff didn't have probable cause to break down the door.

On the street was a trash can. Set out for pickup. Cliff opened the lid. Technically, the trash can was in the utility right-of-way and therefore on public property. Cliff had a right to look in it.

His heart skipped a couple of beats.

On the top were a couple of bags of trash.

Below them were a pair of boots.

Tied together.

Cliff took a pen out of his pocket and lifted them out of the trash bin.

They were wet.

Work boots. Probably a size twelve or thirteen. He lifted them high in the air and looked at the bottom of the shoes.

What he saw caused his heart to do somersaults.

One of the shoes was clearly stained with blood.

***

If Wayne Bowman didn't have bad luck, he'd have no luck at all. Tomorrow morning, the city trash company would come down his street and haul away the trash in his bin never to be seen again.

Instead, he watched in disbelief bordering on horror as the man, Wayne assumed was a detective, held his work shoes in the air.

Would he notice the blood on them? Obviously.

How could he miss it?

Wayne had tried to wash the blood stains off but wasn't able to completely do so. So he tossed them in the trash can and didn't think anything of it. Not believing for a minute that a law officer would be rummaging through his trash and discover them that same day.

He'd been so careful. He'd gone to great lengths to get rid of the white van. He'd sold it to a shop that took care of things like that. They took vehicles apart and sold the parts off. So they could never be traced.

Wayne sold it to them for two grand. A third of what it was worth, but he had to do something. The men in the shop would never say a word about the blood in the seats.

Summer's blood. He'd never be able to get it out.

When the detective came to the house snooping around, Wayne knew it was only a matter of time until he came back. If he wanted to search the van, he'd find the blood, and Wayne would be screwed. So, he made the decision to get rid of it and hope the murder couldn't be tied to him in another way.

Wayne stood in his upstairs bedroom and watched the investigator, who had returned and knocked on his door several times. He wasn't sure what to do. He should probably answer the door. But how could he explain the blood on the shoe?

Did the investigator know about the girl in the park? Not likely. How could they? It only happened the night before.

And he didn't do anything wrong. Well... he didn't report the murder.

How could he?

Eventually, everything would be traced back to him. He should've left well enough alone. He never should've followed the man in the red sports car. Wayne didn't even know his name.

But the rage had consumed him. The jealousy.

The weasel in the sports car had been with Summer the night Bowman killed her. Wayne followed the man for days. He saw him with Summer at the gym. Witnessed them go on a couple of dates. The jerk kissed Summer in the car.

Sending him into a rage.

That's when he decided to kill them both. He almost killed them on the spot.

But he waited.

He followed the man every day. After he killed Summer, he barely let the man out of his sight. Last night, he followed him to the mall. To his shock, the red sports car pulled up beside a girl who was standing outside. Alone. She got in the car with him.

Wayne followed them to a park. He watched from a distance as the man and girl sat in the car. They got out of the car and went behind a building.

A couple minutes later, the man returned to his car. Without the girl.

The man looked around, got in his car, and drove away. Another car drove in at the same time. They saw him in their headlights. Then they left.

Wayne should've left but his curiosity was shooting through the stratosphere. He got off the motorcycle and walked to the back of the building.

It was dark. He could see a figure lying on the ground. He bent down and checked for a pulse. Blood was on his hand. The girl was dead.

He bolted up and went back to his motorcycle and got out of there as fast as possible. The next morning, he noticed the blood on the bottom of his shoes. He tried to wash it off, but couldn't, so he decided to throw them away.

How could he explain it now? Why was he in the park? It wouldn't take long to connect the man in the red sports car with Summer Lange.

How would Bowman explain what happened to the white van? The investigator had already seen the van. He'd ask questions. Bowman couldn't say it was sold. Or stolen. Those things could be verified. He had no plausible explanation.

All roads led back to the murder of Summer.

Now the investigator had the shoes. He'd think Wayne killed the girl. The best thing to do was to get out of there.

He went downstairs and into the back storage shed. He unlocked it. Careful not to make any noise. The investigator was still out front.

He fired up the Harley.

That did make noise. The investigator came running around the side of the house.

Wayne sped off. Past him. Swerved to stay out of his reach.

The investigator pulled his gun, but Wayne hit the gas, and was by him in a flash.

Bowman made it to the street and turned to the right without even looking for oncoming traffic.

He took the fastest road out of town and headed for the midwest.

Maybe South Dakota. The Badlands. Somewhere he could disappear.

10

A few weeks later

Wayne Bowman was arrested in Nebraska and extradited back to Illinois and charged with the murder of Nancee Hale. Ironically enough, he was found in the only state in the region that had a helmet law. He was pulled over by a highway patrolman who had only intended to issue him a warning for not wearing one. When the trooper ran the standard background check, he found the APB Cliff put out on Bowman and arrested him on the spot.

It took a few weeks, but Bowman was brought back to Illinois where he couldn't afford an attorney so one was appointed for him. He also couldn't make bail, so he was in county lockup awaiting his trial which was still a few weeks away.

The evidence against Bowman was overwhelming. Nancee Hale's blood was found on his boot. One of his shirts found inside the house had a blood smear on it as well. A smear the lab determined was made with the index and middle finger on Bowman's right hand proving he touched the body.

The two eyewitnesses who made the 911 call from the park that night, identified Bowman from a line-up and also confirmed his Harley Davidson motorcycle looked like the same one they'd seen that night.

Bowman was also seen on a security camera near the mall where Nancee Hale was last seen by her friends. The cameras didn't show Bowman with the girl but placed him at the mall around that time. Proof enough.

Bowman wasn't talking so he provided no rebuttal for the mountain of evidence.

As a final nail in his proverbial coffin, Bowman offered no explanation for what happened to the white van. Still somewhat of a mystery. Cliff couldn't find a bill of sale or a change in title. It's like the white van had disappeared off the face of the earth. The implication being that the van contained some kind of evidence that was damning to Bowman and he had disposed of it in some manner.

Cliff wished he had the murder weapon. That was probably at the bottom of a lake somewhere. Another hole in the case was that Nancee Hale's DNA or fingerprints were not found on Bowman's bike. He probably washed those off. In the same way he tried unsuccessfully to wash the blood off the bottom of his boot.

Both cases, Bowman's and Clay's, were already in the District Attorney's office and moving through the system. The Lieutenant returned from London and was pleased with both arrests. He was especially beyond thrilled that Cliff had nailed Henry Lee Clay again and that the evidence was overwhelming.

The lab results showed that Clay's DNA was inside and all over Summer's body. Clay's bodily fluids were also found on the bedspread and sheets in her bedroom, proving beyond a reasonable doubt that he was the rapist. Microscopic spots of Summer's blood were found in Clay's condo and on a pair of underwear Clay was likely wearing that night.

Cliff found a credit card receipt for the purchase of the wine. He also got a positive ID from one of the employees at the liquor store who had helped Clay pick out the wine that night.

The employee said Clay was acting nervously which was an added bonus. It didn't necessarily prove premeditation, but a jury might make that leap.

Cliff wished he had the murder weapon in Clay's case as well, but that was easily explained. Most murderers disposed of the weapons. Rarely did a murderer keep a gun or knife around the house for an investigator to find. Thankfully, with the DNA and fingerprint evidence, they didn't need the murder weapons.

Everyone was chomping at the bit to get these cases to trial, especially to avenge the wrongful conviction fiasco with Henry Lee Clay. To restore the reputation of Cliff Ford and the entire department that had been much maligned by the press and other defense attorneys.

It felt like vindication.

Henry Lee Clay killed Tessie years before. Cliff hadn't gotten that wrong. The judge had when he overturned the conviction. The case with Summer Lange wasn't necessarily related to Tessie's case, but Cliff made the connection. Clay was a killer. Once a killer, always a killer.

Cliff sat at his desk one morning when he got the unlikeliest of calls, further providing more vindication.

It was a normal morning. He had taken the last swigs of his second cup of coffee. The phone rang out of the blue. He'd only been in the office for a few minutes and wasn't expecting a call.

An Indiana number. Rather than let it go to voicemail, Cliff answered it.

"Detective Ford," he said.

"Mister Ford. This is Misty Matthews. Do you remember me?"

The name was familiar. It didn't take long for him to remember why. She was Henry Lee Clay's girlfriend. From years ago. The one who provided Clay with an alibi the night Tessie was murdered. Misty testified that Clay was with her that night and couldn't have possibly killed Tessie.

Cliff didn't believe her. Neither did the jury since they convicted Clay of the murder despite Misty's testimony.

She was the last person he ever expected to hear from.

"Yes, Misty," Cliff said, "I do remember you. What can I do for you?"

She hesitated to answer.

"I'm the girl who was Henry's girlfriend. Many years ago."

"I know. I remember. You said he was with you the night Tessie was murdered."

Cliff spoke in a surprisingly gentle tone. Matching her soft-spoken voice. Misty was shy and timid. Extremely nervous. Her voice was shaking.

What she said next caused Cliff to almost fall out of his chair.

"I lied."

"I know."

Cliff could hear her crying now. Soft sobs.

"I'm sorry," she said.

He was not moved by the tears. Witnesses lying was the bane of his job. Above all else, he was in search of the truth. And justice. False testimony contaminated the process.

Even then, he didn't feel angry or the need to condemn. Misty was sixteen at the time. And now she was calling him. To confess. He didn't feel the need to pile on a load of guilt, shame, and condemnation.

"I know he killed Tessie," she said.

"Why did you lie?" Cliff asked, maintaining a soft tone. "Was it because you loved Henry?"

"Oh no. Not at all."

Her strength returned as she said the words emphatically.

"I wasn't in love with him. We barely dated. I was young and naive."

"Then why lie for him? If you knew he murdered her. Tessie was the same age as you. You must've known he'd do it again."

"I was afraid of Henry. He said he'd kill me and my parents if I didn't tell them he was with me that night."

"Ahh. I can see why that was hard for you."

Cliff meant it. Maybe this was the warmth Julia had been trying to pry out of him. He couldn't wait to tell her about this conversation. She'd be proud of him. Misty was a victim of Henry Lee Clay as well. She shouldn't have lied but at least Cliff understood now why she did.

"I was glad when Henry was convicted and went to jail," Misty said. Her tears had mostly abated. "The D.A. wanted me to testify when Henry was trying to get the conviction overturned," she added.

"I know. Why didn't you?"

"I'm sorry. I was afraid. I'm married now and have two children. We moved to Indianapolis to get away from Chicago. I didn't want to get involved. I had no idea that they'd let him go free."

"Well, they did."

The first bit of anger slipped out of his control and came through in his voice. Had she testified, the judge probably wouldn't have let Henry go free. Summer would still be alive. Misty may have had a good reason for not coming back to Chicago, but it wasn't good enough. The bad guys win if the good guys let them.

It sounded like Misty was trying to do the right thing now. Too little, too late for Summer.

"I'm sorry." The third time she'd said it. Almost like Cliff could give her absolution. Which he couldn't.

"The judge was wrong in letting Henry go free," Cliff said.

That was really the bottom line. Law enforcement and judges were supposed to protect the public. If anyone was to blame, it was the judge who ignored the mountain of evidence and set a killer free to kill again.

To be fair, Henry Lee Clay was really the one to blame for Tessie's murder. Not the idiot judge. Not Misty for lying. Not the defense lawyer who misrepresented the facts to the court.

"I feel horrible," Misty said. The tears were behind the words again. "I could've done something about it, and I didn't."

"Why are you calling me now?" Cliff asked. Not in a mean way. More out of curiosity. "What's done is done. We can't go back in time and change things."

"I know. I don't know why I'm calling. Yes I do, actually. When I heard that Henry was arrested again, for the murder of another woman, I felt like I had to come forward and let you know the truth. You weren't wrong. Henry did kill Tessie. I'm sure of it."

"So am I."

"I don't want him to get off again."

"He won't. I'll make sure he doesn't."

"I'm willing to testify that I lied if you need me to."

It took a lot of courage for her to say that.

"I don't see how it would help," Cliff said. "Nothing from Tessie's case is going to be allowed into evidence in this murder case. Your testimony would be inadmissible."

Even without thinking it through, Cliff was fairly certain that was the case. Prior bad acts can be admissible under certain circumstances but, technically, the new judge found Henry innocent of that crime. The judge in Summer's case wasn't going to retry Tessie's case by considering Misty's testimony.

"Okay. I didn't know." She sounded relieved.

"I appreciate the offer. I really do."

"I feel bad about what they did to you," Misty said sincerely. "I followed it on the news. They said you planted evidence and framed Henry. I wanted you to know that I know you didn't."

"Thank you. That means a lot to me."

"Can you forgive me?"

"Of course. If it makes you feel any better, then yes, I forgive you."

Cliff could hear the pain in her voice. This had probably haunted her for a long time.

Maybe he could give her an olive branch of absolution by forgiving her. He took it a step further and defended her.

"Misty, you were a young girl. You were being threatened by a psychopathic murderer who said he'd kill you and your family if you told the truth. I'm sure you were confused. Frightened out of your mind. Henry played on that fear. I don't blame you. I wished things had turned out differently, but I understand now why you did what you did. The past is the past. I wouldn't beat myself up over it if I were you."

"Am I in trouble?" she asked. Her voice was shaking again. "Will they charge me for lying under oath?"

Cliff chuckled slightly, releasing some of the tension he was feeling. This was one of the most intense conversations he'd had in a long time.

"No. The statute of limitations has long since passed. Nobody's going to be coming after you. I promise."

Misty let out a huge breath of air discernible through the phone.

"That's a relief," she said.

Cliff thought of something. A jolt of panic sent the thought into his head.

"Does Clay know where you live?" he asked.

"I don't think so."

"Let's keep it that way. Have you told anyone else what you told me?"

"Only my husband. He encouraged me to call."

"He sounds like a good man. Listen Misty. You protect your precious children and your husband. Don't speak of this again. I'd encourage you to put it behind you. This secret is between us. No one will ever know. I promise that I won't tell anyone what you told me today. I don't want to do anything to put you or your children in danger."

"Should I be afraid? Do you think Henry will come after me?"

Cliff didn't want to overstate the threat and worry her unnecessarily. He didn't want to understate it either. Clay was capable of anything. He might seek revenge if he knew Misty was spilling his secrets now.

"I don't think you have anything to worry about," Cliff said. "You aren't on his radar. He has no reason to come after you. He's got bigger worries. All I'm saying is let's not give him a reason to. You are out of sight and out of mind. I want to keep it that way."

"Me too."

"Thank you for calling Misty. It means a lot to me."

It really did. Whatever lingering doubts Cliff had in the recesses of his mind about Clay's guilt were gone. Henry Lee Clay did kill Tessie. Cliff had gotten it right. Why would he threaten to kill Misty if he hadn't?

"I figured you hated me," Misty said, in a pained tone.

The scared child was back, and her voice was weak and timid again.

"I never blamed you, Misty. Clay is the one who killed that girl."

"I know. I'm sorry."

"There's nothing you could've done to prevent it. It's in the past. All you can do is try to move forward. My job is to make sure Henry Lee Clay spends the rest of his life behind bars. So he doesn't hurt anyone ever again."

"I pray that happens."

"Me too. I'm glad you called. I really am."

Cliff's heart was warmed when he hung up the phone. Misty Matthews had obviously been carrying this burden for years. Cliff was happy about the way he had handled it. He could've been angry and bitter. Instead, he was gentle and kind.

Julia would be pleased with him.

When he arrived home, he didn't get the chance to tell her. Julia was at the door waiting for him. He didn't even have an opportunity to set his briefcase down on the kitchen counter.

"Rita's principal called me again," Julia said in an excited voice. "I went in and met with her. You won't believe what Rita did now."

11

"What did your daughter do now?" Cliff asked.

"So, she's *my* daughter now?" Julia replied, in a snarky but joking voice.

"Yes."

"I seem to remember you were there when she was conceived."

"I was only a surrogate."

They were moving slowly toward the kitchen. Cliff had come home from work and hadn't even had a chance to put down his things when Julia dropped the Rita and principal bombshell on him.

How big a bombshell could it be when it involved a six-year-old? He was ready to find out but was enjoying the banter and didn't want it to stop.

"A surrogate applies to the female," Julia said, playing along. "A surrogate is the one who carries the baby to term on behalf of other parents. That's what I was. Carrying the baby to full-term for your benefit."

"Thanks for the clarification. Let me rephrase. I was a donor then."

"Try telling that to a judge."

"No way," he said. "We're never getting a divorce. Judges hate me."

Julia laughed. "A more truthful statement has never been spoken. You need to stay as far away from judges as possible."

Cliff was at the kitchen counter now and put his briefcase, gun, keys, and wallet on the island. He wouldn't wander far from that position with a six-year-old in the house. The gun needed to go in the safe as soon as he saw his daughter's smiling face.

He already wondered why Rita hadn't come to greet him. She usually came running when she heard the garage door. Always when the backdoor opened.

"Speaking of Rita, where is she?" Cliff asked. Looking around for her even though she obviously wasn't in the room.

"She's not here."

"Did the principal have her arrested for saying 'God Bless You' after someone sneezed? If so, I might be able to pull some strings and get her out of jail on good behavior. That's assuming she's been good in lock up. Which is a big assumption."

Julia's laugh was cute. Not hearty nor full throated, but more of a feminine chuckle. The kind of seductive laugh that drove men crazy. Like she was doing to him now.

"That's funny, Cliff," Julia said. "Good one. Rita's at a sleepover with Angel. I thought tonight could be our date night. You know. We could go out to dinner. I thought I could be the dessert."

"I'm all for that."

Cliff leaned against the kitchen counter and folded his arms in front of him. He could deal with the gun later since Rita wasn't there. Actually, if they were going out, he'd have to take it with him. As a detective, he was required to have his gun and identification on him at all times when he was out of the house. Even on date night.

"Remind me to tell you about a phone call I had today," Cliff said. "It's very interesting."

"Go ahead and tell me."

"No. I want to hear about Rita first. You said you met with the principal. Why didn't you call me so I could be there?"

"That didn't go so well when you were there the first time. The two of you hit it off like a couple of gladiators in the ring. I thought it'd go better if I went alone."

"Did it?"

"No!"

Julia twisted her lips to the side.

"I was wrong. It didn't go any better."

"Tell me about it. I'm anxious to know what happened."

Julia shifted her feet. Like she was bracing to put some emphasis behind the words. She was clearly anxious to tell him as well.

"Rita's teacher showed a video in class. About how the police oppress the masses."

Cliff let out a groan.

Julia reacted. "I know! It's a bunch of crock."

"The police have their flaws, but I'd hate to live in a country without them."

"I agree. The movie was nothing more than a 'Bash the Police' propaganda video."

"Why would they be showing it to preschoolers?"

"That's a good question. I asked Ms. McVade. The principal."

The woman's face popped into Cliff's head. He could imagine the disdain on her face.

Julia continued. Talking at a faster pace than normal. She was clearly still angry about the meeting. "According to the principal, children are never too young to learn how guns and violence are evil."

Cliff let out a huge breath. Blew it out for effect. Shook his head from side to side in disbelief.

"Oh, it gets better," Julia said. "Or worse, I should say. Ms. McVade did not have very nice things to say about your profession."

"What did she say?"

"You are part of the oppressive state that keeps the regime in power."

Cliff shuttered. He could feel the anger rising inside of him as well.

"I'm glad I wasn't there," he said. "I would've lost it."

"I almost did. I'm proud of myself. I raised my voice, but I somehow managed to control my anger. If I'd said half the things I was thinking, I'd be the one in jail right now."

"What does it have to do with Rita?" Cliff asked. "What did she do?"

"I'm getting to that. After the video was over, the teacher asked the students to write one sentence on a piece of paper. What they thought of the video."

"I can't wait to hear this."

"Rita wrote, IT WAS STUPID. In big, red letters. All caps."

Cliff burst out laughing.

"Good for her."

"Rita's teacher wasn't amused. She made Rita stand in front of the class and apologize."

"Now I'm not amused. I'm angry. She shouldn't embarrass our child by making an example of her in front of the class."

"Oh Rita wasn't embarrassed. She stood up in front of the class and said the video was, and I quote, 'left-wing liberal propaganda.'"

Cliff clapped his hands together. He'd never been more proud of his daughter.

"Rita used those words?" he said. "Propaganda. That's impressive for a six-year-old."

Julia let out a hoot.

"Where do you think Rita learned those words?" She put her finger on Cliff's chest. "I told you Rita hears everything you say and mimics it. She's heard you say that very thing more times than I can count. Usually when we're listening to one of those cable news channels."

Those were banned in their house. They hadn't watched the news on any channel for a long time. Other than local news.

Cliff felt a wide grin come on his face. "It is left wing, liberal, commie..."

Julia put her finger over his lips to stop him.

"Don't say it."

"So what happened next?" he asked.

"Rita was sent to the principal's office. Ms. McVade made Rita sit in the corner for the rest of the day to learn her lesson."

"She did not!"

"I swear she did. I was furious. I told Ms. McVade that she will never punish my child like that again without my permission. Which she won't get. Ms. McVade's actions border on the absurd."

"Good for you. I'm proud of you for sticking up to the lady. We need to pull Rita out of that school."

"We don't have to. Rita was kicked out."

"I thought you said the teacher made Rita sit in the corner for her punishment. Why punish her if she was going to be expelled?"

"That was two days ago. Today was when the proverbial 'you know what' hit the fan."

"What happened today?"

"They played the second half of the video. Rita put her hands over her eyes."

"Why?"

"So she didn't have to watch the video. She actually alternated between putting them over her eyes and ears."

Cliff could barely contain his laughter. He could see Rita doing it.

"The teacher told her to quit," Julia said. "She did. You know, I told her to obey her teacher."

"So what's the problem?"

"All the other kids in the class started doing it. The teacher was practically in tears screaming at the top of her lungs for the kids to stop. They wouldn't. The teacher left the classroom. Can you believe that? She left the kids alone, mind you. Five and six year olds. She went down to the principal's office and told Ms. McVade. The principal stormed down to the classroom and read the kids the riot act. She made Rita leave the classroom since she was the instigator. Then called me."

"It's a good thing I wasn't there. I'd have read her the riot act."

"Trust me, I let her have a piece of my mind."

"She deserved it."

"That's when Ms. McVade told me, in no uncertain terms, that Rita was no longer welcome at the school."

"That's unbelievable. This is a public school. We should complain to the school board."

"I intend to. I've been thinking about joining the PTA and bringing it up at one of the meetings."

"I think you should."

"Anyway. I don't want it to ruin our evening. I wanted tonight to be special for us."

"How's Rita doing?" Cliff asked.

"She acts like nothing happened. She's her same old perky self."

Cliff took Julia in his arms. She placed her head on his chest.

"Rita's tough like her momma. She's not going to take any guff off anybody."

Julia lifted her head and Cliff kissed her.

"Where are we going for our date?" he asked.

"I don't know. You decide and I'll make the reservations."

"How about our favorite?"

"Sounds good."

"I'm going to take a shower first and get changed."

"I'll call the restaurant and then join you in the shower."

It wasn't as hard to put the events of the day out of Cliff's mind as he thought it was going to be.

***

Champions Bar

It felt like old times.

Pre-Rita. Cliff actually felt his shoulders relax. He wasn't on call, so he put his phone on silent. He didn't wear a tie, so he actually felt like his neck could breathe for the first time that week.

He wore a suit jacket, but only to hide the gun on his hip. He had on blue jeans and loafers and a white polo shirt.

He almost felt normal. Except for the gun, he was like everyone else in the sports bar.

It felt good.

Julia had a glass of wine and her whole demeanor changed. She appeared to be over the traumatic events of the day. Or if she wasn't, she didn't let it show.

Neither of them probably realized how uptight they'd become over the last few weeks and years. The stress of their jobs and the care of Rita had put them on constant edge. Not that they'd trade their lives or

Rita for anything in the world. It's that they didn't take enough time to unwind. Cliff was realizing that now.

Julia was right. They'd lost a little spark in their marriage.

Tonight was something they should've done sooner and should do more often.

They finished the meal, including a rare dessert, and should've asked for a check, but neither of them wanted the evening to end.

Cliff assumed things were going to be a lot of fun once they got back to the house, but he wasn't in a rush to get there. He was enjoying being out. The ambiance. The relaxed atmosphere. The restaurant wasn't fancy or high priced. Casual. Great food. Packed with customers. TV's lined the walls and baseball games were on every channel.

The din in the room was slightly below a roar and made it feel even more special. Like they weren't alone. Which they weren't. Except for the times when he gazed deeply into his wife's eyes and it felt like they were the only two people in the room.

He loved her so much.

"That was good," Cliff said, smacking his lips and rubbing his stomach.

"I'm stuffed," Julia said. "I don't remember the last time I ate that much. Or drank that much. I can see why wine is addictive. I haven't been this relaxed in a long time. If we had it around the house, I'd be tempted to drink a glass every night."

"A lot of people do."

Julia's eyes narrowed and she got a more serious look on her face.

"You said to remind you about a phone call you got at work today. So count yourself reminded."

Cliff had forgotten. He waved his hand in the air.

"Let's talk about it tomorrow. It's something to do with the Henry Lee Clay case. I don't want to ruin our night together. I'm having a good time with you."

"It won't ruin it for me. I like it when you talk to me about work. It makes me feel close to you."

He hesitated.

He did want to tell her.

He started slowly. "I was at work. I got a call. From Misty Matthews."

"Henry Lee Clay's girlfriend."

"How do you remember that? It was ten years ago. I probably only mentioned her to you once or twice."

"I don't know. I remember names. It's my thing."

"Okay. Anyway. She called me. Out of the blue. That's the last person I expected to be on the other line."

"What did she want?"

"She called to tell me that she lied. That Henry Lee Clay wasn't with her the day Tessie was killed."

"That's huge, but you already knew that since Clay did kill Tessie. He couldn't have been with her."

"That's right. It's good to hear it from her, though. It's further confirmation that I didn't get it wrong."

"It's a little late now, don't you think?"

Cliff could feel the tension rising in his shoulders again. Maybe it hadn't been a good idea to talk about it. They were ruining the mood.

"It is too late," Cliff said, searching for a way to change the subject. "She knows that. She heard about Clay getting arrested for killing Summer."

"Allegedly."

"What?"

"Allegedly killing Summer. He hasn't been convicted yet."

Cliff was suddenly angry. "Not allegedly. He killed her."

"Innocent until proven guilty."

"Why are you doing this?"

"Doing what?"

"You're trying to provoke an argument."

"No. I'm not. I'm simply pointing out that he hasn't been convicted yet."

"Why can't you support me on this?"

Julia leaned forward in her chair. "I have a theory about Henry Lee Clay and Wayne Bowman. They might be innocent of the crimes they're charged with. Do you want to hear it?"

"No! I don't want to hear it. I have no interest in hearing one of your far-fetched theories."

"How do you know it's far-fetched when you haven't heard it?"

"Anything that says Clay and Bowman didn't kill those girls is far-fetched. I've seen the evidence."

"Hear me out. You might change your mind."

"I'm not having this discussion with you," Cliff said, angrily. His voice was raised. So much so that he noticed others looking at them. It wasn't really appropriate to discuss a pending case with Julia. Certainly not in a way that other people could hear it.

"You're so stubborn, Cliff."

"You're ruining our evening, Julia. I told you we shouldn't talk about work until tomorrow."

"I'm not ruining anything. You're the one getting angry. I'm trying to have a civil conversation and you're getting mad at me."

"You're not the investigator for the Chicago P.D."

"I know that."

"I'm the senior homicide detective. It's my job to investigate these murders. Not you."

"Of course. I'm only trying to help."

"I don't need your help."

He saw a hurt look come across her face.

"What do you want me to do, Julia?" he said, lowering his voice to a whisper. "Go in and tell the D.A. that I made a mistake. That Henry Lee Clay didn't kill Summer. That Bowman didn't kill that girl. They'd laugh me out of the office. They wouldn't believe me anyway. A lot of man hours has gone into these cases."

"I thought your job was about truth and justice. Do you want to convict the wrong man of the wrong crime?"

"What are you talking about? Have you lost your mind? Henry Lee Clay killed Summer. His DNA and fingerprints are at the scene. I have a receipt that he purchased the wine. Why are we even having this discussion? I told you I didn't want to talk about it."

"I'm sorry I brought it up," she said coolly. Julia sat back in her chair with her arms folded. The beautiful smile from earlier was replaced with a scowl.

"Not as sorry as I am," Cliff said just as coolly.

"Fine! I'll never discuss one of your cases with you again."

"Now who's mad?"

"I thought you liked it when I told you my ideas."

"I did. I mean, I do. But not in this case. It's personal. Henry Lee Clay is a killer. Misty Matthews confirmed it. Everybody in my office knows he did it. The Lieutenant. The D.A. Why do you think you know better than them?"

She turned her head away. "I'll keep my mouth shut."

"Thank you. That's all I'm asking."

The frost between them was colder than an iceberg.

Cliff motioned for a check.

They drove home in silence. When they got in bed, he kissed her on the forehead and they each turned their backs to each other.

The tension was thicker than a prison yard.

Cliff was kicking himself. The evening hadn't turned out like he had expected. He thought they'd come home and make love. Things had been going so well.

He was angrier at himself than he was at Julia. He made a mental note to never bring up work on date night again.

This was the first night in a long time they went to sleep mad.

He tossed and turned. About two in the morning, he must've been asleep because he bolted up in the bed.

Something had jolted him. What was it? The fight with Julia? The phone call from Misty Matthews?

No. Something was weighing heavy on his mind. Something Julia had said.

"They might be innocent."

Cliff got angry all over again. They weren't. He had the proof.

But why was Julia so adamant about telling him her theory? What did she know that he didn't know?

He tried to go back to sleep but the conversation weighed heavily on his mind.

The next morning, things were different. Julia wasn't mad. They both apologized and made up.

Cliff wanted to hear Julia's theories.

But he was too proud to bring it up again, so he didn't.

12

Three years later

Henry Lee Clay had finally exhausted all his appeals. He was sentenced to eighty years in prison for the rape and murder of Summer Lange. Meaning he'd likely serve the remainder of his life behind bars.

Clay's lawyers had put up a tremendous fight. They put Cliff on trial and ran his name through the mud. Accusing him of every investigative crime they could think of. In the end, the evidence was so overwhelming that the jury came back with a guilty verdict after two days of deliberations.

When the jury didn't come back with a verdict after one day, Cliff had been worried they might have a hung jury. Eventually, he got word the jury had reached a verdict and he rushed to the courthouse with tremendous trepidation. Nerve racking apprehension that the jury might somehow find Clay not guilty.

His worry had been for nothing. His fear turned to exhilaration when he heard the words from the foreman, "We find the defendant, Henry Lee Clay, guilty."

Guilty on all counts.

The judge threw the book at Clay. Noting the extreme viciousness of the crime.

"A man like you should never spend another day outside of a prison cell," the judge said during sentencing. "This is one of the most heinous crimes that has ever come into my courtroom."

The defense had asked for leniency.

"If I could sentence you to a longer sentence, I would," the judge said, dashing any hopes Clay had of a lighter sentence.

Clay's lawyers had vigorously appealed the verdict. Slamming Cliff with every turn of the judicial lever. The appeals courts rejected the arguments and Clay had reached a dead end. No one else to appeal to. If he were ever to get out of prison, he'd have to secure a pardon from the Governor or President, or get his conviction somehow overturned by new evidence.

Wayne Bowman got even harsher treatment from his judge. He was convicted and sentenced to life in prison without the possibility of parole. Probably because his victim was a young girl and he had a pro bono attorney who put forth minimal effort.

Cliff was worried the conviction might be overturned on appeal for ineffective counsel. That argument was never raised since Bowman couldn't afford a high priced appellate attorney and had to use the pro bono one. Who put even less effort into the appeal than he did the trial.

Cliff could finally put both cases behind him. Justice was done. Two killers were behind bars. He'd been vindicated, which was a bonus. The Henry Lee Clay wrongful conviction verdict was a distant memory. Except for the most cynical, an impartial observer knew Cliff was innocent of the accusations and the sixteen-million-dollar settlement was a travesty.

Clay had killed Tessie. The judge had been wrong in overturning the original conviction. Summer Lange was dead because of that judge.

Cliff never spoke of his conversation with Misty Matthews to anyone. Other than to tell Julia about it. He'd promised Misty that he wouldn't disclose her secret, and he'd kept that promise. With Clay behind bars, she could now rest easy that he'd never be a threat to her or her family.

The massive Henry Lee Clay case files arrived from the D.A.'s office and Cliff wanted to be there as they were archived into the closed case room. It felt good to put an exclamation point behind them and have that horrible chapter in his life nothing more than a memory.

Cliff was a man of deep faith. He felt like things had somehow worked together for good in the end. It didn't seem like it on that day when the judge freed Clay and wrongly accused Cliff of horrendous acts. But the truth won out in the end, and Cliff could sleep well at night knowing he'd put two murderers behind bars and had been integrous through the entire process.

Never compromising.

Relentless in the pursuit of justice.

The system had worked in the end. Henry Lee Clay and Wayne Bowman would spend tonight in jail.

Cliff would spend the night with a beautiful woman.

Julia.

Date night.

They'd consistently set aside one night a week for each other. Not always, but most of the time. It'd been good for their relationship. The spark was back. Or at least it was like the pilot light on a furnace. They kept a steady flow of gas running to the flame and it kept the light from going out.

He had never loved her more. And wanted to show her. Tonight. On their date. They were going to celebrate his major victory.

Considering they both had extremely demanding jobs and Rita was nine going on thirty, they were doing pretty well in their marriage. They still lived in the same house. Neither of them had the energy or motivation to move with everything that entailed. So their life had settled into a comfortable routine.

When they let themselves dream, they thought about moving somewhere warm. Julia grew up in Miami and would like to return there someday. Maybe when Cliff retired and Rita was married and out of the house.

The harsh winters of Chicago were the only thing Cliff didn't like about his life.

On the way home, he stopped by a high-end liquor store. In a ritzy strip mall with expensive fancy shops.

When he walked in, he thought he'd entered into another world. Everything was marble. A large chandelier hung from the center over a thick rug with the logo of the store in the center. Mirrors lined the walls and ceilings adding to the effect.

The salesmen wore black suits and ties. The women wore tight fitting dresses with high heels. Within seconds of walking through the door, Cliff was greeted by a man with a thin mustache and a French accent.

"Good afternoon, sir. Welcome to *Georgiana's*. How may I be of service to you today?"

"I'm looking for a bottle of champagne," Cliff said. "Something really nice. What do you recommend? For a special occasion."

"I have just the thing," he said. "Follow me."

He led Cliff toward the back of the store. Navigating through the fancy shelves with glittery bottles of wine on them. The man stopped at one particular area and took something off the shelf and handed it to Cliff.

It felt like he was handing Cliff a newborn baby. That's what it felt like holding it. He suddenly became insecure. Afraid he was going to drop it. He held it with two hands just in case his sweaty palms lost their grip.

What was he supposed to do? Look at it? Shake it? Read the label?

Not sure, he handed it back to the man like it was a hot potato.

The man took it and skillfully sat it back on the shelf. Then pointed to a box.

"It comes in this designer gift box."

The box was jet black. Almost velvety but that was an illusion. An ace of spades logo was on the outside of the box. The same design had been on the bottle as well.

Cliff had to admit that the labeling was impressive and looked expensive. That's what he was going for. Tonight, he was going to splurge to make things special for Julia who'd endured the whole Henry Lee Clay fiasco with him.

"This is an exquisite champagne," the man said in a hoity toity voice. "It's an Armand de Brignac Ace of Spades Brut Gold."

Ace of spades is perfect, Cliff thought.

Maybe it's a sign.

Sort of like the Henry Lee Clay case. Cliff felt like he'd been dealt four aces today. Two anyway. Bowman and Clay were behind bars with no possibility of parole or appeals.

Life was good. All was right in the world again.

"It is a trio of vintages," the man continued. "A special blend. Forty percent Pinot Noir. Forty percent Chardonnay. And twenty percent Pinot Meunier."

"Don't ask me to spell those," Cliff quipped.

The employee chuckled dutifully. At any moment, Cliff expected the man to take out a silk handkerchief and brush something off Cliff's shoulders. Or reach over and straighten Cliff's hair, which was probably mussed.

Cliff suddenly wished he had a breath mint in his pocket. He felt underdressed even though he had on his suit and tie.

"It is a prestigious Cuvée," the man said.

Cliff had no idea what a koo... vay was.

The man continued. "This wine is gentle on the palate. It has a vibrant fresh fruit character. Layers of complexity. It is soft and creamy with a hint of toastiness."

"I like toast."

Cliff quickly regretted the remark. That's probably not what the man meant.

This was all way over his head. He was so far out of his element, he couldn't even see the periodic table.

"The palate is soft and rich with cherries, exotic fruits, a touch of lemon, vanilla, and honey."

"I'd be afraid to drink it."

"I don't understand what you mean," the man said, pressing his lips together in a confused manner.

"Never mind."

"What is the special occasion? If you don't mind me asking."

I put two low life scumbag murderers behind bars for the rest of their lives.

Cliff wasn't about to mention that.

"It is special. It's for my wife."

"Is it her birthday? Anniversary?"

"No. It's because she's so pretty. And good to me. I want to do something special for her. For standing by me all these years. I want to express my love to her."

"*Le grand amour*. True love. Outstanding sentiment. This champagne certainly speaks of love and, shall we say... *Une histoire d'amour*."

"I'm sorry. I don't speak French."

"A love story. An *une déclaration d'amour*. A declaration of your love."

"Exactly! That's what I want to express to my wife. I want to declare my undying love for her."

"Beautiful. I am a romantic at heart." He put his hand on his chest. Cliff thought he was going to burst into song.

"How much does this wine cost?" Cliff asked.

He wasn't sure he wanted to know. He kind of had his heart set on the ace of spades. It sounded perfect.

Cliff didn't see any prices anywhere. It occurred to him that this was the kind of store where if you had to ask then you couldn't afford it. That's probably what the Frenchman was thinking.

Cliff intended to spend three hundred dollars. The same amount Henry Lee Clay spent the night he murdered Summer Lange. Kind of a morbid symbolic gesture on Cliff's part. But something he wanted to do. A redeeming act somehow.

Julia would think it was excessive. Stupid even. It was. But they could afford it. They'd built up their savings. Neither of them spent money other than for the basics. Their vacations were modest. They drove dependable cars. Newer. More expensive than the average. Only because Cliff wanted Julia and Rita to be safe. To not break down somewhere in Chicago. Maybe in a bad area or during a frigid cold spell.

A bottle of wine Cliff had in mind would cost half of one of their car payments. But he was determined to spend it.

When the clerk said three thirty-nine, Cliff said, "I'll take it."

"Like I said, it comes in this beautiful gift box."

"Perfect."

When they got to the counter Cliff pulled out his wallet and handed the man a five-dollar bill. The Frenchman looked at it and then twisted his lips to the side. Obviously confused.

"What is this?" he asked.

"You said it was three thirty nine. Three dollars and thirty-nine cents. I figure there's tax. So I gave you a five."

He looked even more confused.

Cliff started laughing. "I'm joking."

The man chuckled nervously. He still didn't get the joke.

Cliff took the five back out of the man's hand and gave him his credit card.

The man put a bow around the box and Cliff left. He went straight to the restaurant and dropped off the wine, so it'd be chilled that night. The manager was extremely accommodating even though Cliff was bringing his own wine.

Cliff had asked if it was okay when he made the reservation.

This was a new restaurant for them. A surprise for Julia. *Restaurant Le 49*. French. Cliff looked up some French terms for expressing love. Inspired by the Frenchman at the wine store.

Next Cliff went to another store and bought a greeting card. Filled it out in the car before he headed home.

He was running late. Julia was already ready. She was dressed in one of her little black dresses that he loved. He showered quickly, alone, and Julia was giving the babysitter last minute instructions when he walked out of the bedroom ready to go.

Rita and her mother were arguing. The nine year old thought she was old enough to stay home alone without a babysitter. Cliff reminded her that a babysitter would soon be replaced by a chaperone who would follow her around everywhere she went during her teenage years and early twenties. With a cattle prod in his hand in case she got within five feet of another boy.

Rita didn't find it amusing. Cliff thought it was hilarious.

"Where are we going?" Julia asked when they were finally on the road.

"It's a surprise."

Julia didn't like surprises, but she seemed pleased when they pulled up in front of the fancy restaurant and the valet took their car and they went inside. The restaurant was upscale. Elegant. Marble floors. High ceilings with gold chandeliers and gold inlays on the columns.

The mood was romantic and inviting. A pianist played softly in the corner. The lights were slightly dimmed.

The waiter brought out the ace of spades champagne and Julia was impressed. Cliff didn't tell her how much it cost. He didn't want to ruin the evening. He'd tell her tomorrow. Maybe.

Cliff even had the waiter pour him a half a glass and proposed a toast to his *amour de ma vie*. The love of his life.

Julia blushed slightly. Looked at him lovingly. The champagne and atmosphere was working. She was relaxing. This was one of the most romantic things they'd ever done. And they were just getting started.

Cliff tasted the champagne. He wasn't going to spend more than three hundred dollars and not try it.

"The palate is soft and rich with cherries, exotic fruits, a touch of lemon, vanilla, and honey," Cliff said in a butchered french accent, trying to remember word for word what the employee at the store had said about it.

Julia found it amusing to hear Cliff use the word "palate" in a sentence.

They enjoyed the drink together. The waiter let them finish before bringing a menu.

Julia ordered the Escalope de Porc Provençale.

Cliff tried to say it three times in a row to her amusement.

The dish was scallopini with capers, tomatoes, and lemon butter sauce. Cliff had lamb chops with grilled vegetables and pommes frites, which he thought were French fries. Turned out they were potatoes.

Technically, according to Julia, they should've both had fish to go with the wine Cliff had purchased.

They both passed on the dessert du jour.

Cliff gave her the greeting card at the end of the meal. Julia was slowly nursing another glass of wine. The bottle was almost empty.

The card was touching based on her reaction.

"Ahh," she said. "That's so sweet. I love you, too."

Julia preferred personalized cards. So, Cliff had written out some thoughts. The best he could anyway.

"Tonight has been perfect," she said a little later as it became apparent the meal was winding down. The restaurant wasn't full so they didn't need to worry about rushing out of there.

"I wanted tonight to be perfect for you," Cliff said. "It's a special occasion."

"What's the occasion?"

Cliff hesitated. Should he bring it up?

"I got some good news today."

"Tell me."

It seemed out of place considering the atmosphere.

"Today, I got word that Henry Lee Clay's appeal was denied," Cliff blurted. "That's his last one. The case is over."

"That's wonderful, Cliff. That is good news. And worth celebrating." She lifted her glass in the air, took a bigger sip than normal, and giggled like a schoolgirl.

"I'm proud of you," she added.

"Thank you."

Then Cliff said something stupid.

"Do you remember when we had a fight about the Henry Lee Clay case? A few years ago?"

"I do."

"We got in a huge fight when I didn't hear your theory about the case."

"I remember," she said, with a little bit of an icy tone. "Why are you bringing it up now?"

That was a good question. Why was he?

"I'd like to hear your theory now."

"Oh, no... not a chance."

"Why not? Tell me."

"What difference does it make? You said the case is over."

"That's what I mean. What will it hurt if you tell me?"

"I don't want you to get mad at me. We're doing really good. I think that was probably our last fight. The last time we went to bed mad anyway. I don't want to ruin things. We've had a pleasant evening. I want to go home and make love to you."

"We will. I won't let it ruin our night. I promise. I'll be mad at you if you don't tell me."

He smiled widely so she'd know he was kidding.

"Are you sure you want to know?" she asked, hesitantly.

"I'm sure."

"Okay. Here goes. What if Wayne Bowman actually killed Summer and Clay was the one who killed the girl? What if you got it backwards?"

Cliff had only had a few sips of the champagne, but his head started spinning.

13

Cliff rubbed his eyes roughly.

Julia had just dropped a huge bombshell into the middle of their beautiful romantic evening at *Restaurant Le 49*. With the cockamamie theory that Wayne Bowman was the one who actually killed Summer Lange and Henry Lee Clay killed Nancee Hale.

Was it that far-fetched?

He had to admit, he'd never considered the possibility. Something about it rang true.

No way.

Bowman and Clay were convicted by two separate juries. Twenty-four people. The evidence was overwhelming. The judges believed they were guilty given the harshness of the sentences. The appellate courts all confirmed their guilt.

It didn't get any more compelling than that for an investigator.

Not that Julia didn't mean well. But anyone could take a set of facts and make them fit into any number of plausible scenarios. Only one was the truth. Cliff felt certain he'd gotten it right.

He did value Julia's instincts. After they had their fight three years before, back when Julia wanted to tell him her theory the first time, things had been cold between them for a few weeks. Especially on the investigative front. He didn't talk about his cases. She didn't ask. A sort of détente ensued.

More of a cold war.

Then one day, Cliff had a murder case come across his desk. A wealthy octogenarian died. A man on his deathbed was murdered. He'd actually lived longer than anyone had expected. Cliff didn't care. A murder was a murder. It didn't matter if the victim only had one day to live. No one had the right to end his life.

The murderer tried to make it look like the rich man died of natural causes, but Cliff saw right through the ruse. He suspected the heirs. They stood to inherit tens of millions of dollars.

Something bothered Cliff about it. The heirs only had to wait a couple more days and they would've gotten the money anyway. He mentioned the case one night over dinner to Julia. She asked a few questions. He hesitated to answer them, but eventually explained the details.

When he was done, she said emphatically, "The butler did it."

"Was he killed with a candlestick?" Cliff joked, making a reference to a famous murder mystery board game.

"Nope," she said, matter-of-factly, ignoring his comment. "The butler drugged his food."

Cliff humored her even though he dismissed her theory as craziness at the time. He didn't want to get into another fight. Especially since tensions were beginning to subside from the last one.

Turned out, Julia was right. The butler did it. He did drug the man's food. Forensics found traces of a drug called Belladonna in the pantry cabinet. Translated "beautiful woman" in Italian. It's a plant most commonly known as Deadly Nightshade. The drug was common in the eighteenth and nineteenth centuries. Mostly used as a pain reliever, but also as a muscle relaxer. It was even in women's cosmetics.

In small doses, belladonna didn't hurt anyone. However, a single leaf, if ingested, was lethal. The butler admitted to putting a whole leaf in his boss's tea and breaking up a leaf and mixing it with the butter on his toast to be certain it'd do the job.

From that point on, Cliff started asking Julia for help whenever he ran into roadblocks on a case. He never did ask her about her theory related to the Clay and Bowman cases though. That was a subject they had successfully avoided for more than three years.

Cliff should not have brought it up now. They were having a wonderful evening. Everything had been perfect up to that point. The champagne. The French restaurant. Julia said they were making love when they got home.

That's what they should be doing right this second. Not talking about a three year old case that was already closed.

Cliff let out an indiscernible sigh.

The cork was off the bottle of champagne so to speak. Literally and figuratively. No way to put it back in.

The thoughts had obviously been pent up inside her all these years. She'd clearly been wanting to share them with Cliff. To her credit, she'd maintained the same self-control as he had and had avoided the topic.

He hadn't asked and she hadn't opened her mouth.

Until now.

At his prompting. He should've left well enough alone.

Cliff consciously told himself to tamp down any anger he might be feeling. What did it hurt to hear her out? Let her tell him her theory. Bowman and Clay were behind bars. The cases were over. Nothing Julia could say would change that fact.

He gave himself a mental pep talk filled with instructions.

Take a deep breath. Let her talk. Nod your head. Don't be condescending. Don't dismiss her theory out of hand. Be considerate when asking questions. Affirm her. Make her feel loved. Don't blow it. You're going to have a good time tonight when you get home. If you don't say something stupid.

Cliff pursed his lips shut and tightened his jaw. Buckled his proverbial emotional seatbelt and stared at his clearly excited wife so she'd know he was listening.

Julia was nervous.

She smacked her lips together.

"Okay. Let's start with the Summer Lange murder," she said. "The old woman who lived across the street said she heard a scream at nine-thirty-one that night. She went to the window and looked out. She didn't see the red sports car belonging to Henry Lee Clay."

"That's right."

Shut up, Cliff.

He'd be an idiot if he kept interrupting her.

"The rape and murder were violent," Julia said. "More than a hundred stab wounds. Clay didn't have enough time to kill Summer, get in his car, and leave. Not between the time the woman heard the scream and the time she looked out her window."

Cliff couldn't keep his mouth shut. It'd be like telling himself not to breathe. He was an investigator. With an inquisitive mind. He had to interject his thoughts. Regardless of how risky it was to do so.

He made a conscious effort to keep a respectful tone. They were just talking about it. It didn't have to end up in a fight.

"I didn't find the woman's testimony that credible. She's older. I'm not sure she can even hear a scream from her bedroom coming all the way across the street. I also don't know if 9:31 is accurate."

"Still. It took time for Clay to rape Summer, would you agree with that?"

"The defense argued in its opening statement that the sex was consensual," Cliff said. "Rough, but Summer willingly participated in it. Clay's attorney said that when Clay left the scene, she was very much alive."

"That fits with the testimony of the woman. According to her, Clay was already gone when she heard the scream. If he was already gone, he couldn't have killed her."

Cliff felt a rise of anger starting to boil up inside, but he knocked it down with a mental sledgehammer.

Try smiling.

He smiled at Julia. She leaned forward with her elbows on the table. Fully engaged. Studying him up and down for his reaction.

"Okay," he said. "Let's assume for the sake of discussion that your theory is correct. Let's say Clay didn't kill Summer. Why do you think Bowman did it?"

"He was stalking Summer. According to her parents she was afraid of him. He came to her work."

"That's hearsay."

Julia grimaced.

Cliff had been doing so well. Why did he have to be argumentative? A thousand voices screamed inside his head to humor her. Or he'd be sorry he didn't.

"This isn't a court of law," Julia said roughly. "We're only discussing it. You'd agree that Bowman has violent tendencies. If he's capable of killing the young girl, he's capable of killing Summer."

"No doubt about it."

Julia smiled at him.

He was back on track.

"What if Bowman was there that night? Stalking Summer. Watching in the shadows."

"The neighbor didn't see or hear a motorcycle."

"He was in the white van. That's why he got rid of it. It had Summer's blood all in it."

"The old woman across the street didn't mention a white van."

"Did you ask her if she saw one?"

"No. I didn't have any reason at the time to ask. Besides, Bowman wouldn't be dumb enough to park the white van in the driveway. He'd park down the street. "

"Another salient point, Detective Ford. Think about what you just said. Why would Clay park his red sports car in the driveway if he intended to kill Summer? He'd have to know someone would see it."

She paused waiting for Cliff to respond. When he didn't, she continued. Cliff had decided to keep his mouth shut. Julia was making good points.

"When Bowman saw Clay leave, he was infuriated. He could only imagine what went on inside of that house. He was jealous with rage. He went inside the house and confronted Summer. Then killed her. Stabbed her more than a hundred times. Something a jealous ex-boyfriend would do in a fit of rage."

Julia paused again. Cliff didn't respond. He was deep in thought. He'd gone from humoring Julia, biding his time until they could get home, to seriously considering her theory.

Since Cliff didn't interject anything, Julia said, "Why didn't you find Summer's blood in the sports car? Wouldn't it be all over Clay's clothes?"

"The defense argued that point at trial."

"If you stab someone a hundred times, I'd think you'd have blood all over you."

"Wayne Bowman had Nancee Hale's blood on him."

"A slight amount. On his boot and a dab on his shirt. Not much blood. Considering he'd just murdered her."

"It was only one slice to the throat. Not nearly as much blood as the other crime scene. How did Bowman get Nancee's blood on him? It obviously proves he was there that night."

"He was following Clay."

"There's no evidence that Clay was there."

"Did you ever consider it? You only saw Bowman's motorcycle on the security camera. Did you look for a red sports car?"

"No."

"What if Bowman was following Clay? To kill him. He saw Clay pick up Nancee Hale. Followed them to the park. You said a couple saw Bowman in the park."

"They identified him in a lineup."

"What did they say he was doing?"

"Acting suspiciously."

"Exactly. But where was the girl?"

"The couple never saw her. She was dead behind the building."

"Then why was Bowman still at the scene? Why didn't he leave? If the couple saw him, he must've seen them. Why didn't he leave immediately?"

"You tell me. It's your theory."

"Because he wasn't doing anything wrong. Other than following Clay. Which is not illegal. But he was curious. So he hung around the parking lot. He didn't know the girl was dead. He only knew that Clay picked her up and brought her to the park."

Cliff shrugged his shoulders.

"Did you ever ask the couple if they saw a red sports car?"

"It never occurred to me."

"Exactly. The couple drives up. They see the Harley. Call 911. Then leave. Clay leaves. Bowman is curious, so he gets off his motorcycle and walks behind the building where he sees the dead girl. He checks her neck for a pulse. Feels blood. Wipes the blood on his shirt. Accidently steps in the pool of blood. Leaves a footprint on the sidewalk."

"You have a vivid imagination."

Undeterred she said, "Bowman goes home. Notices the blood. Tries to wash it off his boot. He can't. It's stained. So he throws the boots away in the trash. Never in a million years does he think you'll come by his house to question him about the Nancee Hale murder."

"I only did because I was investigating him for Summer's murder."

"Exactly!" Julia said. Pointing her finger at Cliff. "Did you ever find it strange that the two murders were connected by the same two people?"

"It did seem strange. But they weren't connected. Only by coincidence."

"You always say there's no such thing as coincidence."

"Most of the time, that's true. Not a hundred percent of the time."

Julia leaned in even further and lowered her voice to slightly above a whisper. "Here's the thing. And don't be offended, Cliff. What I'm about to say is human nature. It's easy to make the evidence fit the theory rather than the other way around."

"Are you saying that's what I did?"

Cliff should've felt offended, but he didn't. If Julia was right, this was a classic case of prejudging.

"With all due respect, there were a lot of problems in your cases," Julia said. "You never found Nancee's DNA on Bowman's motorcycle. Why not? According to your theory, she got on the motorcycle and rode to the park with him. That means she sat on the back. With her arms around his waist. How does she avoid getting DNA or a fiber of her hair on the bike or on his jacket?"

"The wind blew it off. He could've washed it off. At the same time he washed off the boots."

"Or she rode to the park with Clay. Not Bowman."

"Why didn't Bowman testify on his own behalf at his trial?" Cliff said. "Better yet. Why didn't he cooperate with me when I brought him in? Tell me the whole story. Pin the murder of the girl on Clay."

"Because it would've tied him to Summer's murder. He'd have to explain why he was following Clay."

"He was already a suspect in Summer's murder."

"That's what I mean. Bowman couldn't talk. It would be much better to be charged with the girl's murder than Summer's. Because he didn't do it. Cliff, you said so yourself. Had Bowman had a halfway decent attorney, he would've gotten off. The evidence was flimsy at best. His attorney never mounted a vigorous defense."

"I wouldn't say the evidence was flimsy. I had the eyewitnesses who put him at the scene. I had the blood evidence."

"But no murder weapon and no DNA on Nancee or on Bowman."

"I didn't have Summer's murder weapon either."

"That's because Bowman had time to dispose of it."

"We're getting way off track here."

"Let's get back on track. Why was Bowman still in the park if he'd already killed the girl? Why didn't he hightail it out of there? Instead, the eyewitnesses see him hanging around in plain sight. Who kills someone, then doesn't try to hide from other people in the park who might see him?"

"Somebody who has nothing to hide."

"Exactly. That's reasonable doubt in and of itself."

"It's an interesting theory. But that's all it is. A theory. A version of the facts."

"There's one other thing. Would a sixteen-year-old girl be more likely to get in a red Porsche with a decent looking professional or on a Harley Davidson with a man like Wayne Bowman?"

"You'd be surprised."

"When I was her age, I would've been scared to death to accept a ride from a biker dude."

"You wouldn't have gotten in the car with Clay either."

"No I wouldn't have. But I could see where a curious sixteen-year-old might."

"Either way, it cost her her life."

"A good lesson for all of us. We need to teach Rita to stay away from those situations."

"Don't worry. She'll have a chaperone with her at all times."

"Ha. Ha. Good luck with that."

The tension was mostly gone. Cliff was proud of himself for not causing a confrontation.

"See. I didn't get mad at you," he said.

"No. You didn't. I appreciate you hearing me out."

He saw relief wash over her face. She smiled lovingly at him.

"I appreciate you sharing your theory with me," Cliff said, sincerely.

"Like you said, it doesn't matter now. The two men are in jail. Tomato. Tomato. Six or half a dozen. Same thing. Even if the two are convicted of the wrong crime, they are both murderers and behind bars for a long time. Who cares if they weren't convicted of the right crime?"

"I'm not sure the judges would see it that way."

"You have to make sure they never know," she said, ratcheting up the tone again. "Just drop it, Cliff. We talked about it. Let it go. It's over. They are both in jail."

His investigative mind was churning. Julia's theory made sense. It could've happened that way. Probably not. But it was possible. He was already thinking of ways to investigate it.

Security camera footage for one. He never thought to look for Clay's red sports car around the mall. Or Bowman's white van around Summer's neighborhood.

Would the footage still be available? That was three years ago.

Tomorrow, he'd get to work on it.

Julia must've sensed it.

"I mean it, Cliff," she said. "I know you. Let it go. It'd be a big mistake to start investigating things again. It doesn't matter now. They are not, not guilty. Either way. Leave it alone."

Cliff wasn't sure he could.

14

Illinois State Penitentiary

This stint in prison was going better for Henry Lee Clay than the first one. Relatively speaking. Mostly because of the sixteen million dollars. Money could buy influence inside the prison almost as easily as it could outside. Henry was able to use his wealth to curry favors with the guards and other inmates.

Particularly when it came to protection. Henry was basically untouchable. At any one time, he had a dozen or more thugs watching his back.

It's a good thing he had the money to buy the security, or he'd already be dead. Wayne Bowman was in the same prison, and he clearly wanted Clay dead. Since he was serving life in prison without the chance for parole, Bowman had nothing to lose.

The guards sensed that and separated the two almost immediately. Bowman was housed on one side of the compound and Henry on the other. They were never let out in the yard at the same time.

Bowman was feared by the other inmates. He had the reputation as someone you didn't mess with. Even Clay's security goons kept their distance from him.

Because of that, Clay had to kill Bowman before the obsessed man killed him.

He had a plan to make it happen. Someone in the prison was willing to carry out his plan. Another inmate who also had nothing to lose. Clay was willing to pay almost any cost to make it happen. The going rate for a hit man in prison was five thousand dollars. Clay offered ten times that much.

There was no shortage of willing participants. He'd found the right man for the job. Someone with opportunity and resources. Fearless. Access to any number of sharp objects since he worked in the section that made license plates.

Having Bowman dead was helpful but not the main goal.

The second part of his plan was the most important. That was his ticket out of the hellhole of a prison. Clay's money gave him a few conveniences the other inmates didn't have, but it didn't change the fact that life in prison was miserable. Hardly worth living.

With his hitman in place, Clay approached the second man he needed to make this work. He was in the yard. Standing alone by the fence. Staring out into the oblivion beyond the massive amount of fencing and barbed wire.

Clay approached the man carefully.

Krueger, aka Special K. The K was for killer. Not his surname, Krueger. The man was serving a life sentence for the brutal murder of store clerk at a convenience store. He'd robbed the store, then shot the man just because he could.

Of course, Krueger said he was innocent. Everyone was innocent in prison. Only occasionally, did someone admit to being guilty.

Clay called out the man's name while still a distance away. "Krueger. I want to talk to you."

In prison, you never snuck up on a man by accident or on purpose. That was a good way to find yourself dead or in the infirmary. A man like Clay only approached a man like Krueger if invited. Which he wasn't. He had to tread lightly, and hope Krueger was in a good mood.

"What about?" the mountain of a man said roughly.

"I have a business proposition for you," Clay said with as much confidence as he could muster in his voice.

"Not interested."

"Hear me out. I think you will be."

"Get out of here, before I put your teeth in the back of your throat."

"I got something you want."

That statement could be construed any number of ways. Krueger took it the wrong way.

He was in Clay's face faster than a bullet shot out of a revolver.

Clay was terrified. He wanted to run but couldn't. Krueger was his best chance. All his appeals had been exhausted. He had to find another way out of prison and Krueger was his ticket.

He was getting out of the prison one way or the other. Either walking out a free man or in a body bag. If not a free man, then Krueger might as well put him out of his misery right then and there. Hopefully, his death would be quick and painless.

Clay stood his ground although his legs were so weak, if Krueger stuck his massive finger in his chest, then Clay would fall over backwards. A stiff wind might've knocked him over at that point. That's how unstable his foundation had become.

Krueger was within inches of him. His breath smelled like a horse stable. They weren't exactly eye to eye since Krueger was at least a foot taller. Weighed a hundred fifty pounds more. Hardened muscles. Krueger's fists were the size of Clay's head.

An exaggeration, but it felt that way in the moment.

Clay felt like throwing up. It was all he could do to keep from peeing himself. Either one of those things and he'd lose what little respect Krueger had for him. He might have a little since Clay had money.

Everybody knew Clay was the moneybags. Some used it to their advantage. Curried favors with him. Most couldn't care less. Money meant nothing to men like Krueger.

Power and might were the greater currency in prison.

Clay's security was standing off in the distance watching. He'd told them to stay away. He was on his own. That's the only reason he was still upright. Krueger knew about his goons. Not that he was afraid of them, but he was probably curious as to why this scrawny little weaselly man dared to approach him without his security gang.

"You have nothing I want," Krueger said. "You should turn and walk away while you still can."

"I can get you out of here."

That caused Krueger to laugh. A deep frightening bellow. Not an engaging laugh. Not even taunting. Guttural. Accompanied by a cough likely from years of smoking.

Even Krueger's laugh was intimidating.

"Don't waste my time," he said.

"I have connections."

"Ain't no connections gonna help me get out of here."

"You're wrong. I've got money. I can afford lawyers."

"I have a lawyer. Can't appeal no more."

"There's a way. I can make it worth your while."

"Like I said, I'm not interested. Step away."

"You're not interested in two hundred and fifty grand?"

"Oh sure. I'll build me a condo. Right over there." He pointed toward the main yard. "With a swimming pool," he said sarcastically.

"That's what I'm saying. You won't be in here. I can get you out. You can have that pool on the outside."

"I don't know what you're smoking, but I ain't getting out of here except in a coffin. Which is fine by me. The sooner, the better."

"What about your boy?"

Krueger was back in his face. He grabbed the shirt collar on Clay's gray jumpsuit and lifted him off the ground. The prison guards came running.

"Here me out," Clay said. "Let me down. I'm serious. I can get you the money. For your boy. I can get you out so you can see him."

The guards were on them now. Krueger lowered Clay back to the ground.

"We're fine," Clay said, as the guards were about to tackle Krueger. "We're just messing around. I'm all right."

The guards seemed skeptical, but Clay was the one they were there to protect. They reluctantly turned and walked away after giving them both a warning.

"Let's walk," Clay said.

The prison fence stretched all the way around that side of the compound. They could walk for several hundred yards before they reached the end of it.

Calling off the guards had given Clay some goodwill with Krueger whose attitude had changed somewhat. He seemed willing to listen as they walked slowly away from the main yard.

They had the attention of the man in the tower now. The one with a pair of binoculars and a rifle. He watched their every step.

"What do you want from me?"

"You're Bowman's roommate," Clay said.

"Yeah, what of it? He's got a stick in his crawl for you. You'd better watch your back."

"I want him dead as well."

"If you want me to kill him, you're barking up the wrong tree. I don't like the man, but he ain't done nothing to me. He ain't said ten words to me since we became bunkmates."

"I don't want you to kill him. He's going to be dead soon. It's been arranged."

Krueger chuckled again.

"Good luck with that. There ain't a shard thick enough to kill that bull."

"Let me worry about that."

"Ain't none of my business. What's between the two of you ain't my problem."

"Have you heard of the *Not Guilty Group*?"

"Yeah man. Everybody has."

"They got me out of prison once. I got a sixteen-million-dollar settlement from the city of Chicago for a wrong conviction."

"Good for you. Why were you stupid enough to end up back here?"

"I'm innocent."

Krueger let out a groan. "Yeah right. So am I."

"I'm serious. I really am innocent. I was screwing Bowman's girlfriend. That's why he has it in for me."

"Not a smart move."

"If you saw her, you'd know why I did it."

A lustful grin appeared on Krueger's face.

"Bowman killed his ex-girlfriend," Clay said. "Pinned it on me."

At the time, Clay didn't actually know that Summer had an ex-boyfriend. He had no idea Bowman was stalking them. But he figured it out. After he left Summer's house that night, Bowman went in and killed her. It's the only thing that made sense.

Bowman kept following Clay. Intending to kill him. He was in the park the night Clay killed Nancee Hale. After Clay killed the girl, Bowman must've gotten curious and went behind the building to see what had happened. Accidentally stepped in a pool of Nancee's blood. Got nailed for the murder by that detective, Cliff Ford.

A stroke of fortune for Clay except that Ford nailed him for Summer's murder. A murder he didn't commit. After his conviction, Clay had pleaded his case with the people at the *Not Guilty Group*, who were not interested in helping him. They saw him as a murderer now.

The pretty reporter, Shannon Roberts, was the only one in the world who still believed in him. She'd been to the prison several times to visit. They'd struck up a romance. She was in love with Clay. He was using her to help him get out of jail.

The *Not Guilty Group* said they wouldn't help until all the appeals were exhausted. Even then, Clay would have to come up with new evidence for them to consider taking on his case a second time.

Clay needed Krueger to make that happen.

"Bowman stabbed his girlfriend a hundred times," Clay said.

"Like I said, ain't none of my business."

"What if I make it your business?"

"Oh yeah. $250,000. What do you want me to do? I ain't gonna kill Bowman. I ain't stupid."

"I told you, I've already taken care of that. You don't have to kill anyone. Once he's dead, all you have to do is tell my attorney that Bowman told you he killed Summer."

"I ain't no snitch."

"He'll be dead. You can't snitch on a dead guy."

"I suppose you're right."

"I'll give you two hundred fifty grand to tell that story."

"Like I said, money don't mean nothing to me in here."

"That's the good part. I'm going to get the *Not Guilty Group* to take your case. They're good. They're going to get you out of here. You'll be out in a few months. All you gotta do is stick to the story. Bowman confessed to you."

"They won't believe me."

"You guys are roommates. Bowman ain't alive to say it ain't so. They'll believe you. He told you everything. Talked like a sieve. Wanted to get it off his chest. He saw his ex with some rich guy. Getting it on with his girl. He got jealous. Killed her. Was so mad, he killed the young girl in the park."

"He killed a young girl?" Krueger asked.

"Sixteen years old. Pretty little thing. He slashed her throat."

Krueger let out a flurry of expletives. One common thing ran through the prison. Men who raped and killed children were the lowest of the low. The worst scum. Ironically, Clay was lucky Summer's murder was pinned on him and not the young girl's death or he'd be the one in the crosshairs of every dude in the place. No amount of money would buy him security or a favor.

This was the opening he needed. He'd hit the right nerve.

Clay moved in closer. Nobody was around but he lowered his voice for effect.

"Tell them Bowman told you where the knife is that he used to kill the young girl in the park."

His eyes widened.

"Don't worry. It's not the real knife. I had someone plant it there."

Clay didn't want Krueger thinking he was the murderer. Hopefully, he wasn't smart enough to put two and two together.

Clay continued. "The knife is at a pizza place on Chicago Avenue called Buzzi's Pizza. It's in the men's bathroom. Above the toilet. In the ceiling. There's a knife there in a bag. Along with ten grand. Bowman told you he wanted you to have the money when you got out."

That was actually where Clay hid it. After he left the park, he had to dispose of the weapon. He went into the bathroom and washed it off in the sink. Wiped off the fingerprints. Put all the cash he had on him in the bag. In case he had to run. He figured no one would find it there.

"You tell the *Not Guilty Group* that story," Clay said. "They'll check it out. They'll find the knife. They'll believe you. You testify in court. I'll get off. You get $250,000 now and another $250,000 after you testify."

"That's a lot of dough."

"It'll change your life. I'm going to get you out of here. I'll help your boy until you get out. I'll see that he's taken care of."

"All I gotta do is tell that story?"

"That's it. But wait until Bowman's dead. Then call your lawyer and tell him you want to make a deal."

"My lawyer's worthless."

"He'll get the ball rolling. I'll talk to the *Not Guilty Group* on your behalf. They'll find a hole in your prosecution. Even if you did it."

Krueger smiled widely. Clay took that as an admission of guilt.

"Bowman will be dead soon," Clay said.

"When's that going down?"

"Soon. Hang low until then. Don't let Bowman know anything's coming. Do we have a deal?"

Krueger held out his hand.

"We have a deal," he said as Clay shook it.

Krueger pulled Clay close to him and put him in a tight bear hug. Then held it. Clay could barely breathe. He couldn't have gotten out of the grip even if he tried.

"If you screw me, I'll kill you," Krueger said in his ear.

"I won't," Clay said, barely able to get the breath necessary to get the words out.

He let Clay go but maintained the grip on the hand.

"You're my new best friend."

"Stick to the plan," Clay said. "I'm going to make you a very rich man."

Clay walked away. Thankfully Krueger was on board. Also, extremely glad he was still alive.

This might really work.

15

Cliff had not made much progress in investigating Julia's theory about the Bowman and Clay cases. He had his normal case load to consider. There was no shortage of murders in Chicago.

One particular new case demanded most of his attention. A forty-year-old man, Elmer Foley, was reported missing from work. He worked in a warehouse loading and unloading trucks. He disappeared shortly after the end of his shift. Reported missing when the reliable worker didn't show up to work on time the next morning.

Three days later, his badly decomposed body was found in a dumpster near his work. The coroner estimated that Elmer had been dead for nearly three weeks. Coworkers were adamant they saw him at work three days before. One even said she spoke to him. Security footage clearly showed him on the job.

The mystery and murder were still unsolved. A bunch of rabbit holes made things difficult for Cliff. The list of suspects would fill up a murder book.

Foley was said to be distributing drugs out of the warehouse for a man named Benny Kus. A known drug dealer in Chicago who was suspected of at least a dozen murders. Foley had recently made a trip to El Paso. Presumably for Benny. It wasn't much of a stretch to assume that Elmer went to El Paso to pick up drugs and bring them back to Chicago.

Apparently, Elmer was skimming off the top making Benny suspect number one.

Elmer's wife was stepping out on him with one of her coworkers. Suspect number 1A. Her lover lied about his alibi. Did he lie because he was hiding the affair from his wife or because he killed Elmer?

Security footage showed Elmer arguing with a man a week before on the loading docks. They came to blows. Had to be separated by other coworkers. The man threatened to kill Elmer. Eyewitnesses heard the threats. The man was fired from his job. His alibi didn't check out either. A promising suspect at the top of the list.

Three years before, Elmer hit a girl on a bicycle in a school zone, killing her. The girl wasn't paying attention and had darted out in front of his truck. The officers on the scene determined it wasn't Elmer's fault even though witnesses said Elmer was driving too fast.

Elmer claimed he was going the speed limit and had two hands on the wheel and two eyes on the road. He simply didn't have time to stop. Who knew what was the truth?

The girl's father blamed Elmer. Came to his house one day. Beat Elmer to within an inch of his life with a baseball bat. Would've killed him had a neighbor not pulled the distraught father off of him.

The father spent eighteen months in prison. He got out two weeks ago. He refused to cooperate in the investigation. It was clear he still held a grudge. He didn't have an alibi either. He said he was home asleep.

The neighborhood around the dumpster where Elmer was found was seedy at best. His watch was missing, as was his phone and all the cash and debit card out of his wallet. A nineteen-year-old was seen on a security camera using that debit card at an ATM. Did he steal them off of Elmer after he was already dead, or did he kill Elmer to rob him?

Who knows?

In other words, any one of them could've done it.

How many more suspects were still out there Cliff didn't know about? He was chasing his tail trying to keep it all straight. Which thread should he pursue?

All of them were obvious answers. But that was time consuming. Considering what might've happened in the Bowman and Clay cases,

Cliff was also a little skittish. Trying not to prejudge his cases. Zeroing in on one subject prematurely.

If he were being honest, he was second guessing himself. His confidence had taken a hit. He almost wished Julia hadn't told him her theory. He wasn't as good a detective as he was before she told him. Now he was hesitant. Didn't trust his instincts.

What if they were wrong?

Eventually, he'd get his mojo back, but he needed to prove or disprove her theory before that would happen. That meant he had to find the time to investigate her theory. While at the same time, figuring out how Elmer Foley's body defied Casper's Law.

The law of decomposition. A body left in the open air decomposes twice as fast as if it were immersed in water and eight times faster than if it were in the ground. Elmer Foley's body had decomposed three hundred times faster than that. Or some such percentage. Math had never been Cliff's strong suit.

All he knew was that the coroner was adamant. The time of death was three weeks ago. They'd argued about it.

"I've got witnesses who said the victim was alive three days ago," Cliff had said. "How is that possible?"

"That's not my job," the coroner said roughly. "I don't have to make my facts fit with yours. I tell you like it is and you make your facts fit with mine."

Cliff couldn't.

He had no explanation for Elmer Foley's believe it or not world-record decomposition.

Or an explanation to disprove Julia's theory of murder relativity. Things appear differently depending on your perspective. Looking through her lens, Wayne Bowman killed Summer. Henry Lee Casey killed Nancee. Looking through Cliff's eyes, the opposite happened.

Ironically, if Cliff had arrested Bowman and Clay under Julia's theory, he probably would've gotten a conviction. With the same result. They'd both be behind bars for the rest of their lives. Such was the system of jurisprudence.

Relativity. A jury could be made to believe almost anything if presented in a compelling way by a skilled prosecutor or defense attorney.

So why did it matter? Both men were in jail.

It mattered to Cliff.

Maybe it was an ego thing.

It went deeper than that. Cliff had a deep-seated need to know the truth. He was an investigator. He had to know things. Curiosity killed the cat, so to speak. He might very well be walking into a trap of his own making. He'd always been a "let the chips fall where they may" type of investigator.

He didn't care who killed the victim as long as he got it right.

This was different. The ramifications could be tragic.

But he made time to investigate Julia's theory anyway.

The security cameras were a dead end. Most businesses kept archived footage for one to three months. Big box retailers kept footage for up to a year, in some instances. Home security systems retained video footage from a day to a month. Depending on storage capacity. The Chicago Transit authority kept footage on the toll roads for a period of eighteen months.

Bowman and Clay wouldn't have used the toll roads anyway. Only the dumbest murderers let their faces be shown on those cameras around the time of a murder.

In Bowman's file was saved footage from the mall that was used at his trial. Cliff checked it out of the archives. Another dead end. It was edited and only showed the relevant footage of Bowman cruising the mall.

No sign of the red sports car.

Cliff was kicking himself. All he had to do three years ago was look at all the footage and he might've seen Clay at the mall at the same time as Bowman.

Instead, he was left with no choice. Something he didn't want to do.

Talk to the eyewitnesses.

His Lieutenant would have a cow if he knew. Cliff had already taken a risk logging out the security footage. His name was on the record log in case anyone ever asked.

It'd be hard to explain. The case was supposed to be off his radar. What if it got back to the Lieutenant that Cliff was interviewing witnesses again?

He should drop the whole thing.

Something he couldn't make himself do.

He looked up the name and phone numbers of the couple who'd seen Bowman in the park. He dialed the man's number. It went to a voicemail but had no greeting, so he didn't know if he had the right number for the man. He left a message to call him back on his cell phone. Didn't leave his name or the reason for the call.

Cliff didn't want that on voicemail anywhere.

He had a phone number for the old woman who lived across from Summer's house. He debated on whether he should call or go over there.

After an hour of indecision, he decided to drive by. Better not to leave a phone trail. For all he knew, the woman was dead by now. He'd make a pass by her house and see if he saw any signs that she was even there.

On the way, he tried to convince himself a half dozen times to turn around and drive back to the station. For whatever reason, he kept going until he pulled onto the street where Summer was killed. He hadn't been in that neighborhood since the night of her murder.

It looked the same, except that Summer's home had been sold. To a family. The reason he knew that was because he could see a multi-colored elaborate children's playset in the backyard and a station wagon in the driveway.

Cliff pulled up to Vivian Keller's house and sat in his car for a good five minutes debating on whether or not to knock on her door. After a while, he started to feel conspicuous. At some point, a neighbor might get suspicious and call 911. That's the last thing he needed.

So he got out of the car and walked up to the front door. He rapped on it lightly. Maybe if she couldn't hear him, she wouldn't answer the door.

To his surprise, a young woman answered.

"Hello, I'm looking for Vivian Keller," Cliff said.

He didn't identify himself as a detective. No use giving out his name if Mrs. Keller didn't live there anymore.

"She's not here," the young woman said in a friendly tone. "May I help you?"

"My name's Cliff Ford. I'm a homicide detective with Chicago P.D."

He grimaced on the inside as he said it.

The girl's eyes widened.

"Oh. It's nothing like that. I met Mrs. Keller about three years ago. She was so sweet to me. I wanted to stop by and say hello and see how she's doing."

"I remember that. The murder." The girl pointed across the street.

Cliff looked that way. Then nodded.

"Grandma had to testify," she said. "I heard about it."

"So, you're Mrs. Keller's granddaughter."

"Yes. Sarah."

"It's nice to meet you, Sarah. How is your grandmother?"

"She's doing as well as can be expected. She has her good days and bad days. She's at Northside Nursing Home. I'm sure she'd be sad she missed you."

"I doubt she'd remember me."

"Oh yes, she would. She remembers everything about that night. She still talks about it all the time. She doesn't remember what she had for breakfast this morning, but she'll talk your ear off about that night, if you let her."

Cliff had a sudden urge to get out of there.

"Sarah, it's been a pleasure to meet you."

"Do you want me to tell her you stopped by?"

"That won't be necessary. I was in the neighborhood. Maybe I'll stop by the nursing home. If I get a chance. Thanks again."

Cliff rushed down the sidewalk to the car like a burglar fleeing a robbery.

When he got back to his car, he paused before getting in. He took the opportunity to get a lay of the land. Mrs. Keller's house sat up on a hill. Overlooking the other houses on the street. From her vantage point, she could see both directions. Up and down the street.

Along the driveway of Summer's house was a row of hedges. They were neatly trimmed. Cliff searched the recesses of mind to see if he could remember what they looked like three years ago.

Definitely the kind of place Bowman could've hidden and watched Clay drive up in the sports car.

Further up the road was a vacant lot. An even better place to surveille Summer's house. Bowman could've parked there and watched the house without even getting out of the van. Cliff could picture him doing so. Summer wouldn't be able to see Bowman from her house. But Bowman could clearly see the driveway and the front porch.

It didn't prove anything. A detective could create all kinds of scenarios in his head, if he let his imagination run wild. That's why Cliff had always stuck to the facts.

He was defending himself at that moment. The facts still pointed to Clay being Summer's killer. Cliff had no evidence then or now that Bowman was at the scene.

The only facts he had at the time were Clay's fingerprints and DNA. And the testimony of the old woman who saw Clay's red sports car. The facts aligned like the stars. Any other detective in his department would've come to the same conclusion.

Bowman could've been there in a white van. So could Jack the Ripper. The same men in the grassy knoll who shot Kennedy could've been hiding behind the hedges. Cliff wasn't hired to chase ghosts. He was hired to accumulate facts. Make conclusions. Arrest the most likely suspect. Bowman and Clay were arrested and found guilty beyond a reasonable doubt. Not beyond a shadow of doubt.

Cliff didn't have to prove his case with one hundred percent certainty. He couldn't expect to get everything exactly right every single time. He wasn't infallible. All he could do, was all he could do. And he'd always done that. Gave these cases all he had. Worked his tail off for Summer and Nancee to find their killers.

If he got it wrong and Julia was right, then so be it. He was only human.

He decided not to go see the old woman in the nursing home. It didn't matter to him anymore. With that newfound resolve, he went back to the station. He hadn't been there for five minutes when his phone rang.

"Ford," Cliff answered.

"I'm sorry. Who is this?" a man's voice on the other end of the line said.

"Who is this?" Cliff asked.

"I missed a call from this number. I had a message to call you back."

"My name is Cliff Ford. I'm a detective with the Chicago P.D."

"Yes. Mr. Ford. I recognize your name. We've met. This is Dawson Hawley. My fiancé and I were in the park the night the young girl was murdered. We saw the motorcycle and called 911."

"I remember. Thanks for calling me back."

Cliff suddenly felt nervous.

"What can I do for you Mr. Ford?" the man asked.

"Nothing urgent," Cliff said. "I had a question for you. I was wondering if by chance you happened to see a red sports car that night in the park."

"As a matter of fact, I did."

Cliff's heart skipped a couple of beats. Then began to race.

"A red Porsche," the man said. "The reason I remember it is because he was pulling out of the parking lot when we were pulling in. I mentioned to my fiancé that I wanted a car like that someday. Still don't have one."

"Did you mention the red Porsche in your statement to the police?"

"No. I didn't think it was relevant. I forgot about it actually. Until you mentioned it just now. We pulled into the parking lot. I hadn't even turned my car off. We were going to sit there for a while, but I saw the man and his motorcycle over on the far end of the parking lot. Like he was hiding from something. He was pushing the motorcycle. Like he didn't want to be seen or heard. We might not have seen him except that our headlights were shining in his direction. We took one look and left the parking lot and called 911."

"Thank you for that information. You've been helpful."

"Is the man who murdered that girl still behind bars?"

"Yes, sir, he is. He won't be getting out for a long time."

"That's a relief. That guy gives me the creeps."

"You don't have to worry about him."

"Okay. That's good to know."

Cliff hung up the phone slowly.

Dang it.

Julia was right. Henry Lee Clay was in the park that night. Why? He wouldn't be following Bowman. He didn't even know about him.

Only one thing made sense. Clay was the one who killed Nancee Hale.

16

The conversation with the man in the park left Cliff with a major dilemma.

What if Henry Lee Clay killed Summer Lange and Nancee Hale? Then an innocent man was in prison. Wayne Bowman. Cliff's worst nightmare. He never wanted to be the person responsible for taking away a man's freedom for a crime he didn't commit.

Cliff couldn't stand the thought of someone suffering behind bars because he'd gotten it wrong. It happened. More times than any investigator wanted. That didn't make it any less mentally painful.

Since he didn't know, he had to keep digging. He'd have to visit the old woman in the nursing home. The odds of her having any pertinent information about a white van were slim to none.

But he had to know.

He wouldn't be able to sleep at night if he didn't.

He couldn't care less about Clay and his fate. That's not why he was doing it. Even if Clay didn't kill the young girl or Summer, he deserved to be in jail. Misty Matthews confirmed it. Clay killed Tessie. Lied about it to get out of jail. He should still be behind bars for that murder.

If he was in jail for a murder he didn't commit, then so be it. The city of Chicago was safer because of it. Justice was served in a rare bit of irony. Cliff didn't believe in karma, but this would be an example of it if he did. Clay was getting what he deserved.

Wayne Bowman, on the other hand, might be innocent. That's why Cliff had to pursue it. He wasn't sure how to prove Bowman didn't do it. What would he do if the old woman didn't remember seeing a white van? What if she couldn't tie Bowman to the scene? That was more than likely going to be the case.

At that point, Cliff would have no choice but to talk to his Lieutenant who would be furious. He wouldn't be happy about going to the D.A. and reopening the Wayne Bowman case. Cliff could already hear the Lieutenant's arguments.

How are you going to prove that Clay killed Nancee Hale? All you can do is place his car in the park. That doesn't mean he killed her?

He did.

Cliff was sure of it now. Julia was right. At least about half of her theory. Clay picked up the girl at the mall. Took her back to the park and killed her. Bowman followed him to the park. That's why he was there and acting suspiciously.

Nancee's slashed throat was the same way Tessie was killed.

Cliff knew in his heart that that's how it went down. Proving it would be next to impossible. Julia was sure Bowman killed Summer. It sure made sense. But what if he didn't?

If the lady at the nursing home didn't see a white van, Cliff would never know if Bowman was guilty or innocent.

What a mess!

What if they were both guilty and they both got off because of his screwup?

On the way to the nursing home, Cliff stopped off at a local restaurant for a burger and fries. It gave him time to think through all the different scenarios. All of them led to one outcome.

Him looking like a fool.

If the old woman saw the white van, then Julia was right, and Cliff had gotten both murders wrong. If she didn't, the best case scenario was that Cliff only got one wrong. He was wrong either way.

What would be worse was if Bowman did kill Summer and Cliff got him released from jail because he was wrongly convicted for killing Nancee. And then he couldn't prove that Bowman killed Summer. So he goes free.

No. What would be even worse would be Bowman getting off for the murder of Nancee Hale and then not being able to pin it on Henry Lee Clay.

Then two murderers walked free.

Cliff felt sick to his stomach.

He ate his burger slowly. Trying to figure out a way to avoid going to the nursing home. Halfway tempted to check himself into it.

The thought made him laugh but didn't release any of the tension he felt in his shoulders and chest. He felt like an elephant was laying on top of him.

Was this what a heart attack felt like?

He left half his food and paid for the check. Got in his car and drove to the nursing home. He didn't see any way to get out of going.

Northside Nursing Home was a one level facility with two large wings branching off from one central entrance. Cliff walked in with a purpose carrying a box of chocolates. He didn't take out his badge which would only draw attention to himself. If anyone asked, this was a personal visit. He'd heard the woman was in a nursing home and brought her a gift.

The lady at the front desk was frazzled. Cliff knew from experience that nursing homes were understaffed and overworked. He sympathized with them. He'd rather be crawling through a bed of glass than taking care of elderly patients.

A lot of people would probably say that about his job. They'd rather be changing bedpans than looking at Elmer Foley's three-week-old, decomposed body.

How am I ever going to figure that one out?

A problem for another time.

"My name's Cliff Ford, I'm here to see Vivian Keller," he said in his friendliest voice to the lady at the front desk. Leaving out any mention of his job.

"Sign in, please," the lady said, barely looking up.

A clipboard lay on the counter. Cliff signed the ledger illegibly. No one would be able to identify his name. The lady hadn't asked for his ID and his badge and gun were hidden under his suit jacket. The facility didn't have metal detectors. Only one rent-a-security guard standing off to the side. Bored. He hadn't even given Cliff more than a cursory look.

From the looks of it, Cliff was a business professional dressed in a suit. Half the battle in these situations was looking like you belonged. Cliff acted like he could be Vivian Keller's nephew, even though no one had bothered to ask about his relationship to her.

"Room 110," the woman behind the desk said. "Down the hall on the right."

The facility obviously wasn't worried about security.

Cliff found the room easily enough. The door was slightly ajar. Cliff pushed it open a little further after a weak voice answered his knock.

He entered slowly.

Vivian Keller lay in her bed attached to oxygen. Her hair was mussed, and she appeared frail and weak.

But she recognized him immediately.

"Detective Ford," she said. "What a sight for sore eyes. I haven't seen you in..."

She put her hand to her forehead.

"How long has it been?"

"Three years," he answered.

"Land sakes alive. Has it been that long? Time flies when you're having fun."

She grimaced when she said it. Obviously referring to her plight. The room was modest. No flowers or magazines, nothing to pass the time other than a television on the wall that wasn't on.

Seeing him had given her a burst of energy and her face turned flush as blood rushed through her body from the punch of adrenaline. Her eyes were wide with excitement, and she tried to sit up. Fumbling with the controls of her bed. Trying to elevate her head more.

"Hello, Mrs. Keller. I brought you something. A box of chocolates."

He remembered she wanted to be referred to as Mrs. and not Ms. As far as she was concerned, she was still married, even though her husband was dead. At least she wanted to be identified as such. Cliff respected that.

"Don't tell my daughter about the chocolates," Mrs. Keller said. "She won't let me have sweets. What difference does it make? I'm an old woman. I'm going to die soon. I should be able to eat whatever I want."

"I agree with you. I won't tell your daughter."

"Give me some of that," she said, pointing at the box.

Cliff opened the box, and she took out a piece. Her hand shook as she lifted the chocolate to her mouth and put the whole piece in her mouth. Then let out a satisfied moan.

"Oh. That's good," she said.

"I've actually never met your daughter," Cliff said, "but I did meet your granddaughter."

"Which one? I have seven granddaughters and five grandsons. Or is it... seven grandsons and five granddaughters? I forget."

"I think her name is Sarah. She answered the door at your house. She told me you were here. I came by to see how you were."

That's his story and he was sticking to it.

"I'm okay, I guess. Don't get old, Detective Ford. It's not fun. I hope you don't end up in a place like this."

"I've got a pretty young wife and a beautiful young daughter. Hopefully, they'll take care of me when I get old."

"What's your daughter's name?"

"Rita. Would you like to see a picture?"

Cliff pulled out his wallet and then remembered his badge was attached. Didn't matter. Mrs. Keller already remembered he was a detective.

She invited him to sit down after admiring the picture of Rita. He got the feeling she was humoring him and couldn't see the picture without her glasses and was too proud to ask Cliff to get them off the table for her.

"I can't stay long," Cliff said, after sitting down. "But I do have a question for you."

"Is it about Summer's murder?" she asked, with an enthused smile.

She had perked up even more.

"Yes ma'am."

"I thought you caught the guy."

"We did. Thanks in part to your testimony. About the red car."

"Oh yes. I remember it like it was yesterday. What's your question, Detective?"

"Do you remember seeing a white van in the neighborhood?"

"Many times," she answered immediately.

Cliff's heart did a lap around the room.

"Can you describe it for me?"

"It was white."

Cliff chuckled.

"Of course. I mean, where did you see it?"

"You know that vacant lot up the street and to the left of my house?"

"Yes, ma'am. I remember it."

"It used to park up there. All the time."

"Was it there the night Summer was murdered?"

"Yes, sir, it was. I saw it the same time I saw the red sports car in the driveway."

"Was it there after you heard the scream?"

"Yes. I went to the window and looked over to the house. I didn't see the sports car, but I saw the van."

Cliff wanted to stand and pace but maintained his seat.

"Did you see a person in the van?"

"No."

"What did you do next?"

"I called 911."

"Was the van still there after you called 911?"

Mrs. Keller looked out the window, deep in thought.

"Now that you mention it, I don't believe it was. I think it was gone."

"You said the van was in the neighborhood a lot. Did you ever get a good look at the driver?"

"Oh yes. Several times."

"What did he look like?"

"He had a beard and long hair. Rough looking type."

"Why didn't you call the police when you saw him hanging around the neighborhood?"

"Oh, I did. Several times. One time, somebody came. The police car drove through the neighborhood, but the van wasn't there. I believe Summer called one time as well. They quit coming after a while."

Cliff made a mental note to look for a police report.

The nurse entered about that time with a plate of food.

"Time for your lunch, Mrs. Keller," she said.

"I just ate a few minutes ago, honey."

The nurse looked over at Cliff and smiled. "No, you haven't eaten yet. Mrs. Keller."

"I could've sworn I ate something. What was it? It tasted good."

"No ma'am. We haven't served lunch yet."

"I'm sure you're wrong. I'm not hungry. I'd be hungry if I hadn't had lunch."

Cliff wasn't going to mention the piece of chocolate. She'd clearly forgotten about it.

The granddaughter was right. The woman could remember the murder like it was this morning but couldn't remember whether she'd eaten lunch or not.

Cliff saw an opportunity to excuse himself. Hopefully, Mrs. Keller would also forget he was ever there.

He got in his car but didn't start it right away. He didn't know whether to feel ecstatic or ashamed.

He'd gotten it so wrong. Bowman killed Summer. Clay killed Nancee.

What should he do now?

***

Later that afternoon

Cliff arrived home early. Julia was already there. Rita was in her room doing homework.

"You were right, Julia," Cliff said.

"Of course, I was," she said. "What about?"

They were in their office. She was on her computer. Cliff was trying to think of how to tell her about the events of the day.

"You were right about the Bowman and Clay cases."

Julia stopped what she was doing and looked his way.

"Bowman killed Summer and Clay killed Nancee," Cliff said. "I got it backwards."

"I thought you weren't going to investigate that," she said strongly.

"I spoke to the eyewitnesses on both cases."

Julia let out a groan.

He told her about the two conversations.

"I know. You said I shouldn't. I'm an officer of the court. I have a fiduciary responsibility to make sure I get things right."

"Oh, Cliff! Why would you do that?"

"I testified in both of those cases. I swore to tell the truth, the whole truth, and nothing but the truth."

"That's what you did. You told the whole truth. As you knew it."

"It wasn't the truth."

"It's not a lie if you believe it. Surely you know that, Cliff. You can't be expected to read people's minds. You're not a psychic. You can't look in a crystal ball and see who committed the murders. All you can do is tell the truth as you understand it."

"I'm obligated to tell the truth now."

"That's why I didn't want you to investigate my theory. It would put you in a tough position if you found out I was right."

"I've already decided not to tell anyone."

Relief washed over her face.

"Smart man. I don't think you should."

"I can't run the risk. I promised Misty Matthews."

"What does she have to do with it?"

"Clay threatened to kill her if she told his secret. I told her I'd never tell anyone. I promised. If I open this can of worms, it'll have to come out. If Clay somehow gets off, her life would be in danger."

"So would other young girls. How do you know Clay wouldn't come after Rita?"

"I don't. That's why he has to stay behind bars. No matter what. I can't risk him getting back on the streets. Now I know Bowman is a murderer as well. If we reopen the cases, they'll both walk. I don't think we could get a conviction now anyway. Too much time has passed."

"I agree."

"So what if the lady saw Bowman's white van in the neighborhood. She didn't see him kill Summer. I have no physical evidence that he did. So, what if the man in the park saw a red sports car. That doesn't mean Clay killed Nancee."

"You and I both know he did."

"Yes, we do. But how do I prove it? I don't have a murder weapon. I don't have Clay's car on a security camera, picking up Nancee at the mall. I don't even have a positive ID that Clay was the one in the sports car. It's not like the man in the park got a license plate number. Or could pick Clay out of a lineup."

Cliff's phone beeped. He had a text. He ignored it. Technically he was off the clock.

"If I say something now, they'll both walk. Clay will file another wrongful conviction lawsuit. And he'll win. He'll get another sixteen million. Or more. So would Bowman. I'd lose my job."

"There's not one good argument for telling the truth."

"I can think of one. My integrity. I always try to tell the truth."

"No, you don't."

"Yes, I do."

"When I try on a dress and ask you, 'Do I look fat?' you always lie and answer no."

"That's not a lie. That's the truth. You don't look fat."

"That's not my point. Whether I do or not, you are always going to answer that question the same way. At least, you'd better answer that it doesn't make me look fat. Anyway, we all tell white lies at times. Sometimes it's for the greater good. This is one of those times."

Cliff's phone rang. He looked at the caller ID. His Lieutenant was calling. It looked like the text was from him as well. Marked urgent. Even if he wasn't on the clock, he'd better answer it.

"This is Ford," Cliff said, leaving it on speaker phone for the convenience.

"Are you watching the news?" the Lieutenant asked.

"No," Cliff said. "I'm at home. Here with Julia. What's up?"

"Turn it on."

Julia already had the remote in her hand.

"What's going on?" Cliff asked.

"Wayne Bowman is dead."

17

Cliff's first thought when he heard that Wayne Bowman was dead might sound insensitive to most people. He felt jubilation. A major problem was resolved for him. He no longer had to worry about whether or not Bowman killed Summer. The man was dead and Henry Lee Clay was behind bars.

He felt certain the Lieutenant felt the same way. Those in law enforcement didn't much care when a murderer died. They saw the pain caused to the victims. If they ever grieved, it was always for them.

In some ways it was a relief. It shifted the burden of punishment from the state to the hands of God. That was a good thing. Another ball that no longer had to be juggled. A threat handled. More than one convicted murderer had gotten out of jail and killed a detective or one of his family members. Or arranged a hit from the inside.

With Bowman gone, Cliff could rest easier. For reasons no one would ever know except Julia and him.

The Lieutenant still seemed concerned as he relayed to Cliff the circumstances of how Bowman met his demise. It suddenly dawned on Cliff that he wouldn't have called him with an urgent message just to deliver that news.

Julia flipped through the television channels searching for a local station. Before she found one, the Lieutenant blurted out the source of his angst.

A bombshell of monumental proportions.

Cliff might've fallen out of his chair had it not had side arms on it.

"Henry Lee Clay has filed a lawsuit through the *Not Guilty Group* to have his conviction overturned," the Lieutenant said in his monotone voice. The words still had a chilling effect regardless of the delivery.

Cliff felt a bolt of panic run through him like he'd been hit with a taser at close range.

Motions could only be filed if new evidence had been discovered. The *Not Guilty Group* were savvy lawyers. They didn't file unless they thought they could win.

What's changed? Did they know about the white van at Summer's house?

"I don't understand," Cliff said, trying not to sound as stunned as he was on the inside. "On what grounds do they think they can get his conviction overturned?"

Julia kept looking back and forth between Cliff and the television. One eyebrow raised. She was obviously as shocked by the news as he was.

"Apparently, Bowman confessed to killing Summer Lange before he died," the Lieutenant said.

Cliff let out a discernible groan of disbelief. "Who did he confess to?"

"To his cellmate."

"Well, that's ridiculous. Jailhouse snitches are totally unreliable."

"Be that as it may, that's the story. You are named in the lawsuit. Get prepared to defend every action. Is there anything you want to tell me?"

What was that supposed to mean? Did the Lieutenant know something? Was he digging for information?

The city of Chicago had taken a sixteen million dollar hit on one of Cliff's cases. Some people had clamored for Cliff's firing. The Lieutenant had gone to bat for Cliff, which was why he still had a job.

Would he do it a second time?

Cliff decided at that moment to keep his mouth shut. To never tell what he knew. He'd lose all credibility.

"No sir," Cliff said. "This was a good arrest. I did everything by the book. You saw the evidence. It was overwhelming."

In essence a lie. Cliff couldn't swear in a court of law that Clay actually killed Summer. He had his doubts now.

He had no doubt that Clay belonged behind bars. That he killed Nancee. But he probably didn't kill Summer.

Cliff would almost certainly be called to the stand. Would he lie about Clay killing Summer in order to keep him behind bars?

If he didn't, he could already imagine the ramifications. Clay goes free. Another young girl is murdered. Clay gets another big settlement. Cliff loses his job.

Was telling the truth worth the risks associated with it? Especially the young girl part. How could he let a murderer go free to kill again?

Cliff didn't realize he'd been holding his breath until he heard a voice inside his head shouting at him to exhale and take in another breath.

"Do you have the TV on yet?" the Lieutenant asked.

Julia had the television on the local news station that had broken into regular programming.

From the looks of it, riots had broken out in downtown Chicago.

"Are those riots related to Henry Lee Clay?" Cliff asked, rather than answering the question.

They had to be. Otherwise, why would the Lieutenant be on the phone with him?

"We're trying to get a handle on it," the Lieutenant said. "It was organized on behalf of Clay. By a local reporter, Shannon Roberts. She's the one who led the charge to get Clay off the first time. She's got the 'Defund the Police' crowd all stirred up."

The television station was recording the events in real time. With a helicopter in the air and various cameras on the ground. A large group of protestors blocked the major freeways into downtown Chicago. A group of people appeared to be marching toward the police station. Another large group was assembled at City Hall.

A bevy of reporters were at a makeshift podium where speakers were taking turns bloviating. Cliff recognized some of them as leaders of the anti-police movement.

A picture of Clay's mug shot was suddenly on the television screen. His face was bruised and battered from where he'd been thrown against the wall that day when Cliff chased him down. A red banner ran along the bottom of the screen.

Detective Cliff Ford accused of Police Brutality.

Julia let out a gasp.

Cliff's picture was the next thing on the screen. The Lieutenant was still on the line, but neither of them were saying anything. Both watching the horror unfold before their eyes leaving each of them speechless.

Cliff motioned for Julia to turn up the sound.

A commentator, a so-called expert, was pontificating about the wrongful arrest. The travesty of justice.

Cliff wanted to throw something at the television. He might've if Julia hadn't been between him and the TV.

Cliff would get no sympathy from this station. Any sense of fairness gave way to a salacious narrative. Especially in a city like Chicago, where a loud minority had been clamoring for defunding the police for a long time.

"How did Bowman die?" Cliff asked, when he couldn't stand listening to the commentator anymore.

"Took a shard to the side of his neck. Killed by another inmate."

"I bet you ten dollars Clay is behind it. It's awfully suspicious to me that Bowman is killed and his bunkmate suddenly concocts this story about a confession. I guarantee you these guys are getting paid."

"I hear you. Be that as it may, I need to get you protection."

It was good to know the Lieutenant still had his back. He wasn't getting fired yet.

"I can take care of myself."

"Reporters are going to be camped out in front of your house if they aren't already. It won't take the protestors long to show up there as well. You need to get you and your family to a safe place."

Upon hearing those words, Julia stood up abruptly and left the room. Presumably to begin packing things for her and Rita.

"We can go to Julia's shelter. No one will know we're there."

"I'll send a couple of units to your house to escort you."

"Then everybody will know where we're going. They'll follow us. We'll sneak out the back and head straight to the shelter. If anyone follows us, I'll put on my blue lights and lose them. We'll be fine."

"I'll send a couple of units to the house to watch it."

"Thanks. I appreciate that. That'll also make the reporters think we're still here. I'll leave the lights on. And the television. Make it look like we're still in the house."

"Good idea."

"I'll be in touch when we land at a safe place. I'm sorry this is happening."

"It's not your fault."

Cliff wondered if the Lieutenant would say that if he knew what Cliff knew. He had to put it out of his mind. Right now, he had his family to protect.

Cliff hung up the phone and stared at the screen. He picked up the remote and listened to the reporter, Shannon Roberts, who had a microphone in her hand in front of a burning building in downtown Chicago. It always amazed Cliff that the people protesting violence by the police engaged in horrific violence to make their points.

"Three years ago, Henry Lee Clay won a sixteen-million-dollar civil case against the City of Chicago," Roberts said. "The largest wrongful conviction settlement in the city's history. He spent ten long years in prison for a crime he didn't commit."

"He did commit it, you imbecile!" Cliff shouted at the television.

His heart was now racing around his chest like a dog chasing a rabbit.

"Detective Cliff Ford was the arresting officer in that case," she continued. "He's the same one who arrested Clay for the murder of Summer Lange. It appears that history has repeated itself and that Clay has been wrongly accused again. By the same detective."

She shook her head in disgust for effect.

Cliff wanted to scream at the television again, but her words rang true. Clay probably didn't kill Summer. Cliff had gotten it wrong.

"In his motion to have his conviction overturned, Clay accuses Detective Ford and the Chicago P.D. of targeting him. They didn't consider any other suspects. I've learned that Wayne Bowman was an ex-boyfriend of Summer Lange. He'd been stalking her. I have a transcript of a 911 call Summer made shortly before her murder. She made the call because Bowman was outside her house and she was afraid for her life."

Vivian Keller mentioned the 911 call. Cliff hadn't had a chance to find it. It was on his things-to-do list.

This was a disaster.

Between the reporters and the *Not Guilty Group*, how was Cliff going to keep them from learning the truth?

The television station split the screen. Roberts on one half and the desk reporters back at the station on the other.

"We understand that Wayne Bowman confessed to killing Summer," one of the newscasters said. "Is that correct, Shannon?"

Shannon Roberts had her hand to her ear and her head ducked down like it was hard for her to hear. Cliff could see the utter chaos unfolding behind her. The rioters made him sick to his stomach.

"That's correct," she said. "Before he died, Wayne Bowman confessed to murdering Summer Lange and Nancee Hale."

Cliff was pacing now.

"To refresh your memory," the desk reporter said, "Nancee Hale was the young teenage girl abducted in front of the mall, taken to a park where she was brutally murdered. Wayne Bowman was convicted of that crime."

"Clay is the one who killed her!" Cliff shouted.

How could he make that case now?

He couldn't. That'd be admitting he got it wrong. How could he fight the motion when he believed in his heart that Bowman did kill Summer?

Cliff was skeptical of the jailhouse confession. He interviewed Bowman. Watched him through the entire trial. The man barely spoke five words to his attorney in his defense. He couldn't imagine Bowman opening up to a fellow inmate and spilling his guts.

Even if he didn't, Bowman wasn't around to deny it.

Shannon Roberts continued. "Wayne Bowman told his cellmate that he killed Summer and the girl. He confessed to both crimes."

Now Clay knew the cellmate was lying. Bowman would not have confessed to the killing of Nancee Hale because he didn't do it. Henry Lee Clay did it.

Cliff smelled a rat. Sixteen million dollars' worth of a rat. Clay had Bowman killed. Not hard to do in prison if you had money. Any number of people would be willing to do the deed. People who had nothing to lose. They were in prison for life anyway.

Why would they kill for money?

Because money could buy a lot of conveniences in prison. So, what if an additional murder charge was tacked on. Murderers also had a lust for killing. Some did it for the thrill. For the reputation. Many would kill for the sport. Add money to it, and Clay probably had men lined up wanting to kill Bowman for him.

The cellmate was paid off as well. To lie about the confession. He had nothing to worry about. Who was going to say he was lying? Stick to the story and he was home free.

What did he get in return?

Probably more money. Promises of help to get out of prison. Not hard for Clay to make those things happen. At least the money part. Spend a small portion of his vast fortune and get the man to lie.

Bowman's cellmate was a murderer. What's a lie to him? He told lies more times in his life than he told the truth. All the jailhouse snitch had to do was testify. If he didn't get out for good, participating in the trial got him out of jail for a little while anyway.

He got to meet with attorneys. That got him out of the cell block. He might get a jailhouse interview with Shannon Roberts. Become a celebrity. Who knows all the reasons why Bowman's cellmate would lie?

Cliff had heard enough. He clicked off the television. Roughly. Tossed the remote in his chair. Then remembered to leave the television on for the reporters outside. So, he turned it back on.

He stood and walked over to the window and looked out. A crowd had gathered. The street was practically blocked. Cliff went into the room that held his gun safe. He opened it and pulled out an assault rifle and a shotgun. He took his badge and service revolver out of the safe and clipped them to his belt.

Secured the ammunition he thought he needed, then walked back into their bedroom. Julia had two backpacks on the bed. One for him and one for her.

"Rita's getting ready," she said. "I told her we're going on a short vacation. Let's try not to worry her."

"She's nine years old. She's smart enough to figure out that something's going on."

"I know. All I'm saying is downplay it. Walking around with a shotgun and assault rifle is not going to allay any of her fears."

"I'll put them in the SUV."

Cliff hid the guns and went back inside to hurry them along. They needed to get out of there as soon as possible.

He drove them to the shelter avoiding the freeways and trouble spots. It didn't appear that they were followed.

The shelter had an apartment meant for a live-in supervisor. The position was currently unfilled, and the apartment was vacant. It had one bedroom and Julia brought in a rollaway bed for Rita to sleep in the living room.

Cliff wanted to watch the news again, but Rita was there. Eventually, he decided she was old enough to know what was going on. The three of them settled on the couch in front of the television screen and watched the events in real time.

Cliff's name was mentioned. Rita practically jumped off the couch.

Up to that point, she'd been glued to the set. Cliff wondered if she might go into politics someday. Like her mother, she wasn't short on opinions. Rita was beyond her years in understanding the issues.

"Why are they mentioning your name, Daddy?" she asked.

He decided to tell her the truth. Most of it anyway.

"I arrested a guy for murder. Now they're trying to say he didn't do it."

"If you say he did, then I believe you."

That caused Cliff to grimace. His daughter had more faith in him than he had in himself. Henry Lee Clay might not have killed Summer. Probably didn't. He wasn't about to tell Rita that.

"Look!" Rita said out of the blue.

It caused Cliff and Julia to jump.

"That's Ms. McVade," Rita said as she pointed at the television.

"You have a good eye," Cliff said.

In the crowd of protesters was Rita's former principal. The one who'd given them so much trouble three years before.

After that fiasco, they moved Rita to a private school. For safety reasons more than anything. Cliff had always insisted that his daughter would go to public school. He didn't want her sheltered from the things of the world. She'd have to deal with them eventually anyway.

As Cliff began to have a higher profile in Chicago law enforcement, they decided Rita needed to be at a school with increased security. Cliff had arrested a number of notorious killers over the years.

Henry Lee Clay being one of them.

They'd also considered moving into a gated community. Now Cliff wished they had.

The threat was growing more real by the day.

Cliff had to make sure Clay didn't get out this time. The man would get back on the streets and kill again. Would he come after Rita?

"Turn it up," Rita said.

Cliff had the sound down. He'd gotten tired of hearing the incessant drone of the reporters and commentators berating the police.

Ms. McVade and the other protesters were chanting. Outside City Hall. Holding up signs. *Defund the Police. Abolish Police. Stop the Brutality.*

"What do we want?" half the protesters shouted.

"Dead cops," the other half answered.

"When do we want it?"

"Right now."

Disgusting.

Ms. McVade's sign said something about 150 years of oppression. She wasn't participating in the chant. Thank goodness. She had a little bit of sense about her.

Some of the protesters in the background clashed with police in the background. Things were getting out of hand.

"I don't know how a principal of a school gets away with protesting like that," Julia said. "Not when there's violence involved. Look at what she's teaching the kids by example."

"We live in a different world," Cliff said. "Imagine what our city would be like without police. What do they expect would happen if they fired all of us?"

"It's unworkable in a civilized society. We need the police to maintain order," Julia said.

"These idiots want to take away our guns. Limit our ability to make arrests. Prevent us from using force."

"We'd have utter chaos on the streets of Chicago," Julia said. "These people have no idea what they're asking for."

"Then the bad guys will be the only ones with guns," Rita said.

"My nine-year-old has more common sense than her principal," Cliff said.

The camera panned to a sign.

Cliff bolted up.

The sign had his home address on it.

"I'm going back to the house," Cliff said.

"No, you're not!" Julia said. "It's too dangerous."

"I've got to protect our things."

"I'm not letting you leave. They're just things. They can be replaced. You can't be replaced."

She was right. If he went to the house, what if he got in a confrontation? It'd only make things worse.

Cliff called the Lieutenant.

"Somebody put my address on the television," Cliff said. "Can you get more officers there to protect my house?"

"I've got two there right now. But I'll send more."

"Let them know protesters might be headed their way."

"I will. I'll block off both ends of the street. I can't keep the protesters off the street, but we can try to contain them and keep any vehicles from going in and out."

Cliff slumped back on the couch.

"Is our house safe?" Rita asked.

"Don't worry honey," Cliff said. "It's safe."

Although he wasn't sure if that was true or not.

***

Later that night.

Rita was already in bed. Cliff and Julia were in the bedroom awaiting word from the Lieutenant who had gone to their house.

The television station had shown protesters at his house. Firebombs were thrown at his residence. The firetrucks had been called.

The phone rang.

"I'm sorry, Cliff," the Lieutenant said.

Cliff's heart sank to the bottom of his chest.

"Your house is a total loss. The fire destroyed everything. We had trouble getting the fire trucks in. The protesters blocked the street."

He'd seen them cheering in the streets.

Cliff hung up the phone.

Tears filled his eyes.

Julia was standing next to him. He took her in his arms.

She didn't have to ask.

She knew.

18

Courthouse,

Six days later

For the first time in Cliff's distinguished career as a homicide detective, he intended to lie under oath. He wouldn't characterize it that way. He intended not to tell the "whole truth."

No one else involved in the emergency hearing to overturn Henry Lee Clay's conviction was going to tell the whole truth. Why should he?

The jailhouse snitch who went by Krueger had lied through his teeth. He was the first on the stand. He said Wayne Bowman confessed to killing Summer and Nancee. Krueger even gave Clay's attorney's the location of the murder weapon in the ceiling of a pizza joint's bathroom as proof he was telling the truth. The lab proved the weapon was the one used to kill Nancee but not the one used to kill Summer.

Cliff suspected Clay hid the knife and gave Krueger the location. It fit with Julia's theory that Clay killed Nancee and Bowman used a different knife to kill Summer. One which had never been recovered.

Kruger was as nervous as a mouse in a room full of cats. Cliff was trained to spot liars. This guy wouldn't know the truth if a seal hand delivered it to him in the courtroom. That's what the man reminded Cliff of. A seal at an aquarium. Trained to do tricks on command.

Henry Lee Clay's attorney led Krueger through the tall tale by the nose. Correcting his inconsistencies as they became apparent.

The D.A. had done an admirable job discrediting Krueger but hadn't been able to shake him completely off the testimony. The convicted murderer held up surprisingly well. Considering he was a pathological liar and had been all his life.

He was pressed hard about a quid pro quo but didn't admit that anyone promised him anything in exchange for his testimony. Of course, Clay did. Cliff could see it in the smirk on Clay's face as Krueger stuck by the story.

"I'm only here to tell the truth," Krueger had said. "I want justice to be done. I couldn't stand to see an innocent man in jail for a crime he didn't commit."

Cliff almost laughed out loud when he said it.

Krueger wouldn't know justice if someone slapped him in the face with the constitution. His rap sheet was as long as a two by four.

Cliff expected Krueger not to tell the whole truth. If he had, he'd have admitted that

Clay paid him off. Promised him money. That Bowman never said a word to him about Summer's murder.

Henry Lee Clay's equally smug attorney with the *Not Guilty Group* didn't want the whole truth told. He made a motion at the beginning of the hearing to suppress certain evidence and testimony. Namely any suggestion that Clay might've been involved in Nancee Hale's murder. The defense attorney didn't want any mention of Clay's previous murder conviction. No evidence at all that might've proved Clay really did kill Tessie or Nancee.

The defense attorney didn't want anything revealed in court if it were detrimental to his client. Even if it was true.

A fact everyone knew but no one admitted openly.

The judge ruled in the defense's favor on the motion to suppress, proving that the man presiding over the trial didn't want the whole truth told either. The black robe was supposed to symbolize neutrality and humility. This judge had neither of them going for him.

The judge lied. In his opening statement, he said the hearing today was a search for the truth.

No it wasn't.

If it were, Cliff would be able to tell the court about the white van. That he believed Wayne Bowman killed Summer. About the witness who saw Clay's red Porsche in the park that night. Misty Matthews could come into court and tell the judge how she had lied. That Clay had threatened to kill her if she didn't lie for him.

The judge would hear none of that. The same judge who'd let Clay walk the first time presided over this hearing. From the first words out of his mouth, it was apparent that he was looking for any reason to let Clay walk again.

If the judge were telling the whole truth, he'd admit that he had a bias against the police. That he'd already prejudged this case before hearing any of the evidence. That he was looking for any justification to rule in Clay's favor.

He wasn't about to admit that. He couldn't tell the whole truth. It'd make him look bad.

Even the good guys didn't want the whole truth. The D.A. was fighting hard to keep Clay behind bars and Cliff's reputation intact.

But truthfully, he just wanted to win.

This was a game to the lawyers. They fought it out like a couple of gladiators in the courtroom, then afterwards, set up a playdate for their children to get together. They hobnobbed in all the same social circles. At all the same parties and country clubs. During the break they might even discuss a time to get together for lunch.

Attorneys and judges made up a fraternity. Everyone else intruded into their space occasionally, so they could fund the system and make them feel important.

The D.A. warned Cliff not to say anything damaging to their case. With the caveat of telling the truth.

Wink. Wink.

Please not the whole truth.

"Answer the questions with yes or no," the D.A. had said. "Don't offer any more information than necessary."

In other words, don't tell the whole truth.

A good strategy in the court of law.

The Henry Lee Clay case had caused Cliff to lose faith in the system. Maybe it was the best judicial system in the world. Probably was. But it was full of flaws. If the whole truth did come out today, it'd be a minor miracle. An accident. Every person in the room was working hard to make sure the truth didn't rear its ugly head and turn their agendas upside down.

So, if no one in the courtroom was going to tell the whole truth, then Cliff wouldn't either. Not if it meant a cold-blooded killer of young girls was going to walk out of that courtroom today a free man.

Cliff couldn't risk it.

If the people in that courtroom were in search of the whole truth, then they'd all ask Clay if he intended to kill again. If Clay told the whole truth, he'd say yes.

But that wasn't how the legal system worked. The constitution protected Clay from self-incrimination. For good reason. It should be up to the state to prove beyond a reasonable doubt that Clay killed Summer. Up to the state to prove that the conviction should be upheld.

Cliff would be the sole witness tasked with making that case.

The problem was that Cliff didn't think Clay killed Summer. Not anymore. He'd be more than happy to cede the point and let Clay off for the murder of Summer Lange, as long as Clay agreed that he killed Nancee and to spend the rest of his life behind bars.

All of that was wishful thinking.

Cliff intended to fight like a wounded lion to get the judge to think Clay did kill Summer. For all the young girls of Chicago. Their parents. Sisters. Brothers. Aunts and uncles. Friends.

He swore an oath to protect them. He'd do whatever he had to do today for them. And live with the consequences.

His name was called, and he walked confidently to the stand. Resolved. Steadfast. His conscience was clear.

On a mission. To keep Henry Lee Clay behind bars.

He thought he knew a way to do it. He had a couple of aces up his sleeve.

"Raise your right hand," the judge said. "Do you swear the testimony you are about to present is the truth, the whole truth, and nothing but the truth?"

They'd taken the "so help you God" phrase out of the oath a long time ago.

"I do," Cliff said confidently.

All but the whole truth part.

Cliff sat down and adjusted his suit and tie and tried to keep from staring at his adversary, Anthony Dowling, Clay's attorney, who seemed anxious to get his hands on Cliff. To rough him up. Score some points.

Dowling was one of the foremost criminal defense attorneys in the country. The *Not Guilty Group* was a high-profile social justice firm. With the backing of a lot of high-net-worth individuals. Their efforts were praised nationwide all the way up to the President of the United States.

Cliff didn't necessarily have a problem with it. If the cops made a mistake and arrested the wrong person for a crime, then Cliff wanted that man or woman released from prison. He appreciated the good work of the group.

Not in this instance.

Dowling was already standing at the podium. His shoulders back and head held high. He had been extremely disappointed when the judge ruled that the hearing would be closed. No reporters nor cameras were allowed in the courtroom. Due to the risk. Emotions were still running high in the city of Chicago. The riots had quieted down, but the judge didn't want to stoke the flames by letting the attorneys grandstand for the cameras in the hopes of playing to public opinion.

The only good decision the judge had made so far.

"Good afternoon, Detective," Dowling said, in his most friendly voice. Cliff knew it wouldn't last. "How are you today?"

"I'm fine, thank you."

"You'd be doing a lot better had you arrested Wayne Bowman for the murder of Summer Lange back in the very beginning of this case don't you think?"

"Objection."

"I'm merely stating that I'm sorry the detective lost his house over this," Dowling said.

The D.A., Ed Armitage, feigned outrage. "Seriously. Is this really how counsel wants to start these proceedings? His statement is argumentative."

"Sit down, Mr. Armitage," the judge said. "Objection sustained. Stick to the facts, Anthony."

The judge and the defense attorney were on a first name basis. A rare slip of the tongue showing the personal relationship between the judge and the defense attorney. Back in chambers they probably discussed setting up a tee time.

The judge turned toward Cliff. "I'm sorry that you lost your house as well."

He sounded sincere.

"Thank you, Your Honor."

"Detective Ford, did you ever consider Wayne Bowman as a suspect?" Dowling asked.

"Yes."

"Really? You arrested Henry Lee Clay the next day. You couldn't have given Bowman much consideration."

Cliff wasn't going to take the D.A.'s advice and answer with yes or no when possible. He intended to get in as much information as he was allowed. Everything he could think of that made Clay look bad.

"I met with Ms. Lange's parents the next morning. They put Wayne Bowman on my radar. That same day, I pulled as much information as I could find on Bowman. Prior arrests. DMV records. That sort of thing. I went by Bowman's house. He no longer lived there. I went to his place of work. He no longer worked there. I did everything I could to track him down and question him."

"You didn't have any trouble finding him after you started investigating Nancee Hale's murder, did you detective?"

"By that time, I had a current address for him. He wasn't home, or at least he didn't answer the door. But I confirmed with a neighbor that Bowman still lived at that address."

"That's the same location where you found the bloody shoes? At that same house."

"That's correct."

"And you arrested Wayne Bowman for the murder of Nancee Hale."

"Not on that day. Bowman took off on his motorcycle. He fled the state. It took a few weeks to find him and get him extradited back to Illinois. When he arrived back in this jurisdiction, I arrested him."

"For the murder of Nancee Hale. Not the murder of Summer Lange."

"Like you said, I had the bloody shoes and shirt. He also ran, which is a sign of guilt. I had his vehicle on security tape at the mall. That put him in close proximity to the victim at the time of her abduction. The evidence was overwhelming."

"I'm not arguing with you," Dowling said. "We all agree that Wayne Bowman killed Nancee Hale."

No, we don't.

"We're here today about a different subject. Did you question Wayne Bowman about the Summer Lange murder?" Dowling asked.

"No. By that time, I already had Henry Lee Clay in custody and was satisfied that he killed Ms. Lange. When I went to arrest Mr. Clay, he ran as well. Like I said, a sign of guilt."

So far, Cliff was telling the whole truth.

Dowling looked down at his notes. Cliff took advantage of the pause.

"There's something else," Cliff said. "There's another reason why I was sure Clay killed Summer Lange. Would you like to hear it?"

"Your Honor, could you instruct the witness to let me ask the questions?" Dowling said.

Armitage stood to his feet. "Your Honor, this is an informal hearing. There's no jury. Surely the detective could have some leeway to talk freely. Within reason."

"Mr. Armitage will get his chance to ask questions of the witness," Dowling countered. "I'd like to proceed under my terms."

"I'll allow the detective to speak. Within reason as Mr. Armitage says."

The judge turned toward Cliff.

"What was the other reason why you were certain Clay killed Summer Lange?"

"As I mentioned, Mr. Clay fled the scene when I went to his residence to arrest him. I had to chase him for several blocks before I apprehended him."

"You mean when you threw my client against the wall, smashed his face on the concrete, and beat him up?" Dowling said.

The judge held his palm in the air for Dowling to stop.

"You may continue, Detective," he said.

"After I apprehended Mr. Clay, I advised him that he was under arrest. He said, and I quote, 'I did not kill Summer.'"

Cliff let that thought linger in the air. Dowling wasn't about to object to that testimony. He should've. It was a setup.

"How did Mr. Clay know he was being arrested for the murder of Summer Lange?" Cliff added. "How did he know Summer was dead? It wasn't common knowledge. We hadn't released the information to the general public."

Cliff bit his lip to keep from smirking. He knew how Clay knew Summer was dead. Cliff had told him. When he was on top of him with his knee in his back, Cliff had said, "You're under arrest for the rape and murder of Summer Lange."

Cliff left that part out. He wasn't lying.

Not the whole truth.

It made Clay look guilty.

Dowling was reeling.

"He could've heard about the murder in any number of ways."

Cliff shook his head.

"Summer's body was still at the coroner's office."

"He could have heard it from Summer's parents."

"They'd never met Clay. They didn't know their daughter was even dating him."

"You didn't mention this statement at the first trial."

"I couldn't. It wasn't admissible. I hadn't read Mr. Clay his rights at that point."

"Then it shouldn't be admissible now, Your Honor."

The judge waved his hand in the air.

"Let's move on."

One of those times when you can't unring the bell. The judge had heard it. Nothing Dowling could do about it.

Clay could rebut it in a second. He was the only one who could explain how he knew he was being arrested for the murder of Summer Lange. But that'd mean he'd have to take the stand and testify. Say that Cliff told him. That wasn't going to happen in a million years.

Clay could give that information to his attorney, and he could work it into Cliff's questioning. But Cliff would say that he told Clay that after he read him his rights. Which he did. Before and after.

Still not lying.

Two could play the game. Selective truth telling.

"If I may add another thing," Cliff said.

"Your Honor," Dowling said, holding his hands in the air in bewilderment that he wasn't able to continue his questioning.

I'd successfully thrown him off his game.

"Make it quick, Detective," the judge said.

"Wayne Bowman allegedly confessed to murdering Summer Lange to Mr. Krueger. Not raping her. The jury found Henry Lee Clay guilty of rape. Guilty of assault. Guilty of false imprisonment. Resisting arrest. Assault of an officer."

"What's your point?" the judge asked.

"Those convictions should still stand," Cliff said. "No new evidence has been presented to refute those charges."

"Evidence was presented at the first trial that the sex was consensual," Dowling argued.

Armitage stood to his feet. "No, it wasn't, Your Honor. Counsel for the defense brought it up in their opening statement. But as you know, that's not evidence. No evidence was ever presented that it was consensual. Defense didn't even bring it up at closing. They wouldn't have been allowed to."

"I'm not going to retry the case. Let's stick to the new evidence."

"The detective's point is well taken," Armitage said. "Even if Your Honor should find Mr. Krueger's testimony compelling enough to overturn a murder conviction, it'd be an abuse of discretion by this court to overturn the other convictions. Considering no new evidence has been presented."

"I don't need you or the detective to tell me what I can and can't do. I'm aware of the law."

Cliff's aim in bringing that up was to keep Clay behind bars. Even if the judge overturned the murder conviction, he'd have to let the others stand. Which meant Clay would have to serve out the remaining part of his sentence related to the rape and other charges.

"I'd like to respond, Your Honor," Dowling said.

"No. Continue with your questioning, Mr. Dowling," the judge said.

Dowling looked down at his notes again.

When he looked up, he asked, "Were you aware that Wayne Bowman owned a white van?"

Here we go.

19

At this point in the proceedings, Cliff made a change in strategy. He reverted back to answering all Dowling's questions with a yes or no answer. Whenever possible.

He had to be careful. The change in tone and demeanor would not be lost on the judge who was all too familiar with the tactic. Every attorney worth his weight in salt advised his witnesses to keep their answers simple when on the stand and not to offer more information than necessary.

Cliff had already made the points he wanted to make in the first half of the questioning. He didn't want to say something to screw it up.

Which wouldn't be hard to do. He was walking into a potential minefield.

The white van was problematic.

Cliff knew about it. It belonged to Wayne Bowman and was at the scene the night Summer was murdered. Coupled with the jailhouse confession, the judge had all he needed to overturn the murder conviction.

Not that he needed much. He was itching to set Clay free. Cliff could tell.

So far, Cliff hadn't lied. He was only obligated to truthfully answer what the defense asked him. If Dowling didn't ask the right questions, then that wasn't Cliff's fault.

Now Dowling had asked the right question.

"Were you aware that Wayne Bowman owned a white van?" Dowling had said.

"Yes."

"When did you become aware of that fact?"

"When I pulled his DMV records."

"Did you ever see the van?"

"Yes."

"When was that?"

"When I went by his house."

Armitage jumped in. "Objection, Your Honor. What's the point of these questions? The purpose of this hearing is to determine if the new evidence is sufficient enough to overturn the conviction. Not fish for additional evidence."

"Your Honor, I believe the detective has information that will corroborate Mr. Krueger's testimony," Dowling said.

Really.

Was he bluffing?

Had Dowling talked to Mrs. Keller? Cliff could only assume he had. Either that or he was incredibly intuitive.

"I'll allow it," the judge said, "but get on with it."

"Detective Ford, have you talked to any witnesses in the last thirty days?"

Bingo.

"Yes."

"Please elaborate."

"I spoke to Mrs. Vivian Keller and one other witness."

"Who was the other witness?"

A classic attorney faux pas. Never ask a question when you don't know the answer.

Cliff looked at the judge, then back at the defense attorney. He was setting another trap for Dowling. He'd rehearsed this exact moment a hundred times in his head.

"I don't think I should answer that question," Cliff said.

Dowling was practically beside himself. He let out a huge sigh of disgust. It certainly couldn't have been the response he was expecting.

A witness didn't get to choose what questions he would or wouldn't answer.

"Your Honor, please instruct the detective to answer the question," Dowling said roughly.

"You told me not to, sir," Cliff said meekly to the judge. In false humility.

"I demand an answer," Dowling practically shouted, while pounding his fist on the podium.

"Answer the question, Detective," the judge said.

Armitage maintained his seat but was squirming. Tapping his pen nervously on the table. The Lieutenant was on the front row glaring at Cliff. Probably wondering what in the world was going through Cliff's head.

If he knew, he'd see that Cliff was practically giddy inside. It took all of Cliff's self-control not to allow a wide grin to show on his face.

"I spoke with Dawson Hawley," Cliff said slowly and deliberately. "He said he saw Henry Lee Clay in the park the night Nancee Hale was murdered."

"Objection!" Dowling shouted. "Side bar, Your Honor."

The judge motioned for the attorneys to approach. Armitage bolted out of his seat. The Lieutenant sat forward in his chair and leaned against the banister that separated the seating area from where the D.A. sat.

Dowling's hair was on fire. His arguments were spewing out of him like an erupting geyser.

"Back in my chambers," the judge said when he realized Cliff could hear everything they were saying.

Cliff kept his seat.

Clay glared at Cliff. If he had a knife, he'd probably come across the table and slash Cliff's throat at that very minute. He probably saw his entire plan flying out the window. No way the judge could let Clay walk if he knew the man had been at the scene of the murder of a teenage girl.

Clay could have no reasonable explanation for being there. It didn't take a rocket scientist to know why he was. The low life scum must've sensed his freedom slipping out of his grasp. He kept shaking his head back and forth in disbelief. Panicked.

A few minutes later, the lawyers returned. When the judge was back on the bench a minute or two later, he said, "That last statement will be stricken from the record. I will instruct Detective Ford not to make any references to the Nancee Hale case. You may continue with your questioning, Mr. Dowling."

The judge could strike it from the record all he wanted. Everyone in that courtroom had heard it.

"I told you I wasn't supposed to answer," Cliff said almost mockingly. Rubbing it in. Still laughing inside. "You made me."

Cliff had gotten it in and looked like he was cooperating with the judge's instructions at the same time.

"Why did you visit with Vivian Keller?" Dowling asked.

"After talking to, you know who, I began to develop a new theory in the case. I thought maybe I'd gotten it wrong."

Dowling's demeanor entirely changed. His eyes widened when he saw the opening Cliff had just provided him with. An opening that led through a trap door for his client.

"You believe you got it wrong? That Henry Lee Clay did not kill Summer Lange. That Wayne Bowman did."

Armitage was fidgeting now. The Lieutenant glared even harder at Cliff. They probably saw their case flying out the window.

"That was my first thought," Cliff said pensively.

"What did Mrs. Keller say that made you think as much?"

Dowling had obviously talked to Mrs. Keller. No use lying about it.

"She saw Mr. Bowman's white van at Summer Lange's house that night."

Henry Lee Clay let out a whoop. Slapped his hand on the table. Dowling quickly silenced him. The judge should've admonished Clay but didn't. He was probably as happy to hear those words come out of Cliff's mouth as Clay was.

The Lieutenant was slumped in his chair with his hand on his brow. Like he had a headache. He obviously couldn't believe Cliff would admit that fact. Even if he was under oath.

"Which fits right into what Wayne Bowman told Krueger in the jail-house," Dowling said.

"That's what I thought."

Cliff was about to lie through his teeth. With a straight face.

"It places Wayne Bowman at the scene of the murder of Summer Lange," Dowling asked. "Does it not?"

The inference being that Bowman obviously killed Summer since he was at the house that night. Amazing that the judge would not allow testimony that would make the same inference about Clay being in the park the night Nancee Hale was killed.

The whole truth and nothing but the truth.

Take all the oaths you want. Not today. Not in this courtroom.

"Yes," Cliff said, as Armitage threw his pen on the table in disgust.

Dowling had to be doing cartwheels inside his calculating brain. He'd probably been contemplating how to get Mrs. Keller's recollection of seeing the white van into evidence. He probably had an affidavit from the woman. His first hope was that Cliff would lie and Dowling would impeach him with the affidavit. His second hope would be that Cliff told the truth and put Wayne Dowling's white van at the scene.

Even better than Mrs. Keller's affidavit.

"I now believe that Bowman was there that night," Cliff added.

"Yes, he was," Dowling said, enthused.

Time to go back to speaking in a narrative rather than letting Dowling dictate the questioning. Time to lie. If Cliff had been hooked up to a polygraph machine, the needle would be going back and forth as fast as a seismograph in an earthquake.

"Wayne Bowman had a motive as well, didn't he Detective?"

"Yes. Wayne Bowman was jealous of Henry Lee Clay. Summer's parents confirmed that. He was in a relationship with Summer several months before she was murdered. They broke up. Bowman was obsessed with Summer. He would drive by her house and park in a vacant lot near the house and watch her. Mrs. Keller called 911 at one point. So did Summer."

"Your Honor, I have a copy of those 911 transcripts," Dowling said. He was so excited the papers in his hand were shaking.

"Summer Lange called 911 on several occasions. One instance in which Bowman became violent with her. They were entered into evidence at trial, but I want to make this court aware of the fact that Wayne Bowman was stalking Summer Lange. Which is motive for murder."

Cliff waited for the next question. When the right question came, he'd spring his next trap.

"You should've looked more closely at Wayne Bowman from the beginning, shouldn't you have, Detective Ford?"

"Probably so. But it wouldn't have changed the outcome. Henry Lee Clay killed Summer. He raped her. Then killed her. His DNA was at the scene. Bowman's DNA was never found inside the house. He couldn't have killed her."

"Wayne Bowman was at the scene! He had motive. Opportunity. He confessed to it."

They were talking over each other. Dowling was shouting. Waving his arms in the air in exaggerated motions for effect. The judge pounded the gavel.

"One at a time, people."

Armitage stood. "Counsel should let the detective speak. He asked a question. When he didn't like the answer, he started filibustering the witness."

"The detective can finish his answer," the judge said reluctantly.

"After I talked to Dawson Hawley, I realized that I'd gotten it wrong."

"Gotten what wrong, Detective?" the judge asked.

"Henry Lee Clay killed Summer Lange. Then he killed Nancee Hale."

"Objection!"

The judge pounded the gavel. Harder.

"Bowman was at the scene of both murders!" Dowling shouted.

"So was Henry Lee Clay," Cliff said. "Because he was stalking Clay. Not because he killed either of them. Bowman had no criminal record. He wasn't a murderer. Clay had already been convicted of murder once."

"Your Honor!" Dowling shouted.

The judge pounded his gavel even harder.

"I warned you, detective. You were not to mention Clay's prior conviction, or anything related to the Nancee Lee case. If you persist, I'll find you in contempt of court."

"Bowman followed Clay to the park," Cliff said as fast as the words could come out of his mouth. "Saw him kill the girl. Accidently, stepped in her blood."

"Detective, shut your mouth!" the judge practically shouted.

"Your Honor, this is an outrage," Dowling said.

"I'm going to put a stop to this. I want to see both attorneys in my chambers. Now. Detective Ford, you may step down."

The judge left, followed by the attorneys. Cliff walked by the defense's table where Clay was sitting and gave him the glare of a bear stalking a prey.

That should do it.

No way the judge could let Clay go now. Too big a risk. Even if the judge didn't want to hear evidence related to Nancee Hale, he heard it. It was on the official record.

Cliff had admitted he got it wrong when it came to the Nancee Hale murder. That's okay. Bowman was dead. He wasn't going to be filing any wrongful conviction lawsuits.

So Cliff lied about the Summer Lange murder. In his mind, Bowman did it. Although he didn't have absolute proof. So it wasn't really a lie.

Cliff wanted to pin both murders on Clay. That was his strategy.

Make sure the man never saw the light of day.

He felt confident he had succeeded.

When the lawyers returned, the judge wasn't with them. Armitage motioned for Cliff and the Lieutenant to follow him into a side conference room. He closed the door behind them.

"What's going on?" the Lieutenant said. The excitement had returned to his voice.

"The judge is in chambers trying to decide what to do," Armitage said.

"He's going to have to rule in our favor, don't you think?" the Lieutenant said.

"He doesn't want to. Let's just say that the judge is not too happy with Cliff about now."

"Why?" the Lieutenant asked. "He simply told the truth."

"That's the problem," Armitage said. "The judge wanted to rule against us. He's probably back in his chambers realizing that he can't do that. You ruined his day, Cliff."

"I only want the truth to come out," Cliff said. "I don't care about the judge. After I talked to Mr. Dawson, I realized that Henry Lee Clay killed the girl in the park. That I'd gotten it wrong. We might not ever be able to try and convict Clay of that murder, but now it's on the record. Everyone will know that Clay is a killer."

"You should've seen Dowling's face back in chambers," Armitage said, gleefully. "He knew about Mrs. Keller, but he didn't know about Dawson Hawley. When you sprung that on him, Cliff, he about came unglued."

"He obviously knew the white van was at Summer's house that night," Cliff said. "Because he talked to Mrs. Keller."

"With Mrs. Keller's testimony, Clay was going to walk," Armitage said. "You did good, Cliff. Getting it on the record that Clay killed both of the girls."

"So we're going to win," the Lieutenant said.

"It's fifty-fifty," Armitage said. "This judge was never going to rule in our favor. That was a foregone conclusion. It didn't matter what Cliff said, the judge was going to let Clay go free. Now, he's back there in his chambers thinking about it. If he lets Clay go, knowing he was at Nancee Hale's murder scene, he could get a lot of heat. He would probably get overturned on appeal."

"Let's hope so."

"Cliff also made the point that Clay should go back to prison for the rape charges," Armitage said. "I would've made that argument at the end anyway, but Cliff made it for me. It's a good point."

A knock on the door interrupted them.

The Lieutenant was closest to the door, so he opened it. The Bailiff stuck his head in.

"The judge is ready to rule," he said.

Cliff felt his heart begin to thump in his chest. Detectives were supposed to separate their emotions from their cases. He'd never been able to successfully do it. Never more so than now.

The three of them filed back into the courtroom and took their places. The judge entered shortly thereafter. Walking with a purpose. He practically slammed the files down on the massive mahogany bench.

His demeanor was as serious as a pileup on the freeway. Cliff wondered if his whole strategy was about to crash and burn or if he'd avoided the disaster.

The judge began speaking as soon as he sat down.

"I've been a judge now for more than fifteen years," he said. "In all my years, I've never been more appalled at the actions of law enforcement. Cliff Ford, you are a disgrace to the badge."

The judge looked right at Cliff when he said it. Whatever nervousness Cliff felt turned to rage.

He continued. "You are either the biggest liar that's ever come into my courtroom or you are the most incompetent detective to ever wear a badge."

The Lieutenant stood to his feet.

"Sit down!" the judge said. "Or I'll find you in contempt of court."

"I must speak up, Your Honor. Cliff Ford has worked for me for more than ten years. He's the best detective on the force. He's won more commendations than I can count."

"I said to sit down!"

"I demand to be heard. I will not let you disparage a good detective and a good man."

"Lieutenant, I see where he gets his insubordination. You're as big a liar as he is."

The Lieutenant was shaking his head from side to side. "No. You are wrong if you think that."

"Cliff Ford said for all practical purposes that he got the Nancee Hale murder wrong. Three years later, after Wayne Bowman is killed in prison. Now Ford has second thoughts. Says that he has new evidence that Clay was at the scene. What a crock! I don't buy it for a second. I doubt he even talked to this so-called witness. This Hawley person."

Cliff could feel the heat rising in his body. His heart was beating out of his chest. He barely had the self-control to keep his mouth shut.

"Detective Ford lied to save his own skin. He has a personal vendetta against Henry Lee Clay. Stems from the first case. He didn't like my ruling and was looking for a chance to stick it to the defendant one more time."

It was clear how he was going to rule.

"I find the testimony of Krueger to be compelling," the judge said.

"You believe a convicted murderer over a decorated detective?" the Lieutenant shouted as he stood up again.

"Bailiff, remove the Lieutenant from the courtroom. I find you in contempt of court, sir."

"I find you in contempt. Krueger was lying. Any impartial observer could see that."

The Lieutenant was shouting as the Bailiff practically dragged him out of the courtroom.

After the din died down, the judge said, "I find that the murder conviction of Henry Lee Clay was flawed. New evidence has been presented that convinces me that Wayne Bowman killed Summer Lange. His van was at the scene. He had a motive. His own words prove his guilt. He confessed. This court can't overlook that fact."

Cliff bit his tongue. Like Armitage had said, this was a foregone conclusion. At least Clay would remain behind bars while they appealed the decision.

"As to the other charges, I find the entire conviction flawed. I'm throwing out the jury verdict on the other charges as well. The fruit from the poison tree. Cliff Ford was the poison. As soon as he touched this case, it was doomed for failure. I feel sorry for the families of Nancee Hale and Summer Lange. They deserve better than you, Mr. Ford."

"Your Honor, you don't have the authority to throw out those other charges," Armitage said. "No new evidence was presented related to those charges."

"Watch me. I'm also sealing all the records to this proceeding and issuing a gag order. No one is to speak of what happened here today."

"So, you want to cover it up," Armitage said, risking his own contempt violation.

The judge ignored his comment. "Cliff Ford is a corrupt detective. Who lied under oath today. I wouldn't be surprised if he planted evidence again. Like he did the first time."

"We'll appeal," Armitage said, still standing.

"You do that. If you win on appeal, I want you to know that I will reduce the sentence to time served. Mr. Clay you are free to go with the apologies of the court."

Cliff stood to his feet. He could no longer hold his tongue. "Henry Lee Clay killed Nancee Hale. He also killed Tessie. You're letting a murderer go free. Mark my words, he will kill again. The blood will be on your hands."

The Bailiff had already started moving toward Cliff.

"I find you in contempt of court," the judge said, as he struck his gavel several times. "Thirty days in jail and a one thousand dollar fine. Bailiff, take Mr. Ford into custody."

Cliff held out his wrists. The Bailiff handcuffed him.

He couldn't believe it.

Clay hugged his attorney.

Henry Lee Clay was a free man.

Cliff was the one going to jail.

20

Cliff was stewing away in a holding cell at the courthouse. Feeling a little sorry for himself. Wondering how he'd gotten into this predicament. Thrown in jail for thirty days. His house was destroyed. He would probably lose his job.

Henry Lee Clay was a free man. The worst part of it all. The judge had been so intent on ruling in Clay's favor that Cliff wondered if the man had been paid off. Judges could be as corrupt as the criminals who came before them.

Armitage suddenly appeared at his cell door with a guard who unlocked it and let the District Attorney in. The metal bars clanged when he closed it behind him.

"I talked to the judge," he said. "He'll drop the contempt charge if you come to his courtroom and apologize to him on the record."

"What happens if I don't?"

"He can lock you up for as long as he wants. He said thirty days. He could extend that if you don't show any remorse. Not to mention the thousand-dollar fine. You'll have to pay that before you can get out."

"I guess I don't have any choice then. I'm worried about Henry Lee Clay. I can't protect my family from in here."

"You're convinced he killed Nancee Hale aren't you?"

"A hundred percent."

"You know there's nothing we can do about it now, don't you? I can't try him for that crime. Not when we've already convicted Wayne Bowman for the same murder. That creates all kinds of reasonable doubt."

"I know. I'm sorry I got it wrong."

"I saw the same evidence you did," Armitage said. "I was convinced Bowman did it as well."

"It's my job to get it right."

"Water under the bridge now."

"Except that he's free to kill again. I also found out new evidence about Tessie's murder. Clay killed her as well."

"I never doubted that. What's the new evidence?"

"I'm not at liberty to say. It's compelling though. Hundred percent proof he killed Tessie."

"Doesn't matter anyway. Nothing we can do about that case either. Double jeopardy would apply to that."

"That's why I have to get out of here. Clay killed Tessie. He killed Nancee Hale. He'll kill again. I have to stop him."

"I should warn you as the District Attorney of the city of Chicago and also as your friend that you should stay away from Henry Lee Clay. Don't go near him. You could find yourself right back in court. On the wrong end of the charges."

"Clay needs to be put away for good."

"You're not the person to do it. Whatever arrest you might make will be tainted."

"I'll be careful. But I have to stop him."

"Don't even think about killing him," Armitage said.

Cliff didn't say anything. Not because he was thinking about it. He'd loved to put a bullet in Clay's head. In his dreams. He wasn't stupid. Illinois didn't have the death penalty. Whether Cliff agreed with that or not was irrelevant. There's no crime Clay could commit that would take his life. Only his freedom.

Cliff wasn't above the law. He also wasn't one to mete out his own justice. He was part of the system. As flawed as it was.

They heard the sound of a door opening down the hall. Armitage and Cliff looked toward the noise at the same time.

The Lieutenant was walking down the hallway with a uniformed policeman. The cop took out a set of keys and opened the prison door.

The Lieutenant walked in. This time the guard didn't close the door.

"Come on, Cliff. Let's get out of here," the Lieutenant said.

"Where are we going?" Cliff asked.

"No detective of mine is going to sit in a jail cell because of some idiot judge."

"Will the guards let me leave?"

"You'll walk out with me. I'm the Lieutenant of the Chicago Police Department. Second in command of my department. Who do you think is going to stop me?"

"It's not necessary," Armitage said. "I talked to the judge. He'll drop the contempt charge if Cliff apologizes."

"Over my dead body."

"I can make all this go away."

"I'm making it go away right now. Stand up, Cliff. You're walking out of here. Right now. With your head held high. You did nothing wrong. I'm not going to let you grovel in front of that fool like some kind of hungry pig. We won't give that pile of horse manure the satisfaction."

"If Cliff leaves the jail cell, the judge can issue a warrant for his arrest," Armitage said.

"Let him. There ain't a cop in Chicago that'll arrest Cliff. He's a hero. I don't care what some moron in a black robe says. Cliff's my detective. He works for me. I'm getting him out of jail and putting him back to work. The judge can go jump in the Chicago River for all I care. You tell him that for me."

"I'll do it right now."

"Be sure to mention the words fool, moron, and idiot."

"I'll leave out the horse manure part."

"Leave it out or not. I don't care."

"The judge won't be happy."

"Remind the dishonorable empty headed noise machine in a black robe that he might need Chicago's finest someday. He should think twice before messing with us. I'd hate for a burglar to be in his house and a cop doesn't show up when he calls for one."

"I think I'll keep that between us and forget you said it."

The Lieutenant smiled for the first time. "Let's go Cliff."

Armitage went one direction; they went the other.

"What do you want me to do?" Cliff said, once they reached the underground garage where they were parked.

"Show up for work tomorrow morning. Do your job."

"I will."

The Lieutenant put his hand on Cliff's shoulder and pulled him into a hug. Something he'd never done before.

"Don't give what happened in there another thought, Cliff. We win some and we lose some. Justice doesn't always prevail. If guys like you give up, the good guys win. Henry Lee Clay will be back in jail before you know it."

"That's what I'm afraid of."

***

Armitage walked into the judge's chambers. The black robe was hanging behind him on a hat rack. He sat behind his desk looking over some papers.

"Is your man ready to apologize?" the judge asked.

"I don't think so."

The judge clenched his jaw. Tighter than the saddle on a bucking bronco.

"He refuses."

The judge let out a laugh.

"Why am I not surprised? Let's give Detective Ford thirty days in lockdown to think about it. Tell the detective that I'm not letting him out until he apologizes to me. I'll bring him into my courtroom every thirty days. As you know, I can keep someone held in contempt as long as I want."

"Good luck with that," Armitage said.

"What do you mean?"

"Cliff Ford is not here."

"Where is he?"

"He left."

"What do you mean he left? I ordered him to lock up."

"The Lieutenant came and got him. They walked out of here a few minutes ago."

"That dirty son of a... "

The judge swore under his breath. Then stood to his feet.

"I'll issue a warrant for his arrest."

"I'd advise against that."

"Are you telling me what to do?"

"All I'm saying is that this is a war you can't win. Do you really want to pick a battle with the Lieutenant of the Chicago P.D. homicide division? I don't think so. You don't want him as your enemy."

"Did he threaten me?"

"I'm just the messenger. You take it however you want."

The judge sat back down behind his desk. The wheels were clearly churning in his mind. He knew the meaning behind the words as his face sagged in resignation.

"I'll let it go for now. I'll drop the contempt charge on Detective Ford."

"That's a wise decision."

The first one he'd made today.

***

Later that evening

Cliff appreciated that Julia didn't tell him "I told you so."

She could've said it outright or subtlety. He came home, told her all the sordid details of the courtroom drama, and she listened intently. Asking a few questions and offering nothing but support for Cliff.

He should've listened to her all along. Back before he even arrested Bowman and Clay. Then again when she said he should let it drop.

Actually, as things turned out, Cliff was glad he had investigated her theory. As an investigator, he was always in search of the truth. He thought he knew it now. He wouldn't have known that Henry Lee Clay was at the park had he not talked to Dawson Hawley. He wouldn't have known that the white van was at Summer's house that night had he not talked to Mrs. Keller.

He was still glad Julia took no satisfaction in being right. She didn't gloat one time. Even though he was prepared to take it without getting angry.

Julia knew the sober reality. Henry Lee Clay was free. The worst possible outcome. Piling on her husband could only make things worse between them.

Clay would've gone free anyway. A sobering reality. Even if Cliff hadn't investigated Julia's theory. Clay orchestrated the whole jailhouse confession ruse. Paid off Krueger. Probably paid off the judge. Cliff was convinced something was done behind the scenes to get the case in front of the same judge as before.

What were the odds of that happening?

Slim to none. Yet it had happened.

An unlikely coincidence.

Cliff and Julia were still staying at the shelter. They had nowhere to go. Their house was destroyed. Julia prepared a light meal and Rita finally went off to bed.

The two were sitting on the couch. Neither of them had made one move toward turning on the television set. Cliff could imagine the non-stop one-sided coverage. Shannon Roberts was no doubt gloating on the screen. Cliff had heard a rumor that she and Clay were an item.

Cliff's name was being dragged through the mud at that very moment. No use subjecting himself or his wife to the abuse.

Julia snuggled up against his shoulder. He had his arm around her and pulled her closer. It made him feel better. The smell of her hair. Her warm touch. The taste of her lips when she kissed him earlier. It warmed his heart and was helping the events of the day slowly melt out of the recesses of his mind.

If only momentarily. Maybe if they held that embrace for days, it'd be gone completely.

"I've been thinking," Julia said without even raising her head. "Do we really want to stay in Chicago?"

Her tone was soft and gentle. Almost seductive except for the subject matter.

"This is my home. I was born and raised here."

"I know. It's getting too dangerous. Don't you think?"

"Where would we go?"

"What about Miami?"

Cliff chuckled. Julia was born in Miami. Her parents fled Cuba and settled in Miami. She moved to Chicago with her sisters to go to college. Her parents still lived there.

Julia had said on more than one occasion that she hoped to go back there someday. Years from now. Cliff didn't think that was ever going to happen. He couldn't imagine living anywhere but Chicago.

"You don't think Miami is dangerous?" Cliff asked.

"Not like Chicago."

"Should I look up the murder statistics in Miami?" Cliff asked.

Julia was sitting up now. The relaxing moment had passed.

"I did look them up," Julia said. "Miami is in the top one hundred for murders per capita. But it's way down the list. Chicago has the highest number of murders in the United States."

"That's why I have a job. If you're going fishing, you go where the fish are. If you're solving murders, what better place to do so than in the murder capital of the world?"

Julia tapped his chest playfully. Her forehead burrowed and her eyes narrowed as her tone turned serious.

"I'm not joking, Cliff. We've already lost a baby to riots. Now we've lost our home. What if we'd been in the house when that fire bomb was thrown through the window? We could've been killed."

Julia had a miscarriage after their vehicle was attacked in downtown Chicago during one of the many riots. This was the second time the riots had significantly disrupted their lives.

"I don't know if I want to be a detective in Miami," Cliff said.

"What if you retired? What if you weren't a detective?"

"I'm not even forty."

"You could do something else."

"What? Sell shoes at the mall. This is all I know. I'm good at it."

Julia crossed her feet underneath her.

"Promise me you won't laugh," she said.

"Okay. I promise."

"What about... private investigator?"

She said the words slowly for effect.

"Think about it. We could open an office. I could work with you. We could investigate things together. Wouldn't that be fun?"

"What are you talking about?"

"I was thinking... you and I. Partners. Julia and Cliff, Family Friendly Investigators."

"Why would your name go first?"

"Cliff and Julia, Super Sleuths."

Cliff laughed.

"How about Under the Covers?" he said, humoring her. "Do you get it? Undercover."

Cliff poked her in the side.

"We do all of our best work under the covers," he quipped.

"I get it," she said, twisting her lips to the side in a frown.

"Our tagline could be we get to the bottom of things," Cliff added.

He playfully tried to grab Julia's bottom. She slapped his grabby hands away.

"Stop it. I'm serious. Think about it, Cliff. It'd be fun."

"Do you really want to go into investigations? What about the shelter?"

"You said I'm good at figuring out clues. I've been working at the shelter for years. I'm ready for a new challenge."

"Could we work together? I'm mean in business. Around each other all the time?"

"Why not? We already do that now. I help you on your murder cases."

"We wouldn't be investigating murders. Law enforcement does that."

"I know. I looked it up. We could investigate fraudulent insurance claims. Corporate stuff. They pay big bucks for that."

"That sounds boring."

"We could catch cheating spouses. That wouldn't be boring."

"You've thought a lot about this."

"Do you know what the average high temperature is in Miami in January?"

"What?"

"Seventy-six degrees. That's the high. Do you know what it is in Chicago?"

"I do know. I've been at many a crime scene in the middle of the night in January."

"The average high is thirty-two. Thirty-two, Cliff. That's forty-four degrees colder. We could have a swimming pool. Rita would love it."

Her hands were in front of her. Pleading. Rocking back and forth.

"My parents live there," she said.

"You saved your worst argument for last," Cliff said jokingly.

"You love my parents. And they love you."

"I do love your parents."

"Promise me you'll think about it."

"I'll think about it."

"Thank you, Cliff. I think a change would do us good."

"I said, I'll think about it."

Julia threw her arms around him. Kissed him passionately. He could hardly catch his breath.

She bolted off the couch. Took him by the hand and led him to the bedroom.

"I hear the sex is better in Miami," Julia said, as she pushed him down on the bed.

The sex that night was pretty good in Chicago.

That's the great thing about being married to someone like Julia.

Cliff could have the worst day in his entire career, and she could make it all better in a few short minutes.

***

Four days later

The Lieutenant called Cliff into his office. Then closed the door. The Lieutenant never closed the door. Even if he was chewing someone out. He wanted the other members of the bullpen to hear him.

This must be serious. His face confirmed it.

"Henry Lee Clay has filed a wrongful conviction lawsuit against the city of Chicago," he blurted. Always one to get right to the point.

"That didn't take long," Cliff said. He'd been expecting it. "I'm sure they already had it basically written before the trial."

"I'm sorry, Cliff."

"It's not your fault."

"What I mean is that I need your service revolver?"

"You're firing me. Why? You said things were business as usual. That I wouldn't lose my job over it."

"You haven't lost your job. Not yet anyway. A letter was sent to the police commissioner by a local congresswoman. Requesting that you be fired."

"What's her name?"

"It doesn't matter. She's part of the 'defund the police' crowd. The Chief came to me. I talked him out of it for now. He set up a panel to review your case. It's made up of three people. I don't know who those three people are. In the meantime, you're relegated to desk duty. You can't carry a weapon and can't investigate cases."

"Then what am I supposed to do?"

"Go home and take a vacation. I'm not going to make you sit around here pushing papers."

Cliff and Julia had already decided to take a trip to Miami. To look around. Consider moving. This news might be a big step in the process.

He always thought he'd leave the Chicago P.D. on his own terms. Now it looked like he might not have a choice.

"How long a vacation?" Cliff asked.

"Until the commission makes their decision. These things could take up to six months. They probably won't do anything until Clay's civil case is resolved. They won't want to make a public admission of guilt by firing you."

Those words were like a fiery dart from the devil.

"I don't know what I'll do with myself," Cliff said.

"Learn how to play golf."

"It's November."

"Do whatever you want. I envy you. I'd love to have six months of paid leave."

"No you wouldn't. Catching murderers is in your blood. Mine too. You'd go crazy."

"You'd be investigating my wife for murder. She'd kill me within a week," the Lieutenant quipped.

They both laughed. Nervously. This was a serious matter for both of them. Trying to make light of it was their way of not letting the emotions show.

"Look Cliff. I'll go to bat for you. I told you I would, and I mean it. I'm not going to let them fire you without a fight. But I don't know if I can stop it. These things are political more than anything. I'm going to insist that you're able to keep your pension and benefits. You'll also get a severance package."

"It sounds like you think they're going to fire me."

"Clay won a sixteen-million-dollar settlement. He'll probably get that and more in this new lawsuit. That's a lot of money caused by one person. You. Don't get me wrong. I don't blame you. Clay doesn't deserve a dime. But this is a different climate we live in. The politicians want to cut our police budgets in half. How do they expect us to do our jobs? I'm afraid you may be made a scapegoat. I hope I'm wrong."

"So that's it."

"I'm sorry."

"One second."

Cliff stood and left the office. He returned with a stack of files and sat them on the Lieutenant's desk.

"What's this?" he asked.

"Elmer Foley's file. Since I'm off the case, somebody else can figure out how a man can decompose by three weeks in three days."

21

Several months later

Cliff and Julia decided they were going to move to Miami after Rita finished her semester of school. They didn't want to pull her out in midstream and have her start all over again in a totally different environment. She'd already had to do that once this school year after the fiasco with Ms. McVade in the public school.

Cliff was still relegated to his desk job, although he hadn't been into the office more than a handful of times over the last three months. Mostly as an advisor on difficult cases and to help whoever took over his caseload.

The commission still hadn't ruled on Cliff's firing, but now that Henry Lee Clay received his second wrongful conviction settlement from the city of Chicago, it was only a matter of time until they brought the hammer down on Cliff. The Lieutenant feared the worst. Didn't even hope for the best. He felt like it was a foregone conclusion based on the political environment and the makeup of the commission.

The Lieutenant testified in front of the committee of three and gave Cliff as glowing an endorsement as he could. But the pressure was great to cut out the "bad seeds" in the police force as one of the local politicians had called Cliff during one of the "defund the police" rallies that were becoming more prevalent.

Henry Lee Clay only got five million dollars this time. The city took a hard line with him. He'd already gotten sixteen million for ten years in prison. This time, he served a little over three years of his sentence. So he got a third of the money.

Even then, Cliff would have to work fifty-three years on his current salary to make five million dollars.

Such irony. The commission was debating on whether to give Cliff his paltry pension while Clay received millions for murdering young girls. It was all Cliff could do to keep from letting the bitterness eat him alive.

In reality, he wished the commission would get on with it. The inactivity was driving him crazy. He barely knew what to do with himself. He tried smacking a golf ball around a course once, but that made things worse. He was more stressed afterwards than he had been before he started.

It did give him more time with Rita though. He was able to take her to school every morning and pick her up in the afternoon. She was now attending a private Christian school. Where she wasn't filled with propaganda and security was tight. The students wore uniforms and were allowed to pray before they ate their meals.

The school day started with the Pledge of Allegiance and a prayer. A sharp contrast to what Rita was subjected to before. She had adapted well and made a lot of new friends. She was doing well in academics and shining in a number of extracurricular activities. It had been a good move which was part of why they were reluctant to pull her out of it.

Moving to Miami in the summer was going to be traumatic enough for all of them. Much less if Rita had to do it in the middle of the school year.

Shielding Rita from all the outside static was next to impossible. She still heard things. Cliff had become a polarizing figure in Chicago. A hero to many; a symbol of oppression and corruption to a vocal minority.

At this point, he was past ready to move. The insurance company gave them a big check for the loss of their house and belongings, so they had enough to start over. He was a fighter by nature but was tired of beating his head against the wall. A change of scenery would do him good. He was looking forward to moving to Miami and starting a private investigation agency with Julia.

UCM, LLC.

Under Cover Miami.

Cliff and Julia's private joke. They solved cases under the covers.

A good thing had come from their plight. The adversity of Chicago had drawn them even closer together. Their relationship had never been better.

Same with Rita. They were getting along well. He was on his way to pick her up.

He sent her a text.

Be there in twenty.

Pick me up one block over. Not in front.

So you don't have to be seen with me?

No. I'm meeting a boy. Smiley face attached, so he'd know she was kidding.

Boys are off limits.

I don't think your texts are getting through. Something's wrong with my phone.

Yeah. They're getting through.

How do you know?

He couldn't help but laugh at his daughter's sense of humor. He couldn't believe she was about to turn ten.

Rita sent Cliff ten LOL's all in a row. Then several emojis of a laughing figure with a tear coming out of his eye. It was funny now. It wouldn't be long until Rita was sixteen and it wouldn't be so funny then.

He'd enjoy it while it lasted. Rita was always pulling his chain. A real prankster. She'd suggested a few days ago that he pick her up a block over to stay out of the traffic which was why she mentioned it now as a joke.

Cliff pulled up to the corner where Rita was waiting for him.

"How was school?" Cliff asked, once she settled into the car and before he drove away.

Rita groaned. "I think I pulled a brain muscle."

"I don't think brains have muscles," Cliff said.

"Maybe yours don't. But mine do."

"Ha. Ha. Very funny. How long have you been waiting to tell that joke?"

"A week or two. Knock, knock," Rita said.

She'd started telling a lot of knock knock jokes. Almost nonstop.

"Who's there?"

"A detective."

Cliff grinned.

"Detective who?"

"I'll ask the questions here buddy."

He laughed to make her feel better even though he'd heard it before.

"Did you hear about the detective who dropped his phone?" Cliff asked.

"No."

"He cracked the case."

Rita laughed just as dutifully.

"My joke was funnier," Cliff said.

"Whatever."

Rita rolled her eyes at him. Like her mother did all the time when Cliff said something annoying or that she didn't like.

Cliff put the car in gear and drove off as the banter had come to a natural stopping point. He slowed down when they came to a school zone that was also letting out. Traffic was bad there as well, so Cliff took a side street to avoid it.

"Daddy, did you see that car back there?" Rita said. "The fancy red one."

"No, honey. I didn't see it. What about it? Was it nice?"

"It was in that same spot this morning."

"So?"

"I think it's strange. I've seen it a couple of times. Every day this week."

"You've got your daddy's detective genes. Suspicious of everything."

"Let's go back and look."

Cliff hesitated. Even slowed down. He looked in his rear-view mirror, but the car was already out of sight. He'd have to turn around to check it out. Probably a waste of time. But they didn't have anywhere they had to be, and his curiosity was now piqued. If for no other reason than to humor his daughter.

He missed the thrill of investigating something. He felt the adrenaline kick up a notch at the thought of surveilling a car. Even if it was nothing.

"Why does the car look suspicious to you?" he asked, as he looked for a place to turn around.

"It looks like he's spying on the school."

"He could be waiting for one of the students."

Rita shook her head.

"That's not where you'd pick somebody up."

Thoughts of Henry Lee Clay popped into Cliff's head. He had to check it out now. For Rita's benefit. She might learn something.

What would it hurt?

He did a u-turn at the next opportunity and drove back toward the school.

The car was gone.

"Where is it?" Cliff asked.

"It was parked right there." Rita pointed.

It did seem like a strange place to park a car.

"What kind of fancy car was it?"

"A red sports car."

Cliff's heart did a somersault in his chest.

He'd heard that Clay bought a red Ferrari with his settlement money. He looked over the situation. From that vantage point, the person in the sports car could see the entrance of the school, but it'd be hard for the car to be seen.

The kind of place a stalker might hang out.

An uneasy feeling came over him. It'd been months since he'd felt that angst.

How would he find the car? Was it still around? Did the man in it find a target? Cliff didn't even know a man was driving. The person might be long gone.

Cliff made a mental note to check for the car tomorrow.

He turned right at the stop sign so he was driving away from the school. In the direction some of the kids were walking. He looked down each side street just in case the car was still around.

"Right there!" Rita said. "There's the car."

She had a good eye. Cliff got a glimpse of it as well right before it disappeared around a curve. Not a good enough look to know the make and model. Only that it was red.

He hit his brakes and turned down the street. Going as fast as he dared in the residential neighborhood. He didn't want to lose the car again.

He slowed as he came around the curve.

The red sports car was up ahead.

Moving slowly.

A girl was walking on the sidewalk. The car pulled up next to her. The girl stopped walking and was talking to the person in the car presumably through an open window.

Cliff lagged back so he wouldn't be seen.

The passenger side door opened, and the girl got in.

Cliff let out a groan. Rita reacted with a muted scream.

"Do you think she knows him?" Rita asked.

"I don't think so," Cliff said. "Otherwise, why would she be talking to him? Why didn't she get in the car right away?"

That wasn't definitive. It just didn't look right. Something about it caused sirens to go off inside Cliff's head. He'd relied on those triggers for years. They'd generally served him well.

He did not intend to let that car out of his sight. Until he was sure the girl was safe.

"Let's follow them," Rita said excitedly.

Cliff had every intention of doing so. He lagged back a safe distance where the car couldn't see that he was being followed.

The car was a red Ferrari.

It was stopped at a red light. The windows were tinted so Cliff couldn't see inside. But he could see a license plate number from his location. Two cars behind.

Cliff was in his government issued undercover vehicle. Not his Volvo SUV. So he could run a check on the plates. Find out who owned the vehicle and if he had any outstanding warrants or tickets.

Did Cliff have enough probable cause to stop the car? Technically, he was still a detective even though relegated to a desk job. He had his badge but not his gun. He had the full authority of the law behind him to make an arrest if the need arose.

The dispatcher came back a few seconds later.

"The vehicle belongs to Henry Lee Clay," she said.

Cliff's heart skipped a beat.

Rita let out a squeal. She was familiar with that name as well.

What should he do?

He should call for backup. But he didn't know where Clay was taking the girl.

He could call in his location. Have a uniformed officer pull Clay over. Make sure the girl was okay.

Indecision hit him. This might be an opportunity to catch Clay in the act.

He kept following. Didn't call it in. Decided to wait and see what happened.

Clay made several turns. Cliff stayed right on his tail. Still careful to keep from alerting Clay that he was being followed.

Clay pulled into a park. Similar to the one where he had taken Nancee Hale.

Adrenaline was on full blast now. Cliff didn't have time to think through probable cause. This girl was in danger. He could feel it.

His feelings weren't probable cause.

What difference did it make? He was getting fired soon anyway.

Clay pulled into a parking space. The lot was empty. Cliff took up a position on the street.

Clay got out and opened the passenger side door.

Looked around.

The girl got out.

She looked around as well. Cliff couldn't see her face well enough to know if she was frightened. Her body language looked hesitant.

She looked to be a little older than Rita. Maybe fourteen or fifteen.

Clay had her arm. He led her toward the storage building. The same type of facility Nancee Hale was found behind. It was the middle of the day so no one was around.

Cliff floored it without thinking.

He turned into the parking lot and raced toward the red car. Pulled in behind it. Blocking it in.

The tires screeched when he came to a stop.

Clay turned toward the noise.

The girl tried to pull away, but Clay strengthened his grip on her arm.

She let out a scream.

"Call for backup," Cliff said to Rita. "I showed you how to do it. And stay in the car."

Cliff threw his door open and was out of the car in a flash. He ran straight for Henry Lee Clay who had a knife in his right hand. His left still firmly gripped the girl's arm. She struggled to break the grip.

Cliff tackled him.

Similar to how he'd done that day when he arrested Clay.

Cliff fell on top of him but had not dislodged the knife.

Cliff lunged for Clay's right wrist but missed when Clay shifted his weight, throwing Cliff off balance.

Clay raised his right arm high in the air. Cliff reacted too late.

Clay plunged the knife into Cliff's left shoulder.

A searing pain shot through him. Like he'd been branded with a hot iron.

Clay pulled the knife out sending more pain shooting through Cliff's back and arm.

The girl screamed again. Louder this time.

Clay was on top of Cliff now. He brought the knife high into the air again. This time to inflict a fatal blow.

Cliff could see the evil in his eyes. They burned like black coals on fire.

Clay let out a flurry of expletives. Calling Cliff all kinds of names. "I've been waiting for this moment for a long time," he said, viciously.

Cliff's left shoulder was numb and useless. He couldn't move it. He could feel the blood soaking the shirt.

The angle was wrong. The knife was in Clay's right hand. Cliff had to reach across his body with his right hand to grab the wrist before the knife was thrust into the obvious target. His chest.

Is this how I'm going to die?

Julia's face flashed into his mind. Miami. Rita. UMC, LLC.

Time slowed to almost a standstill.

It seemed like things were happening in slow motion.

Clay clenched his teeth and brought the knife down. Angrily.

Cliff managed to grab Clay's wrist and stop the knife about six inches from his chest.

A struggle ensued.

Clay strained to break Cliff's grip. But it was strong. It had to be, or he was dead. Killed in front of his own daughter. No telling what Clay would do without Cliff there to stop him.

That thought gave Cliff a renewed energy and resolve. He was able to hold Clay off. How much longer could he do so? Clay had the upper hand. The leverage.

Clay changed the angle. So the knife was aimed for Cliff's throat. He grunted as he pushed harder.

Clay was surprisingly strong.

The knife edged closer to Cliff's throat.

A car door opened.

Rita.

"Stay in the car," he wanted to shout but didn't have the breath to get the words out.

He saw a flash of movement.

Rita kicked Clay in the head.

He cried out as the blow was solid. Not enough to do severe damage and incapacitate him but enough to make him release the effort he was bringing to bear on the knife.

"Hey! You little twirp," he said when he looked back to see who was behind the blow.

Clay was distracted. That was all the opening Cliff needed.

Cliff lifted his hips and rolled up and to the left. While still maintaining the grip on Clay's wrist. They rolled to the side.

Cliff was on top of Clay now.

Still clutching his right wrist.

Cliff bent his wrist backward and to the side, hyperextending it.

Clay cried out.

The knife fell to the side.

Cliff released his grip on Clay's wrist and brought his elbow down and across the bridge of Clay's nose.

Knocking him out.

Cliff rolled off of him. Gasping for breath.

"Are you okay?" Rita asked.

Cliff staggered to his feet. Checked Clay for a pulse.

Satisfied, he was no longer an immediate threat, Cliff took the handcuffs off his belt and secured Clay's hands behind him.

Blood poured from the wound on his back. The cut must've been deep. He was concerned he might bleed out.

Rita was by him now.

"Daddy, you're hurt."

Cliff felt dizzy.

"I called for help," Rita said. "I told them an officer was down."

Cliff could hear the sirens.

"That's good thinking," Cliff said.

He fell to his knees.

That's the last thing he remembered.

Everything went black.

22

Cliff had surgery to repair the damage to his shoulder. He'd lost a lot of blood but was never considered critical. He was resting uncomfortably in his room. He'd refused painkillers and his head, neck, and shoulder were throbbing.

The pain medicine made him sleepy and it was the middle of the day. He wanted to be awake. He'd already had a number of visitors. The Lieutenant called and would be by soon with news. Cliff wanted to have his full wits about him when his boss showed up.

Julia and Rita had been there most of the day. Rita was thrilled to be missing school. She met with the investigators and gave her view of the events the previous afternoon. Mostly relating the part where she saved her daddy's life. Something he was probably going to be reminded of for months and years to come.

"The next time you want to ground me," Rita said, "remember that I'm the one who saved your skin."

Cliff looked at Julia who still had a worried look on her face but forced a smile.

"I'm never going to hear the end of this, am I?" Cliff said.

They stayed a little longer, then Julia decided to take Rita to get some lunch. His daughter threw her arms around his neck when they were leaving, causing him to wince. He was counting his blessings that he was still alive to feel the pain.

The Lieutenant showed up shortly thereafter.

"Do you want to play golf today?" he asked, after taking one look at Cliff, who was sitting up in the hospital bed with his arm in a sling. He'd insisted that the nurse take the IV out of his arm and disconnect him from the machines. They'd done so after a short argument.

"I don't think I'm playing golf anytime soon," Cliff answered. "If ever."

"When you get your arm out of that sling, you'll be as good as new."

"I wasn't any good at golf before I hurt my arm. I can only imagine how bad I am now."

"I always said you're the biggest wuss in the department. This proves it."

"The doctor said it'd take three months before I have full use of my arm."

The knife had penetrated all the way to the bone. Cliff was lucky it hadn't been more in the center of his back and punctured his lung or hit his heart. Then it could've been life threatening.

"If you think I'm going to give you three more months off, you're crazy."

"What do you mean? I didn't think I was ever coming back."

"Think again."

"What are you talking about? Did the commission make their ruling?"

A wide smile came on his face.

"I just left the Police Commissioners office. Your suspension is lifted."

"No way! What changed his mind?"

"What do you think? How can we fire somebody who stopped a cold-blooded murderer from killing another young girl?"

"I was in the right place at the right time."

"That girl was lucky you were there. Clay would've killed her."

"I hope he's behind bars. Although, I guess he made bail already."

"We've been busy. We arrested Clay. I should say we detained him. That way we can hold him for a few days. We got a search warrant.

When we went into Henry Lee Clay's condo, we found some interesting things. He kept souvenirs. Lockets of hair and articles of clothing."

"Of the victims?"

The Lieutenant nodded his head.

"How did I miss those the first time we arrested him?"

The Lieutenant waved his hand dismissively.

"It was well hidden. We were lucky to find them. Each condo comes with a storage unit. Clay rented one out. In a business name. That's where we found it. Hidden behind a locker. The hair and articles of clothing were in plastic bags. We haven't run the DNA tests yet to confirm who they belong to, but Tessie and Nancee's names were written on the outside of each bag. He also took a picture of them with his phone. To put with the souvenirs."

"He's a sick man."

"You were right, Cliff. He killed both of them. You've been vindicated."

"A little late now."

"Maybe not. There's more."

"What?"

"Clay wrote a note to himself to transfer $250,000 to an account belonging to Krueger."

"Oh man... Money for the confession."

"Sure looks like it. Get this. Clay never sent the money. He marked through the note. I guess he gave Krueger the shaft. Didn't need him after the judge ruled in his favor."

"What a cheapskate. He has millions of dollars but stiffs a co-conspirator."

"There's more."

"You're full of good news."

Cliff almost didn't feel the pain in his arm or the throbbing in his head. The good news was the best medicine he could ask for. He was glad he hadn't taken the pain medication now.

"On Clay's computer was a fifty-thousand-dollar transfer," the Lieutenant said. "Who do you think that was for?"

"Who?"

"The judge."

"You're kidding. I knew that judge was crooked."

"Yep. He was arrested earlier this morning."

"I wish I could've been there to see it."

"I was there. It made my year."

"That's wonderful news."

"You were right along, Cliff. Clay is going to jail for a long time. We've got the kidnapping and attempted murder on the girl. The assault on you. We've got obstruction of justice. Bribery. Conspiracy. We can charge him with Nancee Hale's murder. Clay is going away for a long time."

"What about his settlements?"

"We froze all his assets. We'll see what happens with them. I don't think the city can get it back, but it might be able to go to a victims' fund. Or a charity."

"At least some good can come from it."

"You did good, Cliff. You're the hero."

"I was just doing my job."

"There's a reason why you are an award-winning detective."

"I haven't won any awards."

"You will for this. You were right all along. Everybody knows it now. It'll be good to have you back in the office. Don't tell anyone, but I missed you."

Cliff didn't have the heart to tell the Lieutenant they were moving to Miami.

Would this change things?

Maybe. He'd have to talk to Julia about it.

"You take care of yourself," the Lieutenant said. "Get that arm healed. Take as long as you need."

The Lieutenant left Cliff to his thoughts. He'd already mentally checked out of his job in Chicago. Julia had been looking for houses in Miami online. Had already told her parents they were moving. They were beyond excited to have their daughter and granddaughter close again.

Under Cover Miami was already in the works. They'd even set up the Florida corporation. He was actually looking forward to it.

Could he leave Chicago?

Yes. He couldn't disappoint Julia. She'd be thrilled that Cliff got his old job back but crushed if he told her he wanted to keep it.

He couldn't do that to her or to Rita. Even their daughter was thrilled to be leaving Chicago for new horizons.

Ugg. How could he be a Miami Dolphins fan? He was an NFC guy. Julia had argued that he could still root for the Chicago sports teams. No law against it in Florida.

He was looking forward to the weather. The thought of a winter without snow or ice or bone chilling cold was exhilarating.

Julia was right. Things were dangerous in Chicago. The events of the last few days were a setback for the "defund the police" movement, but they'd be back. The sentiment wasn't going away.

"Can I at least shoot somebody every once in a while?" Cliff had asked.

"No. Your gun is going in the safe."

It actually wasn't. He'd already applied for a concealed weapons permit. And a private investigator's license. He'd go by and get the actual permits once he was in town. Cliff intended to carry his weapon with him in Miami.

He'd feel naked without it on his hip.

He'd also check in with the Lieutenant in Miami. Maybe they could throw some business his way. Private Investigators often worked with the homicide detectives to solve crimes.

Cliff's mind was spinning with all the possibilities of the new life they were going to lead in Miami. The only interruptions were the nurses coming in and out to check on him. Every time they came in, he asked if he could go home.

"Maybe tomorrow. If the doctor allows it."

He had to fight back the impulse to put on his clothes and walk out of there. Who was going to stop him?

Eventually he started to nod off. A day of quiet and relaxation might actually do him some good. His shoulder still hurt like the knife was still in it. Another day in the hospital was probably a good idea.

A rap on the door woke him. He wasn't sure how long he'd been asleep.

"Come in," Cliff said.

The door opened and a familiar face stuck her head around it.

Hesitantly.

Someone could've given Cliff a hundred guesses as to who was on the other side of the door. He would've guessed incorrectly a hundred out of a hundred times. He had a better chance of guessing the winning numbers for the lottery.

"Ms. McVade. What are you doing here?" Cliff asked.

At first, he thought she was in the wrong room.

Then he thought he might be dreaming. He moved his head from side to side to try to wake himself from the sleep. When pain shot through his shoulder, he realized it wasn't a dream. It was very real.

"I hope I'm not disturbing you, Detective," she said. "I can come back later if I am."

She was there to see him. Why? He couldn't imagine.

"No. I'm okay," Cliff said. Equally hesitantly. More confused than anything. "Please come in."

She was being courteous so he would be as well.

Was she there to berate him? To spout off her "defund the police" agenda. Cliff had been in the news a lot over the last few weeks and months. He'd become a poster child for police brutality and corruption. The news barely mentioned his exoneration.

Ms. McVade came through the threshold but left the door slightly ajar. In case she needed a quick getaway, he suspected.

She stopped at the end of his bed. Dressed like he remembered her. Wearing a pantsuit with a purse over her arm which was folded in front of her.

"How are you doing, Cliff?" she asked.

His defenses were going crazy. Walls were building all around his emotions. He wanted to be cold and aloof. But her tone was endearing and disarming. It'd be extremely rude of him to let his real feelings show.

"I'm going to live," Cliff said as coolly as he could muster. Although, there wasn't even a trace of resentment, anger, or bitterness behind his tone.

"That's what the nurse said. That you were going to be okay. I'm glad to hear it."

How did she even get in his room?

Could anybody just walk off the street and come on his floor? If so, a flock of reporters might be outside his door as well.

Their eyes met.

Not in a stare.

He saw tears forming in both of her eyes. She looked away and blinked twice trying to fight them back.

"I'm sorry," Cliff said. "I don't mean to sound rude, but why are you here? I haven't seen you in months. The last time I saw you, we didn't leave things on the best of terms."

"I know. I regret that. I'm terribly sorry for my behavior."

She sounded genuine.

"Okay. I guess I was a little over the top as well."

"How's Rita?"

"She's good. She's doing well in school. We put her in a private school."

"That's good. I heard about what she did yesterday. She's a very brave girl."

How did she hear? Was Rita on the news as well? Cliff hadn't turned the television on the entire day.

"The girl you saved yesterday," Ms. McVade said. "She's my grand-daughter."

It all suddenly made sense.

"Oh... I didn't know."

"Foolish girl. Getting in the car with that man."

"He was going to kill her."

Several teardrops escaped from her eyes and began to run down her cheeks. She didn't bother to brush them off.

Cliff's tone was gentle and comforting.

"I saw her get in the car with him," Cliff said.

"I know. She was stupid. We taught her better than that."

"You can talk until you're blue in the face. Kids today don't realize the danger. She probably thought it'd be cool to ride in the fancy car."

"She was lucky you were there."

"I was doing my job."

"I feel like a fool."

All kinds of thoughts popped in his head. He wanted to argue with her. Tell her all the ways she was wrong. How we need the police. That defunding the police was a stupid idea. Dangerous even. If her movement succeeded, nobody would've been there for her granddaughter, and she'd be dead.

But he saw no reason to rub it in. It seemed like Ms. McVade had come to that conclusion on her own. That's probably why she was there.

A cathartic moment. Why make her feel worse by piling on?

"Oh well. Water under the bridge."

"No. You were right, Cliff. I misjudged you. I owe you an apology."

"Does this mean you've come over from the dark side?" he said with a smile on his face, so she wouldn't be offended.

"I don't know. Maybe I need to rethink some of my beliefs."

"Not all cops are bad."

"I know that. I've always known that. I was blinded. I thought I was fighting oppression."

"Hey. I'll be the first one to help fight for the little guy. The ones who can't fight for themselves. Like your granddaughter. She needed me to fight for her. To protect her. And I did."

"It was a brave thing you did. Attacking that man. He had a knife. You could've been killed. Look at you. You're in the hospital because of it."

"I'd do it again. A hundred more times. Pretty much every cop I know would've done the same thing. Most of us want to help. We risk our lives to protect the citizens of Chicago."

"I believe you. You didn't have to do what you did."

"We run toward the bad guys. When others run away. Like firemen running into a burning building while everyone else is trying to get out. If you defund the police, you won't have anyone to protect you from the bad guys."

"I know. You're right."

"I'm sorry. I don't mean to lecture you. This must be hard."

He felt a sudden need to change the subject.

"How is your granddaughter?"

"She's shaken up. It was a close call. I don't think she even realized the danger she was in until she saw the knife."

"I'm thankful I was there."

"So am I. I'm thankful you're going to be okay. I don't know how I could ever repay you."

"You coming here today is payment enough. We don't do it for accolades or a thank you. In fact, we don't get them very often. That took a lot of courage for you to come here. It means a lot to me."

She touched Cliff's foot which was under the blanket.

"Thank you again," she said with a tearful smile.

"You're welcome. Thank you for coming."

He couldn't wait to tell Julia. She was going to be shocked. Actually, she wouldn't believe him. She'd say he was dreaming.

He shifted in the bed. A pain shot through his shoulder like he'd been struck by the knife again.

He pushed the button for the nurse. When she arrived, he said, "I think I'll take that pain pill now."

The girl was safe. Clay was behind bars. Ms. McVade was thankful for him. He had his old job and reputation back.

And he was moving to Miami.

If this was a dream, he didn't want it to end.

Epilogue

Four months later

Henry Lee Clay considered himself a lucky man. Even though he spent his days and nights in the Illinois State Penitentiary, things could be a lot worse.

Almost were. Now things were looking up.

Cliff Ford moved to south Florida. His nemesis. The pain in his neck. Kryptonite.

When he learned Ford moved out of the area, he was thrilled. When he got out of jail soon, he'd be free of the nuisance. Things would be a lot better on the outside without Ford around to harass him.

Clay was convinced Ford had been following him the day he picked up that girl and took her to the park to kill her. Such a brazen move on his part in broad daylight. Clay knew better.

Sometimes the urge to kill overrode his common sense.

He had to be more careful. He wasn't a good killer. Took too many risks. That had to change once he got out.

According to his attorney, he'd been facing life in prison. But things fell into place.

It felt like somebody had given him a lottery ticket. A get out jail free card in eight months.

The District Attorney couldn't nail him on any charges related to the girl. They initially charged him with kidnapping and false imprisonment. But the girl got in his car voluntarily. He never actually threatened her or told her she had to go with him. So those charges were dropped.

They couldn't charge him with assault. He didn't lay a hand on her. The fact that he intended to kill her wasn't considered a crime. Not until he actually did it.

The D.A. had no choice but to drop those charges as well.

Clay laughed out loud.

His voice echoed off the prison walls and filled the six by nine by twelve-foot cell. He was sitting at his desk in his prison cell. The television was off, and he had finished reading. He had pretty much anything he wanted at his disposal. Money bought him a lot of privileges in jail. Basically, every guard had a price.

He was laughing at the idiots in the judicial system. Ford. The D.A. The judge. They were morons. The wheels of justice were broken. Not that he was complaining.

The D.A. had charged him with assault of a police officer. Cliff Ford. For sticking the knife in his back.

That felt good.

Along with assault, he was charged with attempted murder. But that charge was flimsy. Ford attacked him. He was defending himself.

According to his capable attorney, that probably wasn't going to fly with the jury, so Clay took a plea. The D.A. asked for ten years; the judge gave him three. He'll be out in twelve months. Easy time to do considering he had been facing the rest of his life in prison.

His accounts were also unfrozen. The settlements stood. Twenty-one million dollars. He'd spent three million on the condo and cars. With interest, he had the full twenty-one back and sitting in his account.

He'd saved half a million dollars by not paying the lowlife Krueger.

What a fool that man was. He didn't have two brain cells to tie together.

Krueger waltzed right into court and lied. Said Bowman confessed. Did it all on the promise that he'd get paid five hundred thousand dollars.

Clay had intended to wire him the money. Kept putting it off. Then he got out of prison and had second thoughts. That had actually been a stroke of luck. They couldn't charge him with a crime because the money had never changed hands.

Clay denied there ever was a quid pro quo and Krueger wasn't talking.

A waste of time for the D.A. who realized it and didn't pursue the charge.

The only worry Clay had was when he was sent to the same prison as Krueger. His attorney had requested Clay be separated from the main population. He didn't want Krueger or one of his thugs to have the opportunity to cut Clay's throat with a knife.

The prison warden obliged, and Clay was put in solitary confinement. A pain. Clay could only go out in the yard for an hour each day. Alone.

Better than being dead, though. Krueger would kill him in a second if he had the chance.

He wouldn't get that chance. Courtesy of the prison who protected him.

Eight more months and he'd be home free. Krueger would rot in jail for the rest of his life. Clay would be on the outside with his millions.

Clay was also charged with bribing the judge. Money did change hands and the D.A. could prove it. That charge could've sent him away for a long time, but he turned state's evidence. The D.A. really wanted to nail the judge who was a bigger fish. He had it in for him and wanted the judge off the bench.

The D. A. could nail Clay but not the judge. He had Clay's end of the transaction but hadn't been able to trace the money back to the judge. They needed Clay's testimony to convict him.

So, Clay agreed to testify against the judge and got immunity against prosecution for doing so.

Clay was the Teflon man. Nothing stuck to him.

So when the dust settled, he had to do twelve months in the slammer. He felt like a lucky man. Actually, he was smarter than all of them. Even the judge who was now facing thirty years in prison.

The D.A. threatened to charge him with killing Nancee Hale but that didn't go anywhere. They couldn't prove he was there that day. Bowman had already been convicted. Had the girl's blood on his shoe. Proving he did was next to impossible.

Clay was on cloud nine. He had millions of dollars in the bank. A Ferrari in his garage. Ford left Chicago and was in Florida.

When Clay got out of prison, he intended to move away from Chicago as well. Some place where there wasn't so much scrutiny. With a warmer climate. Not Florida. Ford was there.

Maybe California. Their laws were even more liberal than Chicago's. Their judicial system was a joke. They were defunding the police left and right. Gutting the police forces in most of the jurisdictions. Especially around the big cities. They were having a hard time filling positions. Morale on the police force was low.

The court system was backed up. The prosecutors were lenient. A perfect environment for a killer.

He could get away with murder there.

That joke caused him to laugh out loud.

He'd gotten away with murder in Chicago. Twice.

As of right now, he didn't have a single murder conviction on his record. They'd both been overturned.

He had eight months to get better at covering his tracks and not getting caught. That's what he spent most of his time reading. Books about serial killers. Trying to learn everything he could from them.

A horn sounded.

Time for lights out.

Clay was tired.

One more day clicked off his sentence. He'd be out of there in no time.

He heard footsteps outside his cell. Probably the guard.

It was. One of the bulky guards was at his cell door. He took out his keys and opened it.

Strange.

"What's this?" Clay said.

"You have a visitor," the guard said.

Who could that be? At that time of night. He'd only had two visitors over the last four months. Shannon Roberts came once a week. He paid one of the guards to look the other way so they could have conjugal visits.

The other was from his attorney. He hadn't been there in weeks. No reason for him to visit Clay. Everything was resolved at that point.

He'd never met with anyone in his prison cell anyway. Certainly not this late at night.

The guard left the prison door open and disappeared from sight.

A huge figure appeared in the doorway.

Krueger.

A panic shot through Clay like he'd stuck his hand in an electrical socket.

"Alone at last," Krueger said.

He had something in his right hand.

Not, Not The End

Thank you for purchasing this novel from best-selling author, Terry Toler. As an additional thank you, Terry wants to give you a free gift.

Sign up for:
Updates
New Releases
Announcements
At terrytoler.com

We'll send you a copy of *The Book Club*, a Cliff Hangers mystery, free of charge.

READ MORE BOOKS FROM TERRY TOLER

Jamie Austen Thrillers

Read all the Jamie Austen Thrillers. They must be good.
They've been number one on Amazon in ten different countries.
Click on the link below.

THE JAMIE AUSTEN THRILLERS (12 book series)
Kindle Edition (amazon.com)

https://amzn.to/3vmPUy7

Cliff Hangers Mystery Series

Who wants to read a good mystery? We've got you covered! Read the Cliff Hangers where homicide detective, Cliff Ford, solves crimes in Chicago, with help from his wife Julia. These books have everything Terry Toler is known for. Page turning suspense, a hint of romance, and an ending you won't see coming.

The Cliff Hangers Mystery Series (4 book series)
Kindle Edition (amazon.com)

https://amzn.to/36WX3go

About Terry

Terry Toler is an Amazon international # 1 best-selling and award-winning author. He writes clean fiction with a message and life-changing nonfiction. He's a public speaker, entrepreneur, and has authored more than forty books.

Sign up for his newsletter where you'll get free stuff, exclusive content, and news of releases and promotions. He can be followed at terrytoler.com.

If you like his books, please take a few minutes to leave a review on Amazon. We really appreciate it. It helps draw more readers to his books. Thanks!